I0762499

THE REVENGE PARTY

EMILY LYNN PAULSON

THE REVENGE PARTY

Cover design and typesetting by Covered by Kerry LLC

Library of Congress Cataloging-in-Publication Data
Available on request

ISBN 978-1-959524-17-5 (hardcover)

First edition 2026

10 9 8 7 6 5 4 3 2 1

For all the women who know exactly who this is about.

ONE

KATHERINE

"Come on, it's eight-thirty," I called upstairs.

Halfway into the school year, you'd think mornings would run smoother, but no. The kids inherited their father's talent for lateness, no matter how many times I tried to drill it into their heads in my mother's singsong: *If you're not early, you're late.*

I opened the dishwasher and groaned at the chaos inside. Bowls stacked where glasses should go, utensils pointing dangerously upward. Someone had shoved a cutting board in sideways as if physics were negotiable.

Everyone's version of "help" always left me irritated, and lately, I fixated on these petty things because they felt manageable.

"Your mom is a planner," Shane would say, defending me against their teasing. "She knows how to get things done."

But dishes could be rearranged. A marriage couldn't.

The kids trampled down the stairs in a wave of noise and damp hair.

"Quick breakfast, and then you need to get on the road," I nagged. Elliott and Ethan shuffled to the table. They shoveled food into their mouths, shoulders broadening before my eyes. They were so much smaller back when Shane entered our lives, even though it was only a few years ago.

"Emma," I said, watching my daughter drown a waffle with syrup. "Don't get on the highway without stopping because you're already past empty, and the light is on."

"I know, Mom." Emma rolled her dark brown eyes, lined with black, and made more dramatic by her new eyebrow ring. I wasn't the biggest fan of the face piercing, but I feigned approval and had to admit it fit her personality. "God, you act like I've never driven a car before."

"The last time you ran out of gas, you called me at midnight from the side of I-5. Remember?" Their commute was thirty minutes each way, and I was the only one who appeared to care. *Fail to plan, and plan to fail* was another mantra my kids failed to pick up on.

"That was one time."

"Elliott," I said, ignoring my daughter. "Jackson's mom will give you a ride home after Robotics. You can meet us at Ethan's basketball game if you'd like."

"Or you could just get your driver's license," Emma added. "Oh, wait, I forgot. You failed the test like four times."

"Shut up, loser." Elliott threw a muffin wrapper at his sister and missed, his aim as poor as his parallel parking skills.

"Okay, that's enough." I made a mental note to schedule

him for an eye appointment. "You should get on the road. Gas station, Emma, and do not forget."

"Mom, *God*, I got it." She picked up her bright pink tote bag, and the boys shuffled behind her.

I passed out bagged lunches, complete with little notes. Though the kids acted embarrassed, I knew they appreciated it. And I'd never stopped because it was the one small way to reach them before the world did.

"Love. You. Three." I leaned in to kiss each cheek. Ethan was the only one to accept my smooch.

"Current favorite," I whispered, earning a half-smile.

Choosing favorites was off-limits in theory, but it was our family joke, their standings changing by the day, sometimes the minute.

I waved as they climbed into Emma's SUV and drove away. As the Puget Academy Cheer bumper sticker got smaller in the distance, my anxiety returned, automatic as breath.

The house fell into a silence that once felt peaceful but now only emphasized how alone I was with my thoughts. I turned off the stove, plated my breakfast, and waited for my husband. A fresh cup of coffee sat on the counter, ready for him.

I pictured him upstairs doing what he always did before a big day: putting on the version of himself the world expected. Polished and steady. And that was the problem.

When you marry steadiness, you believe you can finally breathe—you can relax into the drumbeat of security. Yet I was crawling out of my skin.

"Morning, babe!" Shane rushed downstairs, close-cropped

salt-and-pepper hair still slightly damp. He pulled a tailored jacket over a slim-fitting Oxford shirt, a blue that brought out the color of his eyes. I smiled at him. Some things were better left unsaid.

Somebody once told me that if you put a penny in a jar every time you had sex as a newlywed, and then, on your first anniversary, started taking a coin out each time, you'd never empty the jar. I'd proved the theory right in my marriage to the kids' dad. We didn't even sleep in the same room after a few years. But I was sure it wouldn't be true with Shane and me; we would have emptied the jar halfway through the second year, no question. We burned through the honeymoon stage like we had something to prove.

Then the proving stopped.

"Morning," I said, breathing in his fresh, out-of-the-shower scent as he wrapped his arms around my waist, kissing me on the forehead. It felt good, warm, a habit, easier than standing there with space between us. I let myself have the moment. I needed it.

"Do you want breakfast?" I gestured to the extra egg I'd made, just in case, trying not to seem like too much of a pushover, though I knew he'd say no. Intermittent fasting was his newest health craze, following the celery juice phase that ended a few weeks ago.

"Thanks, this is good." He raised his mug and took a sip, then shifted his eye contact from me to his phone.

"The McFadden campaign needs some repositioning." He didn't look up, and I was grateful. "Damage control."

"You coming to Ethan's game tonight? Seven?" I kept my voice light.

He gave me the broad, charming smile I fell for. The one that made everyone trust him. "Wouldn't miss it."

That was the Shane I loved. The man who cheered on the sidelines of Ethan's games and remembered my mother's birthday. The man whose steady confidence was solid ground after years of instability. He'd made me feel seen when I was invisible, secure when I was deep in debt. Falling in love with him was easy.

Which is what made everything since feel so hard. Maybe I was the one who had gotten it all wrong. Again.

I looked down to see a text from Emma.

K, fine u were right, I ran out of gas...

Crap. I called, and she picked up immediately.

"Don't tell me you told me so." Emma had one of those voices that instantly gave a visual of her facial expressions.

I clicked my tongue. "Where are you?"

"By the Starbucks off MLK. I'm not dead. Yet."

"Very funny," I said. "Put your hazards on and wait for Triple-A."

Shane looked up, always listening even when he pretended not to. "Out of gas?"

"Yes," I said, irritation spilling from my voice.

"I can go."

"What about your meeting this morning?"

He smiled, no lecture, no frustrated sigh. "It can wait."

I'd spent so long doing everything alone that help still felt like a shock. Like I was taking something that didn't belong to me anymore.

I moved to the sink so he couldn't see my face, the questions rising to the surface, the doubt swirling behind them.

"Thank you." I turned back to him, but he was already grabbing his keys.

"See you tonight," he called as he headed out the door, reversing his too-flashy-for-my-taste Porsche down the driveway, speeding off to help Emma.

I sent a message to Puget Academy to let them know the kids would be late again and checked the clock. Then I heard the familiar sound of teeth on fabric.

"Where did you get that, you rotten girl?" I asked, high-pitched, pulling the chewed-up tube sock from my dog's adorably guilty mouth.

Piper loved socks so much that we'd had one surgically removed from her, but she hadn't learned her lesson. I never thought I'd be one of those people who paid for sock-removal surgery, let alone own a dog. I remembered Ethan saying in a tiny kindergarten voice when we got her, "But mom, you don't *wike* dogs." But that wasn't exactly true. I simply never understood "dog people." Then I divorced their dad, and my desire to please the kids was so strong that I caved to their request while visiting a neighbor fostering puppies.

I picked up the smallest girl of the litter, with a funny white spot over her left eye that looked like an angry eyebrow, and overnight, I became a dog person. I was pretty sure I liked dogs more than people.

"We will go for a walk after lunch, okay?" Piper wagged her tail as she followed me to my office, taking her rightful place on the plush bed at the foot of my desk. Specks of dust from her wagging tail danced in a sunbeam, rare for January, streaming through the panoramic window.

I sat and admired the expansive Seattle skyline. This house was a monument to Shane's success with soaring ceilings, imported marble, and custom everything. When the kids and I first moved in, it thrilled us. I'd tiptoed like an impostor through rooms that belonged in a magazine spread. Perhaps that feeling was intuition, rather than insecurity.

From this height, the city looked ordered and manageable, with ferries tracing paths across the bay and traffic flowing in patterns. Up here, I could pretend my life had the same structure. If I squinted, I could almost see our small two-bedroom across the bay on Alki Beach with the temperamental heater and forever-broken washing machine, where the kids and I lived before moving here. I'd sunk into self-pity back then—broke, divorced, single, with three little kids—focusing on what we lacked instead of appreciating the happiness we had.

My fingers absently twisted my wedding ring. "So, you'll always remember you're mine," Shane had whispered when he slipped it on. I found it romantic then. Lately, I'd woken from nightmares where it tightened in my sleep, cutting off circulation until my finger blackened and fell to the floor.

Stop spiraling, Katie. I pulled my hair into a bun and scanned my calendar for the day. I opened a spreadsheet, each cell color-coded and cross-referenced. Organizing was calming, giving everything a place. Even things that didn't want one.

This afternoon, I needed to finish details for a graduation committee meeting, a class party, emails to vendors for the Sutton Stars charity auction, and hopefully make it to the gym in time for my noon class. Every January, I felt the crunch of all the things I'd said "yes" to at the beginning of the school year, and year after year, I kept saying yes.

My phone lit up, and a Google alert for Sutton Strategy filled the top of my screen. There were more and more of them lately.

Moderate Republican McFadden and His Not-So-Moderate-Takes—Smart Strategy, or Selling Out? – By Anna Dollarhide

A side note in the piece made my scalp prickle: murmurs that Sutton Strategy was "positioning for higher office." Whose? No one said.

I'd always ignored politics; what was the point in a blue state like Washington and an even bluer city? But Shane had dragged politics into our home, our dinner conversations, and my children's classrooms. My eyes were wide open, and I couldn't close them.

I'd watched him strategize and shift beliefs long enough to learn an important lesson: getting what you wanted sometimes meant playing by rules you hated.

Piper huffed like she'd heard enough and hopped down from her bed, trotting to the door.

"I surrender," I told Piper, who jumped up after me, knowing I'd again given in to her furry charm when I grabbed the leash. "The party planning can wait, I suppose."

It was silly of me to resist a rare sunny day during Seattle's most extended season: a nine-month winter. I grew up here; I was used to it. I didn't even own an umbrella. That's how Pacific Northwest I was.

I walked past Shane's office on the way out the door. Locked, as always.

It was such a small thing, but I knew better than anyone that in a marriage, small things could mean so much more.

We hurried down the driveway. "Wait, Piper, wait," I begged as my impatient dog pulled my shoulder practically out of its socket, and another text popped up. It was Shane.

> Got Emma gas. But going to be a late night with the McFadden team tonight, will miss the game, be home late. Don't wait up. Love you.

A standard, responsible text, the kind of message a decent man sent so his wife wouldn't worry. Before I could respond, another text.

> Don't forget to take your medication today. You seemed off this morning.

I glared at the screen. I thought I had things handled, but I was wrong.

I was running out of time.

TWO
ISABELLA

I didn't have an orgasm until I was twenty-six years old.

I am twenty-six years old.

Outstanding timing, truly. Like discovering your favorite restaurant the week before it closes, or getting a text right as the battery dies. Or, in my case, finally understanding what all the fuss was about roughly five minutes before deciding to weaponize it against the man responsible. Because everything changed when I met a man who'd mastered the art of making people feel exactly what he wanted them to feel—in the bedroom or at the ballot box.

My body count isn't low, so it wasn't a lack of experience. I'd been with enough mediocre men to write a field guide on PacWest Fuckboys in their habitat. You don't know what you don't know, you know? But then it happened. Oh, did it happen! The warm build between my legs, spreading to my thighs, deep in my belly, and then EVERYWHERE ALL AT

ONCE AND OH MY JESUS CHRIST, IS THIS WHAT I'VE BEEN MISSING?

The first time, I almost cried. Not from the pleasure, though that was fucking incredible, but because I'd found his weakness. And he'd found mine—a loop we'd both exploit, repeatedly.

Like three nights ago, his breath hot against my neck as he whispered things that should have felt romantic. Afterward, lying in the tangle of hotel sheets, he checked his phone with the same intensity with which he'd focused on my body, and I remembered it was a transaction, just not the kind he thought. He thought he was buying my loyalty with orgasms. Cute. I was collecting evidence and getting off at the same time. Multitasking.

"Isabella, we will be in the conference room. When the team arrives, do you mind bringing them in?" He flashed the smile that had been working magic on me since I started working here in September. "And give these to Davis and Tim, please."

He handed me two stacks of files, fingers brushing mine longer than necessary.

Today's meeting was crucial. McFadden's campaign was at a crossroads. His rhetoric was getting more extreme, but his fundraising numbers were surging. The team was convinced they could push further to the right and still win the general gubernatorial election.

"Will do." My skin flushed as his hand slyly grazed my hip when he walked by. His eyes told me he'd noticed the lack of a panty line. It was our little game.

Except my body's response wasn't a game; heat bloomed

where he touched me, muscle memory overriding common sense. I hated that he could make me want him even as I plotted against him.

An office romance was iconic. An office revenge? Shakespeare.

"Here you go, Neil." I heaped a stack of papers onto our data director's desk.

"Thanks, Isabella." Neil gave a thumbs-up. I liked Neil. Easygoing, half-retired already in his head. His endless motivational quotes—"Failure means you're one step closer to success!"—were more sitcom laugh track than strategy, but harmless. Smart in his own way, the kind of man who'd survive any regime change by being useful but unmemorable.

My phone lit up again.

I love it when you don't wear panties to work, Bells. How am I supposed to focus during our meeting?

The truth? I never wore underwear. Branding, not foreplay. Panty lines were the enemy of a good silhouette, and looking expensive was half the battle when you were broke as hell. But I was happy to let him think it was for his benefit. A lie by omission, something I perfected long before him. Men love believing everything women do is for them. Sure, buddy. It's all for you.

I slouched in my chair and returned a text without looking:

Not sure, but I can't wait to see you try.

Sexting was its own drug. The pet names, the thrill of typing things I'd never say to his face. Every text was another hit of dopamine. The lows were traumatic, but the highs? Inject that shit directly into my veins.

"Have something for me?" Davis's voice startled me as he sidled up to my desk. His shoulders were tight from another day of directing a campaign he clearly hated. I closed my text messages and redirected my thirsty thoughts.

"Here you go." I handed him his stack, a different kind of electricity sparking through me. "Two o'clock with the McFadden team."

"God, I hate this guy," Davis muttered, flipping through pages.

I rolled my eyes. McFadden was a tech bro-turned-wannabe governor. Rich, smug, no political experience, but plenty of arrogance to think he deserved power. Every meeting with his team was a masterclass in why men shouldn't be allowed to run shit.

Davis lingered a little too long, and I didn't mind. He was one of the few people my age in a company full of Xers and boomers. We'd become the kids' table cousins, side-eyeing and sharing looks across meetings that said, *Can you believe this shit?* His presence was comfortable, not consuming like my boyfriend's, who took up space like it belonged to him. Davis touched my arm before he walked away, which I didn't hate.

"Thanks, Iz. I'm grabbing a coffee downstairs. Want one? I need to escape before I have to listen to McFadden blabber on about how climate change is overblown."

Oooh, a caffeine jolt would be great before the meeting.

Keurig swill didn't compare to a seven-dollar latte from the lobby cart.

"Meet you down there in a sec."

On the way to the elevator, I passed the glass-walled office the CEO used when he wanted to be seen, with sweeping views of Elliott Bay and the Space Needle. Framed headlines of old electoral victories lined the walls, dating back to the firm's progressive heyday and ending with centrist sellouts and an orange-tinged presidential hopeful. His laptop sat at an angle away from the door, as always.

It was a stage, set to impress, intimidate, and control. And it worked, even on me.

I never expected to be the cliché assistant girlfriend. Yet here I was, living every HR violation in the handbook.

I'd played hard to get for a few weeks after I started, just long enough to seem professional, not long enough to lose him. I'd planned the timing down to the day when he pinned me against a cold parking structure wall three months ago.

What I hadn't planned was how my knees would actually buckle. How my breath would catch when he whispered that I was different from the others.

Past the strategy room, where Patrick, our compliance and loyalty director, led a brainstorming session, I paused at the whiteboard and read the bullet points: parental rights, curriculum transparency, and protecting children's innocence, which was all coded language to appeal to McFadden's growing far-right base.

"Perfect demographic overlap," Patrick was saying, circling a region on the map. "Parents in these districts are primed for the message."

My eyes snagged on two words: medical freedom. The exact phrase my mom used to justify never taking us to the doctor.

I'd seen that freedom up close—my dad coughing blood in our living room while my mother gave him herbs, refusing to take him to the hospital. I was twelve. Young enough to believe her but old enough to know something was wrong.

Now, here I was, helping market the same fear-mongering BS. But unlike my parents, I knew how the sausage was made. And I was going to use that knowledge to take what was rightfully mine.

I walked away before anyone could notice me there or imagine what I was thinking.

Davis let me cut in front of him in the longer-than-usual line at the coffee cart, gently touching the small of my back as he gestured me forward.

"Thanks." I was hyperaware of the space between us.

We made small talk about local music venues. Shocked I hadn't been to Neptune, he promised to take me "as friends." We both knew what that meant.

Back in October, a few weeks after I took the job, Davis had invited me out with the team. Karaoke at Yen Wor—a.k.a. the Young Whore. Classy. I was sure they were pulling a prank on the new girl, but no. Neil sang a version of "Can't Help Falling in Love" that Elvis himself would have wept over. Davis and I kissed that night, too. One drunken, stupid kiss outside the bar, rain misting our faces while we waited for our Ubers.

For three seconds, I was a person instead of a conquest. Then I'd pulled back, laughed it off, made some dumbass joke about tequila, and spent the next month avoiding him. I regretted it. All of it. But sometimes I wondered if he still thought about that kiss. I did. More than I should. Especially during nights staring at hotel room ceilings, wondering how I'd ended up there. But I still never questioned my reason why.

A group of navy-suited men marched toward the elevator bank. "Think they're McFadden's guys."

"Or finance bros. Either way, white old boys' club," Davis said.

He wasn't wrong. As the lone Black person in the office, he'd told me about how he'd been tapped for his expertise in 2020 when equity suddenly mattered—fitting for a company where I was one of only two women. Neil once suggested we put out a press release bragging about how we'd "doubled female hires" when I arrived. Not a joke. These guys were sweet, competent, and clueless about why that was horrifying.

"I hate this new direction," Davis groaned. "The latest ad was embarrassing."

"You don't believe in McFadden's tough love approach to homelessness?" I held my hand to my chest in false outrage.

The latest ad featured Bruce McFadden striding through a homeless encampment, disgusted, promising to clean up the streets of Seattle with threats of mass arrests.

"Compassion has failed," the voiceover intoned. "It's time for accountability."

If not for this job, I might have ended up in the encampment he wanted bulldozed. We'd been a paycheck away from that reality more times than I cared to count.

Davis smirked. "I believe in data and compassion. Two things McFadden seems to have a troubled relationship with.

But what I believe doesn't matter. We go where the money is right now."

"Right now? You see this changing?"

He didn't answer, just checked the clock, his jaw tight. Whatever he was thinking, he wasn't ready to share it, not with me.

"Shit, they're going to beat us."

"They're early. Tammi can stall." I had zero guilt in letting another group of basic dudes wait; they could use the practice in patience.

"If this meeting goes badly, Whistler is going to be a bust."

"Ah, right, the wiener roast ski weekend. I've heard about this," I said. "Isn't the boss a little out of place with you and your college buddies?" Tales of Davis and his frat brothers' annual ski weekend were office legend, some male-bonding ritual that apparently couldn't be missed, and I found it odd a dude pushing fifty would want to tag along.

"Yeah, well, I don't have much of a choice," he said.

"True." Our CEO tended to insert himself into things, despite the outcome, taking up space, demanding attention to center himself, and taking any "no" as a personal slight.

With a few minutes to spare, we collected our drinks—a tall flat white for Davis and a triple Americano with cream for me—and hurried to the elevators.

Davis's lips curved. "How do you sleep after drinking that?"

"Like a baby with a weighted blanket."

He continued side-eyeing me. *Is there something in my teeth? Is my dress unzipped?*

"What?"

"You're not as sneaky as you think, Bells." His eyes locked with mine when he said it. *Bells.*

The door opened on our floor. He leaned close. "Be careful with him."

Then he disappeared into the conference room, leaving me cold with his warning.

What did Davis know about danger?

Also, if he knew the nickname, he'd seen the text. Embarrassing. Erotic. Both.

"Psst…Izzy." Tammi peeked out in the hallway, breaking me from my hot embarrassment. "Waiting area. And they're all doing that thing."

"What thing?"

"You know. The alpha-male, check-our-watches-simultaneously thing." She mimicked their movements.

I snorted. "God, *men.*" I smoothed my skirt. "How do I look?"

"You could sell sand in the Sahara."

"Thanks." I laughed. "I think."

I took two long chugs of coffee, gathered my files, and strode into the waiting area.

McFadden's team stood in their carbon-copy suits with American flag pins, polished shoes, and the enthusiasm of men compensating for, well, smaller things. They'd arranged themselves in a loose semicircle, each one trying to take up more space than the next.

"Right this way, gentlemen." I led them through the office toward the conference room. My strut was extra. Let them think I'm a decoration. Let them underestimate me; that was the real power. People revealed things to pretty faces they'd never tell their equals. Why stay mad at it when I could use it to my advantage? To survive, I had to use deception to escape a world built on it.

Inside the conference room, his voice was clipped: "I don't care what the polling says. Make it happen." But the second he saw me, he softened and sold the illusion.

"There's my secret weapon." His tone was professional enough for clients who all pretended they hadn't been staring at my ass.

No wonder Davis had figured us out. The question was, who else knew?

I smiled, all charm and teeth, and slid into my chair at the back of the room. I pulled out my notepad, like the perfect, dutiful assistant, taking minutes.

He dove into the presentation, commanding the room with the same confidence he brought to everything. The men hung on his words. He was selling them a path to victory, painting a picture of Washington State turning red.

Soon, I could leave this world of spin and manipulation behind. All the lies, late nights, and moments of selling my soul would be well worth it.

And what a fun climb to the top it would be, watching Shane Sutton fall so hard he'd never see the ground rushing up to meet him.

THREE

KATHERINE

"Mom, they killed my article," Emma's voice cracked as I circled Pacific Place for the third time, hunting for parking. "Principal Morris said we can't publish it."

My hands tightened on the steering wheel. "Wait, slow down. What article?"

"The one I've been working on for weeks! About school funding and where the money goes." Her voice climbed higher. "Morris said it's too controversial right now."

I could picture her, curled behind her locker door, phone clutched like a lifeline, hair swept in front of her face.

"Emma, honey, I'm sorry. That's unfair—"

"Mom, I did everything right." A wet, miserable sob broke through. "I cited my sources, and I used public records. But big-mouth Brock blabbed to his mom, and she complained it wasn't appropriate for a student paper."

I swallowed hard and pushed down the urge to tell her uncomfortable conversations were how people learn, then realized I'd been avoiding those same conversations myself. I found a parking spot on the third level and pulled in carefully, letting Emma cry. Moments like these were rare, and I tried to hold on to them.

Interactions with my daughter had been icy lately, and, at times, even combative. I'd been told it was part of the process, when children were ready to spread their wings, pushing your buttons to the brink of "good riddance, kid," and if so, she was right on schedule.

She continued. "Mr. Carlisle told me to dig into it, that it isn't okay for them to silence journalism, even if it's a school paper."

I heard the echo of every woman who'd been told to be quiet and accept things as they were, including myself. Then I heard the words my mom would have told me: *let it go.*

"Em, listen to me, okay?"

She was crying hard.

"Mr. Carlisle is right. Your article being killed doesn't make it wrong; it makes it important."

"But no one will see it now. No one will know what I found—"

"Then find another way to tell the story," I said. "You did the work. Truth doesn't change because someone is uncomfortable with it."

A sniffle. "You think so?"

"I mean it, Em. The hardest things are almost always worth it."

It was the advice I wished my own mother had given me, instead of the lifetime of lessons in nodding, smiling, and swallowing my anger.

She let out a shaky breath. "You're right. Thanks, Mom."

"Do you want me to come home? We can skip the movie?"

"No, have fun." Another sniffle. "I want to be alone. Bridget and Dad said they were going to bring me some ice cream."

Times like these made me grateful for loving bonus parents and the village we'd built around our kids despite the messiness of divorce.

"Okay, Em. Snuggle with Piper. Maybe take a long, hot bath. I'll be home in a few hours, but call me if you need me, okay?"

"Thanks, Mom, you're the best. I love you."

Aww, current favorite. "Love you, too, sweetie."

It never got easier listening to my children cry. The bigger they grew, the more their pain mirrored my own, and the more I grieved being unable to shield them from it. But Emma would endure. She always had.

With Emma, everything was a *first* first. The boys' milestones would come too, but never with the same sharpness. What undid me wasn't the firsts but the lasts. I couldn't recall the last time she asked me to braid her hair or read her a bedtime story. The last time she smiled with braces or begged me to cuddle. Those moments slipped away quietly, only recognized once they were gone. Parenthood was a series of invisible thresholds, each one breaking your heart.

Pacific Place stretched before me, nearly empty on a weekday afternoon. The place Shane loved to showcase in his ad messaging, proof of "radical left decay." I walked past a boarded-up spot where a kids' shoe store used to be. Yes, it was quieter these days, a casualty of the pandemic like countless other shopping centers, but nothing that the exaggerated photographs Shane's firm circulated, with overwrought captions about crime and despair.

I looked around at an older couple walking hand in hand, teenagers at the boba shop, and a mom pushing a stroller past the Apple store. Not thriving, but certainly not destroyed. Adapting.

The truth, as always, was more complicated than Shane's narrative allowed.

"Katie!" Claudia waved me over. I picked up my pace, and she pulled me into one of her signature bear hugs the moment I was close enough.

"Your tits look amazing in that blouse."

"That's why I wore it," I said.

At five-foot-one to my five-foot-ten, her head pressed directly against my chest, making crude jokes inevitable. Our humor had never grown beyond eighth grade, perhaps a rebellion against the perfectionist mothers who raised us. We were daughters of Dexatrim and SnackWell's, of *Buns of Steel* and Victoria's Secret catalogs. I had always assumed that by my forties, I would stop counting calories and cursing the mirror, but here I was, still negotiating peace with my reflection. My mother, well into her sixties, still refused ice cream, lest she "get fat." There was little hope of my accepting body positivity.

"If you've still got it, flaunt it while the world burns." She linked her arm through mine and steered us toward the concession stand, and I ordered our usual: large popcorn, extra butter, two Diet Cokes, Sour Patch Kids for me, Milk Duds for her. The teenage clerk rang us up with indifference.

"Hey, before I forget, I need to talk to you about Chris's firm and the Sutton Stars Fundraiser…"

"Did they settle on the vacation package donation?"

I'd been counting on the week in Cabo valued at five grand, the kind of prize that drove bidding wars at silent auctions. I'd already designed the display card and planned where it should go in the lineup.

Claudia grimaced, avoiding my eyes. "That's the thing. They're pulling out entirely."

"What? Why?" I asked, flinching, not out of anger but disappointment. I stopped mid-step, forcing a couple behind us to swerve out of the way.

"Chris says they can't be associated with Sutton Strategy anymore. Not with this—" she lowered her voice, even though no one was listening, "pivot."

My mind raced. I'd sent out the programs already, promised sponsorship recognition. Chris's firm, Davidson & Associates, was listed as a Gold Level donor.

"They're a progressive firm, Katie. It was one thing when McFadden decided to run as a Republican, but now? With all his anti-vax nonsense?"

I deflated. The dog-eared copy of *The Real Anthony Fauci* that had appeared on our bedside table last week suddenly made sense.

"I know. I get it."

And I did. I wasn't a MAGA wife. That wasn't what I signed up for. Sure, I'd traded Doc Martens for ballet flats somewhere along the way, and the girl who used to date hackers and sneak into warehouse shows was long gone. But I had never swung to the other political extreme either. I was happy to be in the middle. The middle was supposed to be safe. Yet here I was, apologizing for Shane's politics to my best friend, watching sponsorships evaporate because of choices I never made.

"Chris feels terrible. He really does. But he can't have the firm's name associated with someone pushing McFadden's agenda, even if the event is ultimately for a good cause." She squeezed my arm. "I'm sorry."

"I know. It's okay. I'll figure something out." I took the popcorn from the counter. "I always do."

"Oh, I'm sure you will. You're a pro," Claudia reassured me, with the faith I rarely had in myself.

Truthfully, I was no professional, merely a talented amateur with a lifelong compulsion for planning. For as long as I can remember, I loved planning events. My Barbies and My Little Ponies were in a perpetual celebration when I was little. I always volunteered for the prom planning committee in school, and my kids' birthday parties may have been more fun for me than for them. Orchestrating beauty had always soothed chaos. Control over small things helped me ignore how much of the big picture was slipping through my fingers. Like a formal career. A marriage that lasted. My general self-respect.

"I just don't get it," Claudia said. "When you and Shane first met, I thought we were all aligned. I loved how he championed hybrid schooling during COVID. He seemed so reasonable."

I clenched my teeth. Reasonable was not a word that belonged anywhere near Shane's politics anymore. The speech he gave back then may as well have come from a different man.

"What I don't understand," Claudia went on, "is the strategy. McFadden can't possibly win. Washington hasn't elected a Republican governor since 1980. I was an embryo."

"1981," I said. That was back when Shane's father ran the firm. When Sutton Strategy had principles.

"Whatever. The point is, why align with a losing candidate? Especially one this extreme?"

"Shane would tell you Sutton Strategy has always been bipartisan." I was so tired of rehearsing these lines with our circle of progressive friends. "But I do wonder if there's something bigger going on."

Claudia's face softened. She had read me like a book since the YMCA childcare over a decade ago, when we were both pregnant and exhausted, clinging to the sanctuary of those two allotted hours of kid-free bliss. One day, she declared, "Facebook told me we should be friends." And that was that. I told her everything. Almost everything. Some things still felt too shameful to admit, even to her.

"Well, if you think there's something bigger going on, you need to find out."

"And how am I supposed to do that?" I pretended to focus on the popcorn.

"Break into his phone."

I choked on a kernel. "What?"

"I'm serious, Katie." She didn't flinch. "Remember when Chris was acting weird about that 'business dinner,' and I found out he was planning my surprise party?"

"Yes, and you told me you overreacted and felt like a psycho."

"Because it turned out to be innocent." Her brow was raised. "Are you getting surprise party vibes from Shane?"

Was I?

No. The vibes I was getting were much worse. And they weren't just vibes. But I couldn't tell Claudia what I knew. Not yet, anyway.

"Shane's private, especially about his phone."

"Red flag." Claudia sipped her soda. "Katie, you're too good at making excuses. You are the ultimate Virgo."

Was that what I was? Devoted? Or afraid? Maybe both. "Everything's fine" had been my motto for as long as I could remember.

Claudia opened the theater door. "Katie, peek at his phone. Maybe it isn't some grand master plan. It could be a change of opinion. Or maybe he's too obsessed with testosterone supplements and dirt biking to make rational decisions."

"Mountain biking," I corrected. It was one of Shane's many outdoor activities.

"Same thing." She flicked her fingers dismissively. "Oh, speaking of stupid-ass hobbies, did I tell you Chris bought a sixty-year-old truck last week? Orange of all colors! Hideous!"

"Boys and their toys," I deadpanned. Our sports shed was already crammed with gear I couldn't describe or understand, each hobby more like an excuse to escape than a joy. He used to bore me with every detail of his adventures, but lately he offered vague summaries when I asked.

Claudia plopped down in the seat next to me. "Maybe they're all having midlife crises. Chris can't accept that Josie's about to leave for college."

I arranged my face into what I hoped was a commiserating smile while mentally calculating how much money I'd need if I had to support three kids on my own. My savings wouldn't last a month. Thank goodness I had some college money saved, at least enough to get the kids started.

My Emma and Claudia's Josie were inseparable besties, both awaiting college acceptance letters, which was part of the stress my daughter often took out on me. Emma dreamed of California, while I hoped for the University of Washington, so she'd be local. I didn't tell her my opinion since it would likely cause her to find the farthest school possible out of stubborn spite. Perhaps even overseas or on a different planet.

The thought terrified me more than I wanted to admit. Emma would be gone come fall. My first baby. The house would be so empty.

If it was even still my house by then.

I opened the Sour Patch Kids and tossed a few in my mouth, letting the sweet-sour burst distract me.

"What does Linda think? Have you told her?"

"My mother?" I laughed. "Shane could burn down her house, and she'd ask what I did to provoke him."

Claudia knew. She'd been on the receiving end of Linda's judgment enough times through the years.

But it was more than disappointment. My mother had taught me to doubt myself. I used to call her, back when the kids were little, when Eric and I would have petty arguments about nothing, as married couples do. Back then, I believed mothers were supposed to take their daughters' sides. She'd listen, but then judge instead of actually hearing me, and then redirect. Had I considered his perspective? Was I being unfair? Ungrateful?

Eventually, I stopped calling, hoping she'd say the words she'd never said her entire life: You're right, he's wrong, you deserve better.

And every constant dismissal of my reality had taught me that I was on my own. Always had been.

"You know, I wonder if Shane might be concerned about Fred," Claudia suggested. "Men don't always know how to process family health stuff."

I chewed slowly, momentarily confused by the change in topic. "Shane's father, Fred? What about him?"

"Oh..." Claudia's eyes grew wide. "Shit. I shouldn't have said anything."

"Claudia." She was a nurse at the heart clinic.

"You know I can't." She cleared her throat. "Patient privacy and all that."

I gave her a pointed look. "Well, you already said something, so spill it."

She sighed and leaned closer. "Dr. Clark thinks Fred's not taking his prescribed medication. He mentioned some new supplements he's on instead."

"What kind of supplements?"

"I don't know. Something his wife's been giving him, apparently."

Of course, it was Nancy. Shane's mother, with her essential oils and distrust of Big Pharma, the endless parade of wellness products.

But I pictured Fred a few weeks ago, at Christmas, nodding off in his chair and excusing himself early from dinner. Perhaps there was more to it.

"I shouldn't have told you," Claudia said, concerned. "I could lose my job."

"I won't say anything." I promised. "But I'll keep an eye on him." Though I wasn't sure that was true. They were Shane's parents, not mine. It was out of my hands.

The lights dimmed, and the triumphant music swelled through the theater. My thoughts were everywhere but on the big screen. Emma's heartbreak, my event procurement, my marriage, and now Fred's health. What else could happen?

The opening credits had barely finished when my ringtone cut through the silence. "Damn it." I fumbled with the volume button, knocking my candy onto the sticky floor. The theater was nearly empty, with an unbothered elderly couple seated far below us, but I still flushed with embarrassment.

It vibrated again. And again.

I looked at the screen.

UW HOSPITAL

The letters glowed, and my jaw locked. Hospitals never called with good news. Not repeatedly.

"Oh, no!"

"What is it?" Claudia clutched the armrest as I jumped up and shuffled down the aisle. Every horrible scenario entered my mind as I raced toward the exit. Emma got in a car accident on her way home, Ethan fell on his skateboard, or Elliott had an allergic reaction. An eternity of worries compressed into seconds until I pushed through the theater door into the empty corridor. I took a deep breath.

"Hello?" My voice sounded panicked, as if it belonged to someone else.

"Katherine Valentine? I'm afraid there's been an accident."

FOUR

ISABELLA

Davis shuffled to my desk again, stressed to the max, as rain hammered the office windows like it was trying to break in and drown us all. Seattle's atmospheric river, which sounded low-key fake, had everyone on edge.

My third cup of coffee sat cold on my desk. I'd been staring at the same email for twenty minutes. I was barely functioning, but Davis couldn't sit still for more than thirty seconds.

"Iz, can I get your help? Again?" He braced himself like he expected me to hit him.

"I'm having trouble tracking down the details for the latest mailer messaging. Did Shane talk to you about them? Text you anything?"

I shook my head. Shane and I texted constantly, but usually about when and where to fuck, not campaign strategy.

"Shit. I've been trying to get Shane's voicemails from his

phone, but maybe it's dead or something. I need to check in with Katie about it."

Katie. Katherine. Shane's wife. The one he swore for months he was leaving. The woman he claimed was ruining his life, making him miserable, driving him to seek comfort elsewhere. All the talking points from the cheater's playbook.

I glanced toward the flooded window again, where I could make out the Four Seasons through the downpour.

When you're the secret, date nights mean hotel rooms. Neutral ground. An affair hiding inside a hundred others. Fun, reckless, intoxicating.

Water streaked down the glass like tears the building was crying for all the shitty decisions made inside it, including mine. Room 1847. I could still remember the number, which was pathetic. Shane had ordered champagne I couldn't pronounce and told me Katherine hadn't touched him in months. The sheets were Egyptian cotton, and the lies were bargain-bin cheap. That day was unforgettable because, *hello,* Four Seasons, but also because he'd promised me that he was leaving his wife. Exactly what I'd needed to hear.

"Can I help? I can stop by the hospital and find the phone myself?" The words were out before I realized how dumb they sounded.

"And who are you going to say you are? His coworker? His mistress?" Davis snapped.

The word hung in my head. *Mistress.* Like I was some corset-laced paramour waiting for my married lover to return from the war. Why wasn't there a similar term for single men who boned married women? Besides "lucky," apparently.

Shane was the one with the obligation, not me. I was young, single, and nobody's side piece in my narrative.

Mistress felt like another word for victim. And I wasn't here to become just another one of Shane Sutton's victims. I was here to make him mine.

"Don't call me that."

Davis studied me with those dark brown eyes that saw too much. "What would you prefer? The other woman? Girlfriend? Future Mrs. Sutton?"

I glared, deciding if he was being cruel or brutally honest. Probably both. Davis had a talent for delivering the truth with enough gentleness that you couldn't hate him for it.

"You know nothing about us."

He softened for a fraction of a second—not with concern, which I could have handled, but with something worse: pity. The same look people gave me as a kid when my mom begged on the street, and they'd drop a quarter in her cup and glance at me with those sad eyes. *Oh, poor thing, and you deserve better, but I'm not going to do anything about it personally*. I hated it then. I hated it now.

"I know more than you think, Iz." He lowered his voice.

"What does that mean?"

Davis straightened and rubbed the back of his neck. "Nothing. Forget it. I'm stressed about this whole thing."

But the seed was planted. He knew about Shane and me. What else did he know?

"Yeah," I said. "Same."

Davis gently placed a hand on my shoulder, and I tried to ignore the warmth it sent down my arm. "Sorry, Iz, not trying to be a dick. I appreciate you wanting to help. This is not ideal."

"You say that like we're handling a bad Yelp review and not a nearly dead man." My mouth moved faster than my filter. "But yeah, totally, we're fine. Everything's fine."

Nothing was fine. Nothing had been okay since that call from the mountain.

"I wish this were all over," Davis mumbled before walking away.

Shane's life was on the line. He'd taken tumbles before on his wild adventures; his body was a scrapbook of scars, each one with a story he loved to brag about. But this time was different. Backcountry skiing in a restricted area triggered a slough, a mini avalanche, nearly suffocating him. Poor Davis witnessed the whole thing in horror, and by the time the ski patrol found him, Shane had been buried for almost twenty minutes. CPR kept him alive in Vancouver, and they medevaced him to the UW Medical Center, where he'd been in a medically induced coma for the past week.

If Shane died today, all the sneaking around, the lies, the waiting, would have been for nothing. Months of my life I'd never get back. I knew what people might think about me, about me dating the boss. They'd call me a homewrecker, as if the house hadn't already collapsed by the time I showed up with a sledgehammer.

But nobody else would understand how Shane was my path out. My chance at stability. My family's safety. Everything I'd craved since childhood.

He was my ladder out of the pit I'd been born into.

I wasn't stupid enough to think it was love, but I was desperate enough to believe it was worth it.

I opened my phone and performed my masochistic ritual, clicking on Katherine's Facebook profile. Shane didn't have an account, and I kept my distance from personal social media while running Sutton Strategy's accounts. It was a slick cover for surveillance for feeding the obsession I couldn't shake.

I didn't need to ask what Shane saw in her; waif-like and tall and blonde, like she'd walked off a fashion runway in Milan and accidentally landed in Seattle. I scrolled through smiling photos, the most recent, a selfie of her and the kids opening Christmas gifts. Perfect mother. Perfect wife. I'd memorized her life in fragments: the artistically posed family Christmas cards, the candid beach photos where she still looked flawless. Their wedding photos, with Katherine glowing and Shane's parents beaming next to them.

It was a family dynasty with roots so deep you could burn the tree down, and it would still grow back. I was a dandelion in comparison—scrappy, invasive, something people spend money on to destroy.

I scrolled to my favorite photo, the only one I was in, the first time I saw Shane in person. A fundraiser at their home in Magnolia, where I'd been hired as a server. It surprised me how attractive I found him, almost twenty years my senior, though he didn't look it. Fit and confident, the kind of guy who commanded attention without demanding it. By the end of the night, he'd offered me his card and suggested I apply for the role of his assistant. It was so easy. Too easy.

I should have known then. Nothing good ever comes easy.

I switched to my messages; Mom, and the most recent

photo she sent of her and Pop. They were standing in front of the greenhouse, squinting into the sun. They looked happy. Tired as hell, but happy.

"Tammi, I'm not feeling well. I'm going to head home," I whispered over our receptionist's desk, glancing back to see Davis, head down, working, praying I didn't pass anyone in the parking garage. Everything in this office reminded me of Shane. The stale smell of the elevator, where we'd make out between floors, turned my stomach. The cold, hollow sound of the parking structure, where we'd sneak kisses when nobody was looking, made me want to jump off the side of it.

I drove out of the parking lot of the Seattle Bay Tower, breathing for the first time since Shane's accident. Behind me, the building rose into the gray sky like a middle finger. The further away I drove, the easier it was to breathe. My wipers fought a losing battle against the atmospheric river, which was straight-up a lot of fucking rain.

I could complain about many things here. The shitty weather, the expensive housing, but traffic? Never. Gridlock or open road, I loved being in the car. It's where I did my best thinking. Maybe it was nostalgia, the way I escaped my tense living situation growing up.

My daydreams as a young girl weren't of Prince Charming or becoming a veterinarian. They were about waking up with a mother who didn't believe the government was trying to poison us and a father who didn't wear a tin foil hat…literally. I'd dream of school friends and birthday parties instead of being homeschooled at the kitchen table in a converted barn with plywood walls that never kept out the cold.

I'd been plotting my exit before I ever knew my life wasn't normal.

Perhaps I could find a new job, forget about Sutton Strategy, and leave Shane, Katherine, and Davis behind. Walk away clean, start over somewhere else. Change my name, dye my hair. There were always other ways to make money, like waiting tables, hustling, and petty theft. Skills I'd mastered out of necessity. But none would get me the payout Shane could.

I turned up the volume when "Did Something Bad" popped up on my playlist. Almost without realizing it, I was pulling off I-5 onto 520 toward the hospital, where I was definitely not supposed to be heading.

No, I couldn't stop now.

Forget Davis's mistress comment. I would waltz my way into the hospital, even if only to glimpse Shane. Sign in as family, fake a name. What are they going to do, demand DNA?

In the car, I rehearsed what I'd say if confronted. I was the assistant, checking on my boss. Or I was his cousin from out of town, just arrived. I was delivering important documents. The lies came easily, each one a small brick in the wall I was building between Katherine and Shane to get him to leave her. Sometimes I caught myself believing them.

I entered the hospital, scoured the directory for the ICU, and passed the lobby café. As soon as I saw her, adrenaline shot through me like a lightning bolt.

Katherine. The woman I'd been avoiding. The woman who had secrets of her own.

I ducked behind a large marble pillar that reeked of Purell. Katherine sat at a corner table, posture too relaxed for someone with a husband in a coma upstairs. Across from her sat a man with his back to me, broad-shouldered and tall, wearing a forest green jacket with the collar flipped up.

I moved behind a large potted plant, close enough to see her face clearly. Her eyes were puffy and red, but she was smiling. Actually smiling. He squeezed her hand. Like they'd done it a thousand times before.

Shane had insisted Katherine was cheating. I'd nodded along, filed it away as another manipulation tactic, making himself the victim, but this? This was real.

Here she was, a perfect wife and mother, getting cozy with another man while her husband fought for his life. I pulled out my phone and snapped a photo. Ammunition. Insurance.

They stood, and I maneuvered around the pillar to stay hidden. When they stopped, the man took her arm and pulled her in for a hug. They lingered.

Then he walked toward the exit, while she sauntered toward the ICU.

My mouth went dry. Bold move, meeting your lover in the same hospital where your husband battled for survival.

From one man to the next. Playing both sides. The hypocrisy gagged me.

Shane was right about Katherine all along, and now I had proof. I raced back to my car.

All I needed was for Shane Sutton to wake up.

And finally divorce her.

FIVE

KATHERINE

I shuffled down the corridor toward Intensive Care. Two weeks of sleepless nights had made this route as recognizable as my own hallway at home, past vending machines humming like dying insects. The indefinable hospital smell permeated everything, clinging to my clothes and hair when I left, though I seldom did. Time bent strangely here; Monday bled into Tuesday. Or was it Wednesday? I checked my phone. Friday. I'd worn the same sweater three days in a row.

I settled into the vinyl chair that had molded itself to my body, and the cushion wheezed beneath me. Shane lay motionless, his once-commanding presence reduced to this broken figure. His face was swollen with bruises, his head partially shaved, with tubes disappearing into his mouth. The ventilator pushed air into his lungs, chest rising and falling in an unnaturally perfect rhythm. I still couldn't reconcile this fragile shell with the man who once dominated rooms with charisma, who made decisions affecting thousands with unwavering confidence.

The extent of Shane's brain trauma would remain unknown until they weaned him off medication, which they hoped to do soon. Amazingly, the rest of his body was in excellent shape, with no broken bones, only slight frostbite that might affect movement, and questions about nerve damage.

My phone rang. It was Ethan.

"Hi, sweetie—"

"Mom, it's not fair; everyone is going," Ethan interrupted with teen outrage.

I had expected this call. "I know, bud. I'm so sorry." The Puget Academy Football Retreat payment had slipped through the cracks on top of Elliott's orthodontist appointment and picking up Emma's cheer uniform at the dry cleaners. All things others could have done if I'd let them. But I wanted things done right, so I did them myself. Always. If the situation were reversed, and I were nearly dead in that hospital bed, the world might very well have screeched to a halt.

The room spun, a snow globe in someone else's hands. I was failing at the one thing I always believed I did well: keeping the family machine running.

"I know Shane is hurt, but Mom, we still need you!"

Before I could respond, I heard my mother in the background. "Give me the phone, sweetheart."

"Katie?" The shrillness of her voice slid straight under my skin. "I assumed I'd hear from you before now."

Oh, fun, a guilt trip, as always. "A lot going on, Mom."

"How's Shane?" The question I answered daily.

"No changes since yesterday," I said.

"No changes mean he's not getting worse. I'll take that. Ethan tells me about this retreat payment—"

"I'll fix it," I shot. "I always fix it."

"Yes, but if you came home more often—"

"Mom, I need to be here."

She paused, then softened her tone. "Bert and Patty send their prayers. I've been praying too. Every morning and night."

I bit back the response I wanted to give. My mother knew I was agnostic, something she treated as a phase even after decades, sending me Bible verses "just in case" and assuring church friends I was still seeking. She never missed an opportunity to remind me what she believed I was missing.

"Mom, prayers are great, but what the kids need is—"

"I know, I know," she interrupted. "But a little faith wouldn't hurt you, Katie. In times like these, we need something bigger than ourselves to lean on."

The ongoing disagreement drifted between us, with her certainty opposing my doubts, her rigid beliefs against my messy questions. We were experts at skirting around what mattered. I swallowed my retort—another battle for another day.

"I talked to Nancy. Oh, the poor thing, she's sick over this. They love that boy so much," she said. "Imagine your only child near death. It's so sad. If anything happened to you, oh, I don't know what I'd do."

"Fred and Nancy are staying strong," I said. Shane's mother was as overbearing as mothers came, but I would never pretend to understand another family's wounds. I was still deciphering my own. I'd tried several times to get Fred alone to check on him after what Claudia told me, but Nancy kept him close, like a protective shadow.

"Oh, by the way, I threw in a load of laundry for you."

"Thanks, Mom. You didn't have to do that." The words were automatic, even as I winced inwardly, picturing my colors bleeding into whites. I wanted to beg her to stop touching my laundry, but the thought of seeming ungrateful was worse than quietly redoing it later.

I wouldn't describe my mother as helpful, though she certainly would. When the kids were younger, she'd offer to lend a hand but complain about lost sleep and how exhausting they were. Her help was often more work than her absence. But if I didn't take her up on her offer, she'd worry herself sick, and I'd hear about that, too.

Still, I tried to be appreciative. She made sure nobody slept in, and no doors were left unlocked. The kids were self-sufficient, and their father handled the rest. I'd returned home a few times to replenish clothes, shower, and leave again, spending most of my time at Shane's bedside. I yawned. "Please don't leave out any socks," I begged.

"Are you eating? You looked a little thin when I saw you."

Couldn't end the call without a backhanded insult. "Mom, I'm fine. I need to go, okay?"

"Okay, love you, sweetie."

"Love you, too."

I ended the call, and an email alert appeared. ***URGENT: Special Meeting for Curriculum Integrity.***

I dropped my head back. It was Melanie Anderson, the PTA president, who everyone privately called "Melania" for her Stepford-adjacent perfection and her unwavering belief that her opinions were facts. She was the type who preached purity while dropping racist comments, shooting up Botox and Ozempic, and hustling supplements. And the same woman who kept Emma's article from being published.

Dear Concerned Parents,

It has come to the attention of several members of our community that certain materials being assigned in upper-level English and history classes contain divisive content inappropriate for our children. Some include graphic sexual content and promote anti-religious messaging that has no place in our school.

In the interest of transparency and to protect the innocence of our children, we will hold an emergency session this Thursday at 2 PM to form the Puget Academy Parents' Coalition. We believe that parental rights are paramount in education, and that parents—not educators with woke agendas—should determine what our children are exposed to.

We hope you'll join us in this vital work of reclaiming our schools.

In partnership, Melanie Anderson

The buzzwords leaped off the screen like trained seals,

each one a tiny, infuriating echo of Shane's recent work. I could hear the smooth, charming tone he used when coaching clients. Hell, I'd heard this exact pitch at the dinner table.

Meanwhile, Melanie's son, Brock, who regularly got in trouble at school for drug and alcohol infractions and a streaking incident, was calling books and articles inappropriate.

How rich.

I closed the email before I could do something stupid, like reply. Let them have their little coalition. One more fire burning too close to home.

I pocketed my phone as a way-too-cheerful nurse greeted me. "Mrs. Sutton?"

"It's Valentine," I corrected for the millionth time. Shane had wanted me to take his last name, but I loved mine. It was one of the beautiful things my parents gave me.

"Sorry, Ms. Valentine." She handed me a deceptively heavy bag. "These are some of Mr. Sutton's belongings that arrived."

"Thank you." I was happy to have a project to anchor me in this time warp.

I pulled out his phone, which was long dead, and stared at it before plugging it in. What secrets did it hold? A few weeks ago, I'd planned to search it, convinced he was hiding more than I already knew, a suspicion that now felt trivial.

The black screen reflected my tired face. I pressed the power button, and the Apple logo glowed white, followed by a feverish cascade of notifications. It was too much. I set it aside.

I pulled out his wallet and flipped through it, making a

mental note to alert the banks that the cards were no longer missing.

I took out a watch and his company badge and saw his wedding ring in a small plastic bag. Had he taken it off? Or had someone else? I squinted to read the engraving of our wedding date: 2-14-2022. Valentine's Day. Our inside joke now soured.

I had no intention of getting married again, but Shane had swept me off my feet when he'd proposed the year before. He made a corny joke about Valentine's Day being "my day," and I pretended I hadn't heard that joke hundreds of times. People said we were rushing, and maybe we were, but with him lying in the hospital bed, weak and vulnerable, for a moment, all I saw was the man I'd fallen for.

"Don't die," I whispered.

His phone rang, startling me. I craned my neck to answer it, still tethered to the wall.

"Hello?"

"Oh, Katie! Hi, how's Shane?" Davis, Shane's coworker, had the same question as everyone else. *The* question.

"He's the same, not better or worse."

"Let me know as soon as he wakes up. Obviously, we're all... we're all worried about him over here."

"Yeah, for sure." The phone continued chirping and buzzing against my cheek as more emails and texts loaded.

"Anyway," Davis continued, "I've been trying to remote dial to get his voicemail, but it hasn't worked."

"Yes, the nurse gave it to me just now. Can I help?" I sounded more upbeat than I meant, grasping for tasks to keep me busy.

"I'll come get the phone myself." His voice was tight and urgent.

"I'm happy to listen to his messages—"

"No!" He interrupted, then continued with forced calmness. "I mean, it's complicated. Legal stuff. I'll be there in twenty minutes."

Cold crept up my neck as the call ended. Why would he want to battle rush hour traffic to drive across town when I could look through Shane's phone myself?

"Davis, I really don't mind."

"I'm already on my way. Just…don't look at it, okay? Please."

The line went dead.

I was absolutely going to look at it.

How had Claudia put it at the movie theater? *Set my mind at ease?* I could use some significant mind-easing. "This will be helpful for everyone," I whispered to my unconscious husband.

I held the phone above his face, feeling ridiculous but desperate. To my surprise, the facial recognition worked despite his swollen features and the tubes obscuring half his face.

It unlocked with a cheerful chime, obscenely bright in the sterile silence.

I opened his messages, heart pounding so loudly I was sure the nurses would hear it. Davis's voice had triggered an alarm I couldn't ignore.

I browsed through work messages and client communications, finding nothing out of the ordinary. Then a name caught my eye.

Linda. My mother.

My first thought was oddly mundane—an anniversary surprise? But as my eyes focused on the words, the mundane shattered into sinister.

... worried about Katie. She's been acting paranoid lately...

I blinked, sure I'd misread. I scrolled up to find context, but instead found message after message between my husband and my mother about me.

Blood rushed in my ears. I read and re-read the messages, desperately hoping I'd misunderstood.

Linda, I'm really worried about Katie. She's been acting paranoid lately, accusing me of things, following me. I think it's getting worse. Do you think she might be hiding something?

Oh dear, I've noticed, too. She's not herself. Do you think she's drinking too much? I worry, because of Bill...

Bill. My dad. They were comparing me to him at his worst. My mother and my husband, the two people who were supposed to protect me, were conspiring to make me doubt my own mind.

It reminded me of how he'd dismissed former employees: "They're unstable," he'd say. "Emotional." The same man who once advocated for mental health support was privately using my anxiety against me.

I was simply another opponent to manage.

I backed out to the main message list before I could fully process the betrayal, and another name caught my eye.

Hey, it's Chelsea. I'm at the bar.

Where are you??

Did you seriously stand me up?

SENT VIA ONTHESIDE.COM

The hyperlink glowed blue. OntheSide.com. What the hell was that?

I clicked it, and a browser window opened, loading a website with a sleek black interface and tagline: *Discreet connections for discerning professionals.*

A dating site.

Shane's profile loaded automatically, still logged in. The photo showed him from behind, shirtless, muscular, and artfully anonymous.

Username: Seth_Seattle.

Age: 42.

Status: Widowed.

Fake name, fake age, and widowed.

I scrolled through his profile with numb fingers. His bio was a masterpiece of fiction:

Successful businessman looking for connection after loss. My wife passed three years ago, and I'm ready to move forward. Seeking someone genuine, drama-free, who understands that discretion is essential. Let's make the most of our time.

Passed three years ago. When we were newly engaged and

living together. He wasn't lying by omission; he was actively telling women I was dead.

The matches section showed dozens of women. Dozens. Each with flirty messages, each clearly believing they were special to him. Page after page.

I clicked on Chelsea's to piece together their connection. The timestamp of their planned date was the night of his accident.

She'd waited at the bar. He'd never shown up because he was buried in snow.

I scrolled and scrolled, taking screenshots.

Rhonda in Tacoma. Abby in Portland. Ruby in Vancouver. Each one with contact information listed, with months and months of messages.

The sounds of the heart monitor filled my ears—beep, beep, beep—like applause for Shane's performance. The only proof he was still alive and breathing. Still capable of more damage.

I wished he wasn't.

I heard footsteps in the hallway.

Davis.

I closed the OntheSide website and navigated back to a message thread between Davis and Shane, leaving it open on the screen. Then I collected my things. I wouldn't be staying one more night in this purgatory with that comatose asshole.

"Katie." Davis was out of breath, flushed. His eyes went immediately to the phone.

I held it in front of his face so he could see the screen.

Katie called the office looking for you. She's getting suspicious.

She believes what I tell her.

Sweat beaded on his forehead.

"Katie, I can explain—"

I slapped the phone into his hand, hard enough to hurt. "Save it."

I pushed through the exit doors into the February cold, the shock of it welcome. Shane was worse than I ever knew. But I finally had the evidence I needed; the proof that I wasn't losing my mind.

SIX

ISABELLA

Irritating plastic needles scraped against my forearms as I yanked fake tree branches out like my life depended on it. Neil made me wait until February 1st to take the office Christmas tree down for some stupid-ass reason—something about clients appreciating tradition. *Whatever.* Today, this monstrosity was going down.

I hated Christmas and every festive symbol of it. Wreaths, trees, tinsel, candy canes, all of it. It was so over the top. I'm sure it had to do with my lackluster Christmases. My mom broke the news to me early on that Santa was fake and doubled down, with Jesus being a ruse, too. So, yeah, the holiday season and its icons were a big lie about lying liars. Ironic, considering my job and my relationship were built on spin. And here I was deconstructing a tree that cost more than my car.

"You took that down fast, Lassie!" Patrick joked as I pushed the giant box into the utility closet. He always leaned into the accent when he spoke to me. Whenever he called Neil an *Eejit* or yelled at the *Banjaxed* copy machine, I'd burst into laughter, which made Shane annoyed, as if fun itself was a threat to productivity.

I'd never admit it out loud, but the office was lighter without Shane. Less stress, more fun. Parents' out-of-town energy.

Tammi caught me tossing a stack of Make Christmas Great Again posters in the trash.

"That was a flop, wasn't it?" She laughed.

I snorted. One of Shane's worst ideas yet. The man who insisted on conventional media presence had no clue his audience was watching TikToks, not TV. But hey, his dinosaur approach meant job security for those of us who could actually reach voters under fifty.

Even Patrick and Neil, the boomers among us, knew Shane's approach was, well, *old.* Politics today was all algorithms and rage bait. It's why he relied on young assistants like me to translate boomer-speak into content that wouldn't make Gen Z voters cringe themselves to death.

"Clark Davis, is there a Clark Davis here?" A deliveryman called into the lobby, awkwardly next to a stack of boxes with "Repeal Climate Commitment" stamped on the sides. Another day, another headache.

"It's Davis Clark," Davis corrected, jogging over, emerging from the strategy room with frustration, telling me his recent meeting hadn't gone well. "Trust me, I know it's confusing. My parents thought hyphenated names were too mainstream, so they just…didn't pick."

Davis was Shane's favorite "overcame adversity" story: two

last names, no stable home, a full-ride scholarship funded by Sutton Stars.

"Whatever it is, sign here, please."

Davis surveyed the boxes. "Fuck." He threw his head back. "These are for the climate initiative and were supposed to go to the Puget Coalition office."

Tammi tilted her head. "I thought we weren't taking on that initiative?"

"We weren't, but McFadden's team wants us to rebrand their environmental stance as conservation-minded instead of climate skeptical," Davis said.

"Wait." Tammi scowled. "So, we're reversing the climate policies we literally promoted last election?"

"Yeah," Davis said, not elaborating, though his face gave the honest answer. "Iz, I'm sorry to dump this on you, but I've got fires here. Can you bring this downtown? They're already four days late."

He peeled off his jacket, and sweat plastered his shirt to his biceps. A dangerous idea crossed my mind—what if Shane never came back? Davis was right here. Available. Hot as shit. My brain went straight to rebound. *Chill!*

I pushed the thoughts away immediately. No. Shane was my ticket out. Davis was a complication I couldn't afford.

"No problem, I got it."

"You're the best, Iz. I owe you. I'll run them to your car."

He picked up the box and walked away, shoulders slumped. I was sympathetic, though I couldn't help but wonder why he stayed if he hated the new direction so much. His love-hate thing with Shane baffled me. He'd tell you Shane saved his life, which I thought was a bit dramatic. A decade ago, when Davis was in the Sutton Stars scholarship program, Shane took him in as an intern, then as an associate, and now as the campaign director. Ten years of job growth on paper, that looked like ass-kissing in person.

Then again, who was I to judge? We all had our reasons for being here, our private calculations of what we were willing to gamble for a chance at something better. Also, Davis looked really good when he was stressed, which was information my brain had no business cataloging, but there it was anyway.

I sat at my desk, preparing to leave, and grabbed my phone. I opened Messenger and read my mom's last text.

Pop's numbers aren't good :(

We needed more time and more money. And I was running out of both faster than I could hustle. I typed back:

Hang in there <3

I switched to Facebook and opened Katherine's profile. Her recent status was cryptic: **Ready for new things in the new year! Bring it on.**

But there were no new updates on Shane since I spied on her at the hospital last week. I scanned through the comments and read one from her bestie, Claudia Davidson: **Here for you, always xo.** Did Claudia know something I didn't? Had Katie already moved on with that dude I saw her with in the hospital? My throat tightened at the thought of going back home empty-handed after I'd promised Mom I'd find a way to help.

I tossed my phone in my bag and headed through the office. "Tammi, I'll be back."

She peeked around the dozen flower arrangements and gift baskets, fresh arrivals from people stopping in daily. The Sutton name carried weight in Seattle, mostly from Fred, who'd built the firm. Shane had filled me in on every detail of his origin story, loving to narrate his rise, while I avoided sharing. If there was a banner or a podium, he wanted the Sutton name on it. Though with the new direction from progressive to fascism, the name Sutton was becoming more and more tainted.

"You got it," Tammi said. "See you tomorrow."

I opened my car door and heard a distant voice. I spun to find a petite woman outside the parking garage near the street. She waved as if I should know her. Maybe a reporter. Was that Anna Dollarhide? She had been lurking outside the building lately, trying to gather dirt for her latest hit piece. I walked closer, the cement echoing with each step.

She gripped her purse strap nervously. "Are you Shane's new assistant?"

"Uh, yes." I kept my distance. "Have we met?"

"I'm Jessica Banks."

"Isabella." I instinctively put my keys in my hand to strike. She was shorter than I was, with clear skin and fine lines around her eyes. Floral dress, ballet flats, tight bun. She looked like she'd left a church craft circle, but my nerves spiked anyway.

"Can I help you?"

"I know it's weird showing up like this, but I read about the accident, about Shane." Her voice trembled. "I tried to come into the building, but…"

I suddenly remembered where else I'd seen her face: on the "do not admit" sheet at the security desk.

"Why are you here?"

She reached into her purse, and before I could react with a key-stabbing to the face, she pulled out a card and handed it to me. "Shane Sutton is not a good man."

No shit, Sherlock. I already knew everything about Shane. *Didn't I?*

I took the card from her hand, which listed her name and phone number. My mouth went dry. "What do you mean?"

"You know exactly what I mean." Her eyes held mine, searching. "The late nights. The hotel rooms. I know you're not just working for him."

The blood drained from my face. "I don't—"

"Please." She held up her hand. "I'm not judging you. I was you, Isabella. Until I wasn't anymore."

A shiver ran down my spine, stealing my words.

"My advice is to get far away from him while you can. Davis Clark, too." She pointed to the card. "Get out before you end up like the others." Who was she scared of? Shane? Davis? Me?

The doors of the parking garage opened, and the security guard appeared, startling us. Before I could turn around, Jessica was scurrying away, dress flowing in the Fourth Avenue breeze. I stood by my car, unnerved and confused. What the hell?

"Wait. Jessica," I shouted as she crossed the street. It was like chasing the horror-movie extra who'd seen the monster nobody believes exists. Except in this case, I was the skeptic and maybe the next victim. "You can't drop that on me and leave."

Her words played over and over in my head. *Shane Sutton is not a good man. Davis Clark, too. Get out before you end up like the others.*

The security guard approached me. "You okay, miss?"

"Yeah, I'm good, thanks."

I opened my car door and sat in the front seat, staring at Jessica's card.

My mom always taught me that information is power, but in this case, I was powerless as all hell.

Or was I?

SEVEN

KATHERINE

"He went on and on about how much he missed the love of his life. Made a whole show of it, and I swear, there were tears."

Rhonda's smooth, buttery voice came through my car speakers.

"Yep. A professional liar," I said.

It was surreal discussing my husband's sexual exploits with a beautiful stranger who knew the taste of his skin as well as I did. I should have felt rage or jealousy, but instead, I had a morbid fascination, as if I were discussing a character in a film rather than the man I'd shared my bed with. Rhonda was one of my new acquaintances, thanks to my well-laid husband. Soon to be ex-husband.

"He sure had me fooled. I mean, they all lie, but this prick takes the cake. Figures he's in marketing. He's a true marketing genius for his dick," Rhonda mocked.

"Yep. Create a narrative, stick to it, discredit anyone who questions it," I said. "He's been using the same tactics on me."

Rhonda clicked her tongue. "You know, for someone who just learned her husband had a secret stash of mistresses, you seem remarkably…clear-headed."

I laughed. "Clarity comes when you realize everything you believed was a lie."

And everything was. To me, to Rhonda. They'd met up for dinner one night when he told me he had a client meeting and told her it was a conference. He hid behind fake meetings and campaign trips, using outdoor adventures as covers for indoor escapades. A biking trip in Colorado turned into a rendezvous with MileHighClubKim, a ski trip in Montana was where he met MollyinMT, and a rafting trip segued into a booty call with YakMack in Yakima. There was a time when his mysteriousness was sexy, like I'd won the affections of a man too important to be fully known.

Turns out I didn't know him at all.

I'd talked to almost every woman in his digital rolodex since I found it, and they all echoed the same thing: they had no idea "Seth" was still married. His wife miraculously resurrected from the dead. Every conversation confirmed my worst fears. Shane was a narcissistic, abusive asshole, and worse than I ever realized.

I'd known there were women before me, plenty of them. Shane was the ultimate bachelor. But he said he was willing to give all of that up for me.

Then he proposed, and I fell for it. All of it.

His last assistant, Jessica Banks, showed up at the house

once, distraught, right after I moved in with him. I'd asked if he'd been unfaithful to me. We'd only been together a few months at that point, so knowing me, I would have let it go. But Shane swore up and down she'd been well before my time, then became obsessed with him, jealous, unable to let him go.

"Never again," he'd promised. "No more assistants. I've learned my lesson."

I believed him because, back then, I believed everything.

And he kept that promise. No assistants until the most recent one he hired last fall. I thought maybe he'd grown out of the temptation. Little did I know he had dozens of women online to entertain him in between. The sneaky behavior I'd chalked up to changing politics was more complicated than I'd realized. How Shane managed to keep up the ruse for so long without me noticing was impressive and horrifying.

"Thank you again for chatting with me, Rhonda. I know it's weird, and I'm sorry it's under these circumstances."

"It's my pleasure, Katie. I'm glad you told me, and I'm glad you are leaving that piece of trash."

We said our goodbyes, and I pulled my car off the Queen Anne exit. I wasn't hurt or jealous; I was completely and utterly unfeeling, which made it easier to go through the motions. As of this morning, Shane was still unconscious, so my silent wish that he wouldn't wake up could still come true. Death would be simpler than divorce. At least the life insurance policy was solid. The thought made me sick with guilt, yet I couldn't deny the calm imagining a world without Shane in it: no messy divorces, no fights in court.

What filled me with dread was breaking the news to the kids, and worse, telling my mother. She admired Shane's public image as an all-American, God-fearing, churchgoing person. He had her wrapped around his finger more than I ever realized. I hadn't spoken to her since I found her texts with Shane, and I couldn't stomach hearing her justify him. She believed in till death do us part, and I had yet to keep a relationship intact. She taught me to be agreeable and not make waves. To top it off, Shane's mom, Nancy, was her bestie, which was another awkward dynamic I'd have to navigate.

I pulled up to the Davidson's house next to a large, rusty, orange Ford F-150 with temporary plates and walked to the door. I welcomed the interruption from my spiraling thoughts about impending poverty. If anyone could pull me out of panic, it was my brutally honest best friend, who was right more often than I wanted. She'd been my anchor through my last divorce, too.

"I want to rip that douchebag's dick off," Claudia blurted, flinging the door open.

"Well, line up because it's probably inside someone else at his rate."

"Gross," she snorted. "You see Melania's email?"

I groaned, which was its own answer.

"I know, she sucks." Claudia threw her head back. "But not if we have anything to say about it. You coming to the meeting on Thursday?"

"I don't know. Maybe." Likely not. I had enough battles to fight for the moment.

We moved from the foyer, and I sat at the kitchen table as she put dishes in the sink. "Hey, speaking of dicks, you know Todd Anderson? I hope it's okay, but I gave him your number. He's easily the hottest single dad at Puget Academy."

"Claudia, what? It's way too soon!"

"Oh, come on, live a little, Valentine! What a great outlet."

"He's Melanie Anderson's ex; that's a huge red flag."

"Yeah, but he left her," she said. "Plus, he's a Scorpio, which should make it spicy. I can live vicariously through you again."

"I'm sure you would." Even when I dated lightly before Shane, she thrived on every PG-13 detail. She might be right. Shane indulged while we were married. Perhaps it was my turn. And she wasn't wrong about his hotness. "Hot Toddy" was his secret nickname among the moms at school.

"Chris will be down in a sec, but…" She wiped her hands on a dishcloth and looked at me sheepishly. "There is something else I need to tell you."

"Oh, no, what now?"

"I found a vape pen in Joshua's backpack, and he said he got it from Ethan."

I dropped my head to the counter. "You've got to be kidding me."

"I know, I wasn't going to say anything about it, but—"

"No, of course, I want you to tell me," I said against the cold quartz.

Chris bounded downstairs and kissed Claudia, then turned to me. "Hey, Katie."

I picked my head up and gestured out to the driveway. "That truck is fucking hideous."

"See?" Clauda said.

"It's a classic!"

Chris and I moved to the living room, and I plopped down on the couch across from him. He pulled paperwork out of a file and set it between us.

"I'm really sorry about this, Kat—"

"Me first. I need to get through these questions." I pulled my planner out of my purse, filled with pages of color-coded notes.

"Okay. Go ahead." Chris knew better than to argue.

"All right, is it possible to invalidate the prenup?"

That was the question and the problem, the reason I'd stopped myself every time I considered packing up and driving away. I'd get nothing if I initiated a divorce: no alimony, no share of Sutton Strategy, nothing. The righteousness I once had signing the document—*Look how evolved I am! How not-gold-digger!*—now sat like a chokehold. *A formality*, he'd said. So, I wrote my swirly signature and put my initials on page after page. I suppose nobody marries with the end in mind. I'd believed in forever once, so desperate to prove to everyone, my mom, my friends, myself, I could make marriage work this time, and I wasn't the failure my first divorce suggested.

"Under some circumstances," Chris said.

"Like?" The question came out more desperate than I meant.

"Duress, lack of disclosure, something unconscionable." Chris folded his hands. "If Shane had any assets you didn't know about when signing, or if he coerced you in any way, even subtle psychological pressure, we might have grounds. Washington courts have sometimes invalidated prenups when one party didn't have full financial disclosure."

My mind raced. "He always kept his investment portfolios separate. He said it was 'too complicated' to explain. The Sutton Stars program is separate, too."

Chris scribbled on his legal pad. "The scholarship program? Tell me more."

Sutton Stars, Fred's creation, Shane's public proof of generosity. "There's not much for me to tell. Shane operates it himself."

"Interesting. Mixing nonprofit finances with personal assets can create vulnerabilities. We should investigate that." Chris jotted something else down. "It's a start."

My phone rattled again on the table. Fred.

"Do you need to get that?" Chris gestured toward my phone and handed me a paper with sticky arrows, officially hiring him as my lawyer. Again.

"I'm going to let it go to voicemail." I signed paper after paper. "It's Shane's dad."

Chris looked up. "How's he taking this?"

I gave a half-shrug because I wasn't sure. I hadn't spoken to them in the past week, ignoring their calls. How do you tell grieving parents who almost lost their son that he was an absolute abomination as a husband and human? As much as I hated his guts, Shane was their child, and someone had to care for him. It certainly would not be me.

The voicemail popped up, and I set down my pen. "One sec."

I listened. Fred's voice was strained and weak. "Katie, hi, a few things. First, Nancy's becoming obsessed with Shane's accident… thinking the ski patrol was negligent and that the rescue team took too long. You know how she gets. I wanted to make sure you're prepared in case you hear from her or visit the hospital. Also, I want to discuss some financial concerns with you, not in front of Shane. We miss you, honey. Okay. Bye."

Chris looked at me again. "What is it?"

I shot him a flat stare and deleted the voicemail. "Nothing. One of Nancy's dramatic outbursts."

"Mother-in-law from hell?" Chris grimaced.

"You have no idea. She's convinced the world is constantly conspiring against her perfect son." She couldn't accept her golden boy being reckless enough to ski in a dangerous zone, so she was searching for someone to blame. "Next week, it will be some other imagined slight."

"Sounds like a piece of work. Guess you won't miss her," he said, as if there was some silver lining, and I suppose he was right. "And Fred? What's he like?"

"Oh, he's much different. Kind. Respected." Though silently, I worried about his health, and now, his financial concerns.

I finished signing papers, and Chris stacked them in a neat pile. "Well, that's it for now. I'll have the team start on discovery. Once Shane wakes up, he may cover his tracks, so we need to move quickly."

My phone rang again, the hospital this time. They called multiple times a day with updates. Maybe this would be the answered prayer.

"This is Katie Valentine."

"Hi, this is Janey at the UW Medical Center ICU. I'm so pleased to tell you that your husband has regained consciousness. He's awake."

Fuck.

EIGHT

ISABELLA

"Isabella." Tammi's voice stopped me before I could reach the elevator. She glanced at her watch, then toward the conference room where McFadden's team had filed in. "Got a minute?"

I followed her to the small kitchenette. She closed the door behind us and started fiddling with the coffeemaker. "What's up?" I said. Nobody ever wanted a "minute" to share good news.

She measured coffee grounds and kept her back to me, moving slowly, like she wanted to look casual if anyone walked by. "I've been at Sutton Strategy for eight years. I've seen people come and go, especially women in certain…positions."

My guard went up immediately. "What are you trying to tell me, Tammi?"

She turned to face me. "Izzy, I like you. And I've been where you are." She lowered her voice further, almost a whisper now. "But…there's a reason I've been stuck at the same position so long. So, if I were you, I would have an exit strategy. And document everything. Make sure you have proof."

She passed me a cup. "Proof of what?"

The door burst open. Davis. "Hope I'm not interrupting anything important." His eyes moved between us.

Metal clicked against porcelain. I looked down into my coffee cup, where a small brass key sat.

Tammi's smile reappeared. "Making conversation about our schedule today." She opened the door and walked out as if she hadn't dropped a bomb in my lap. Or coffee cup.

Davis searched me for clues. "What was that all about?"

I hesitated. "She's having some issues with her husband. Girl stuff. Personal."

"All right." He couldn't hide his skepticism. "You get those documents dropped at the Puget Coalition office?"

Oh, no.

I was so distracted by Jessica in the parking lot that I completely spaced it.

"Oh, my God, Davis."

"Izzy." He threw his arms out in a fake act of surrender.

"Shit! I'm so sorry. I swear, I'll go right now. I'll zip down there. I'll blame myself. I'm leaving right now. Tammi can cover for me in the meeting."

"Fine." He stomped out of the room.

I pocketed the key and set the cup on the table.

I waited five minutes, then peeked in the conference room and made sure the whole crew was deep in conversation. Neil and Patrick lectured on "election integrity" using PowerPoint slides. Davis sat in the back, bored. I took a deep breath, grabbed a random folder from my desk, and walked toward Shane's office as if I belonged. If anyone asked, I was dropping off documents.

I went straight for the desk. Nothing remarkable—pens, paper clips, a half-empty pack of nicotine gum. I moved to the next drawer. More office supplies, some business cards. The bottom drawer was locked. I pulled the key from my pocket, inserted it in the lock, and heard the satisfying click.

Inside was a single manila folder labeled "McFadden + Sutton. Senate midterms." McFadden plus Sutton? *Was this a campaign strategy for Shane himself?*

I flipped through the pages of polling data, demographic analysis, and messaging frameworks. One page, in Shane's handwriting, made my jaw drop:

> *Family Man Narrative - Key Talking Points:*
> *Parents = most engaged base (Book bans? Curriculum transparency? Medical freedom?)*
> *Shane Sutton: Not just a stepfather, but a man who saved a broken family.*

If Katherine and her children were props—stage dressing for Shane's secret agenda, then why would he leave her? Why didn't I know about this?

I continued turning page after page, snapping photos, unable to process what I was seeing. McFadden pushed all the Make America Healthy and Family Freedom nonsense; the only reason a conservative governor was making any headway in Washington state was that. It was all part of a bigger plan:

policies that pretended to be about health or children but were all about control.

No wonder Shane had aligned himself with shifting politics. He was helping to elect McFadden so he could eventually get himself elected.

"What are you doing?"

I nearly jumped out of my skin. Davis was in the doorway with his arms crossed over his chest.

I slammed the drawer shut. "Jesus, Davis. You scared me."

My guilt was not subtle.

"That doesn't answer my question." He stepped inside, closing the door behind him. The click of the latch sounded like a snare. "Why are you going through Shane's desk?"

My mind raced for a plausible excuse while Davis moved closer. His cologne distracted me in the worst possible way.

"Iz. What are you doing?"

"Nothing," I lied, slipping my phone into my pocket. "Being nosy, I guess."

Davis sighed. "I know things have been complicated since Shane's accident. But going through his private things will not help anyone." His voice softened. "Especially not you."

"Won't it?" I blurted. "What if he's not who we think he is?"

Davis huffed. "Izzy, Shane absolutely isn't who anyone thinks he is. But please, don't push. I want you to be safe. I know you think you can handle him. But please." He guided me out of Shane's office, closing the door and locking it.

He was either covering for Shane or protecting me. Or both.

"You'd better get those docs dropped off." He guarded Shane's door. "Wouldn't want to disappoint your boss."

I raced down Fourth Avenue, late and spiraling. Stupid. So fucking stupid. How had I forgotten the one thing Davis explicitly asked me to do?

The Puget Coalition office was only ten minutes away, but traffic had other plans. I tried to merge in the carpool lane unsuccessfully, missing the exit, and found myself driving toward my old neighborhood, the one I tried to avoid. Winding through the wet streets back to the on-ramp, I passed Grover High School, my little sister's old school.

It was a boring brick building that looked like any other school built in the 1960s, but it was a symbol of a life we'd fought for.

There, she bloomed, shedding the skin of our parents' paranoia. Her days at school were exciting, nothing like the hours of my parents' version of homeschooling at our barn-wood table. She went to football games and gossiped about boys, talking about forever and sophisticated relationships as if they were tangible things you could hold in your hand. Teenage life was something she navigated like a native, while I was a tourist, forever on the outside looking in. In many ways, she was more worldly than I was.

My own education in the opposite sex was a clumsy, fumbling thing. Back-of-a-pickup-truck encounters with farm boys who smelled of hay and cheap beer. A string of forgettable faces from dating apps. Sex was about survival, a tool.

Then came Shane Sutton, the man who unlocked something else in me. It wasn't just an orgasm or pleasure; it was the discovery of his weakness. A secret weapon. He offered me an investment in my transactional model of the world. And fit perfectly into my plan.

But Davis…Davis was a bug in the code. That one drunken kiss at a karaoke bar wasn't part of a strategy, and it had nothing to do with friction and everything to do with chemistry. We had a connection.

Or was it a test? A way to see how much I knew, so he could report back to his master. Shane's most loyal soldier, pretending to be a friend. Either way, Davis wasn't a liability I could afford.

Finally, I snaked my way back on the road going north and navigated to the PAC office, leaving the past behind once again.

I parallel-parked badly—one wheel definitely on the curb—and lifted the boxes from my trunk. The building was nondescript, sandwiched between a corporate law firm and a trendy poke bowl place. Small steel letters spelling out "Puget Coalition" above glass doors. Professional and polished. The kind of front that made people not ask questions.

As I approached, the door swung open.

A woman stepped out—mid-forties, brunette hair in a sleek bob, and a severe RBF. She wore a camel-colored coat, a designer handbag swinging from her elbow, and oversized sunglasses despite the gray sky. Everything about her screamed money.

She turned sharply and speed-walked toward a white Range Rover parked at the curb. Before getting in, she glanced back over her shoulder—not at me, but past me, scanning the street like she was checking if anyone else had seen her.

The Range Rover pulled away fast enough to make the tires squeal slightly.

Weird.

I shook it off and pushed through the doors.

Inside, the office was aggressively beige. Cream walls, blonde wood furniture, motivational posters about "grassroots movements" and "parental empowerment." A receptionist sat behind a curved desk, typing furiously, phone wedged between her ear and shoulder.

"Uh-huh. Yes. The donation cleared this morning," she was saying. "Tell him we'll keep the connection quiet. Last thing we need is reporters sniffing around—" She looked up, saw me, and her expression shifted instantly.

"Can I help you?"

I hoisted the boxes. "Delivery from Sutton Strategy."

"Oh, perfect! Set them there." She gestured to a table against the wall, already returning to her call. "No, I'm still here. Yeah, just someone dropping something off."

I placed the boxes down carefully, trying not to look like I was eavesdropping, even though I absolutely was.

Donation…Connection…Keep it quiet.

My phone rang. Davis.

"Hey, I got them dropped off. I'm literally walking out right now. I'm sorry again—"

"Shane's awake." He blurted. "I'm headed to the hospital. Can you hold down the fort at work?"

The floor tilted beneath me. The call ended.

I was already moving, boxes forgotten. The receptionist called after me—“Miss, you need to sign”—

I didn’t stop.

NINE

KATHERINE

"I brought gummy bears and rage." Claudia passed me a bag and twisted open the cap of her water with her teeth.

"I shouldn't have to choose between my kid's English class and someone else's politics."

"Melania's got a PowerPoint." Claudia glared toward the stage where Melanie Anderson adjusted her laptop. "She's about to TED talk us into banning books."

The auditorium was standing room only, full of familiar strangers, our school community in polite uniforms. I recognized faces meeting me with pitying looks. Everyone knew about Shane's accident. Nobody knew I'd spent the week cataloging his affairs instead of hoping for his recovery. My stomach twisted thinking about the conversation ahead and the words I'd have to say: *I want a divorce.*

I shoved a handful of gummy bears in my mouth to try to shut my brain up.

Melanie faced the crowd with a binder bigger than both my wedding albums combined and a seamless mouth of the whitest veneers I'd ever seen.

"Thank you for coming," she trilled. "We're here because parents matter."

Claudia leaned in. "We're also here because her son has an F and she'd rather ban the assignments he can't pass."

The projector hummed to life, and Melanie's opening slide appeared with book covers and the words explicit, sexual, divisive floating above them like clouds.

"Oh, for fuck's sake," Claudia muttered.

"As parents, we have a sacred duty to protect our children's innocence and our parental rights," Melanie said, bright and practiced. "And lately, I've heard from many of you that what's happening in our classrooms doesn't align with our values."

She clicked to the next slide—a list of book titles. *The Handmaid's Tale* at the top.

My jaw clenched. Elliott's favorite book. The one that had sparked a deep conversation and an insightful report; he happened to get an A on it.

"These titles are being assigned in our upper grades," Melanie continued. "We simply want age-appropriate, wholesome materials for our children."

Hands shot up. The microphone went first to a man I recognized from drop-off—fleece vest, the kind of guy who referred to his wife as "the ol' ball-and-chain."

"My daughter brought home a short story that uses the f-word," he said. "She's only sixteen."

"Your daughter definitely knows the f-word, buddy," I said under my breath.

Claudia snorted, and her hand hit the air. "Have any of you read the books on the list? Because if we're banning everything with sex and anger and violence, we're banning *Romeo and Juliet*, the Bible, and the school board minutes from last month."

Ripples of laughter surrounded us.

"I'm not opposed to literature." Melanie's fists were balled at her sides. "I'm opposed to indoctrination."

That word. *Indoctrination.* Right out of one of Shane's campaign ads for McFadden.

I shouldn't. I really shouldn't.

Maybe it was thinking about Emma, whose article was killed for asking uncomfortable questions, or about the way Melanie used the exact phrases Shane used when he was manipulating people. Melanie wasn't the problem, I knew that. She was a proxy, a smiling foot soldier in a war waged by men who wanted to control what women knew and said. Like my mom. My rage wasn't for my daughter anymore; it was for myself.

"These books ask our kids to think," I yelled, much louder than I'd planned. "Don't tell me this is about innocence when it's all about control. Because some helicopter parents can't have uncomfortable conversations with their own kids."

Melanie's face soured. "They contain sexual content that—"

"They contain reality," a voice called from the back. I turned. Todd Anderson. Melanie's ex.

Hot Toddy.

"Our son is going to encounter sex and violence in the real world, and I'd rather he learns about it from Atwood than from the internet."

He caught my eye and winked. My face flushed, and Claudia elbowed me.

Melanie ignored his comment, instead clicking to another slide that showed out-of-context quotes from the banned books, words isolated to look as shocking as possible. "This is what we're talking about. Our children deserve protection—"

More hands went up. Another parent stood. "You want to ban *Beloved*? Toni Morrison? A Nobel Prize winner? But *Lord of the Flies*, where children literally murder each other, that's fine? What are the criteria here?"

The room fractured. Melanie was losing control.

She held up her hands and forced a smile. "Of course, we want our children to be educated. That's why we'll be forming a review panel to ensure—"

"We have one," Claudia yelled. "It's called the English department. They have degrees in this. Let them do their jobs."

Another man in the back shouted, "This is why we need McFadden as governor."

The room was chaos now—parents arguing, teachers trying to interject, someone's phone ringing with a hilariously on-point tinny rendition of "The Star-Spangled Banner."

By the time we all filed out, with nothing accomplished, the gummy bears were gone, and my heart was beating out of my chest.

"You were perfect." Claudia squeezed my hand. "And you'll be perfect at the hospital, too."

I hoped she was right. If I could stand up to Melania, maybe I could stand up to my husband.

I turned into the hospital parking kiosk to pay, and had déjà vu while swiping my debit card. I imagined the screen reading declined and panicking, searching for loose change in the cracks of the seats. Men in my life had a track record of wrecking everything financially. My father, my ex. Then the screen read approved, and the barrier to the parking garage lifted.

We would be okay for a while, I told myself. I had a bit of savings, and the kids' college accounts were full, but I'd need to make some serious changes soon.

My phone chimed as I parked. It was Brenda, my former boss.

> I got your app. You can start next Monday if you're ready. Will be good to have you back with us!

Thank goodness! Real work again instead of being someone's unpaid grunt.

I'd emailed her yesterday to see if she had any open positions. I kicked myself for turning down her job offer last year. Like everyone else, I'd been laid off during the pandemic, but when things reopened, I could have returned to the job I enjoyed and was good at. Instead, I merged lives with Shane, who told me I didn't need to work. As usual, I supported my husband's career ambitions instead of my own.

Thank you, Brenda!

I collected my purse and walked into the hospital to end my marriage. I still wasn't sure if I had it in me to break up with a man fresh out of a nearly three-week coma, even knowing what Shane had done. I couldn't even tell someone when they had food in their teeth or if their fly was open.

Maybe it wasn't too late to change course, wait a few days or a week. Or forever. My tired brain ran with the idea. Pretend I'd never answered his phone, pretend things were fine. It could be fine, couldn't it? What if his accident had rewired his brain, erased the monster, and left behind the man I thought I'd married? People changed after trauma, didn't they? Brain injuries could alter personalities entirely. Yes, a new man, a new brain, a complete factory reset. We could forget about the website, the indiscretions, his bevy of beauties, and rediscover the man I married, my Shane.

Or Seth. Who was he again?

My resolve returned by the time I approached the nurses' station. No. I couldn't forget. I wasn't my mother. She'd been the queen of keeping up appearances, no matter the cost, apparently, even a behind-my-back relationship with my husband.

A nurse with dirty blonde hair and round cheeks met me with a grin. "Oh, good, he's been asking for you!"

I didn't speak. How had he kept me straight from the others? I matched the nurse's pace, practically speed-walking toward his room.

"Talk about a true miracle," she said. "You must be relieved."

Her face lit up with happiness I couldn't match. Yesterday, I'd hoped he'd never wake up. Today, I hoped he would be awake enough to understand me, but still comatose enough not to respond.

"Yeah, what a relief," I said, entirely unrelieved.

"The news crews were here earlier," she added. "Mr. Sutton is a big celebrity. We had to ask them to leave—hospital policy."

Great. Shane's public persona was being amplified and washed while his private life remained hidden.

Nancy and Fred beamed at me from the room when I entered. "Katie!" they said in unison.

"It's so good to see you!" Fred shuffled toward me.

I expected him to look frail after what Claudia had told me, but his ash-gray skin shocked me. The spark that once separated him from Nancy's coldness was dim. His posture stooped, worry carved deeper into his face.

"How are you, Fred?" I said, casually, as if I wasn't secretly evaluating his declining health.

"Hanging in there." His voice was thin.

"We missed you, Katie. Where on earth have you been?" Nancy interrupted. "Other people from the office have been here, but not you. His wife."

I wanted to flip her off. If only she knew about all the others, the whole harem of women who believed they were special to him, too.

"I'm sorry I haven't been in touch. This week has been…a lot." An understatement like another lie.

"Oh, honey, we understand." Fred shot Nancy a warning look.

"The governor-to-be himself sent flowers. Such a kind man." Nancy gestured to a massive arrangement in the corner. "And three state senators called. Everyone's so concerned about Shane."

I wondered if Fred knew how much his son had corrupted the Sutton legacy, both professionally and personally. He had to. And based on his appearance, with sunken cheeks and red eyes, he was as devastated as he was ill.

I walked toward Shane's bed and looked at his face. There he was. The man I recognized, yet didn't know at all. "Shane." I sounded empty, and I was.

"Hi, baby." His voice was coarse and low, quieter than his usual booming volume.

"We will give you some time." Fred strolled behind Nancy as she shuffled out.

Shane was less fragile than he had been the last time I saw him. His face was still swollen, and his eyes had rings of black and blue, but he was there, the man I fell in love with. The eyes I'd once trusted, the smile that charmed me, and the lips that lied more than I'd ever uncover.

I sat next to him, unsure where to put my hands, trying not to disturb anything.

"Are you in pain?"

"Pretty drugged up, the goooood stuff," he slurred. "Davis filled me in; McFadden's polling numbers are climbing." He was still thinking about politics and his public success. Not even a *How are you? How are the kids?*

He might have expected me to show joy that he was alive, but I couldn't. I was furious. For years, he'd played me for a fool. He'd looked me in the eye thousands of times and lied, and I'd believed him because I wanted to. He wasted years of my life, stole my peace of mind.

The invisible picket line of all the other women he'd lied to lit my fury even more.

I took a deep breath and faced him. "Shane, I think we should…" My planned monologue turned to ash on my tongue. Instead, I heard myself say, "I spoke with Rhonda."

His face became unreadable.

I folded my arms. "Do you remember who Rhonda is?"

Again, nothing. Not a word, a nod, a sound, or a breath. His silence was infuriating. I had a whole speech memorized about how he was a wonderful part of my life, but we had to go our separate ways, and we could wait until he was well enough to split. I couldn't say any of it.

"Katie," he soothed, as if speaking to a child. "You're confused. The doctors warned me this might happen."

"Warned you about what?"

"That the stress might affect you." His hand reached for mine, the same hand that had caressed other women. "That you might say…strange things. Imagine things." His thumb stroked my wrist. "This must have been hard for you."

I pulled away, rage boiling in my chest. No, this was another one of his manipulations, as if the doctors were diagnosing my marriage.

"Strange things? Like finding your profile on OntheSide.com? Or strange, like the hotel rooms? Or the lies to my mother?"

His features hardened. "Katie, sweetheart, you're not making sense—"

"Oh, is that so, Seth?"

The name hung between us like a grenade with its pin pulled.

His gentle façade vanished instantly. He met my eyes, almost resigned.

And there he was, Shane Sutton stripped away to the manipulator beneath.

I let out a shaky breath. "This is for the best. You'll be happier single, and I'll help with logistics. I'll talk to your parents—"

"You won't talk to anyone, Katie."

I sprang to my feet. "Excuse me?"

"We're married, Katie. That was the deal."

"What deal?"

"You tell anyone what you know, what you think you know, try to destroy my reputation, I'll destroy yours."

He spat each word with pure malice.

"My reputation? I didn't do anything wrong, Shane." My stomach lurched.

"I told you never to look at my phone," he hissed.

"Shane, it rang when you were—"

"I'm telling you, not a fucking word, or our kids will pay." His pupils dilated, his cheeks blotched.

"Our kids? You mean my kids?" I backed away. The phantom army of women vanished. I was alone with a stranger wearing my husband's face.

The cardiac monitor beeped faster.

"Emma's college applications? You know how many connections I have through Sutton Stars? One phone call. Elliott's stock trading accounts? I set those up, remember?

And Ethan," he sneered, "you know how impressionable teenage boys can be. How easily influenced."

"Shane, I—"

"I have friends everywhere in this city. The media, the courts, the schools. Decades of relationships, favors. People who can make or break futures with a call. Don't forget who I am, Katie. Don't forget what I can do."

The room shrank around me. The man I married, the man I trusted with my children, was threatening them with the same confidence he once used to promise love.

"You wouldn't."

"Don't try me." His eyes held mine, and I saw the emptiness behind the charm.

I turned and raced out of the room, barely reaching the bathroom before vomiting.

I gripped the cold porcelain, my body emptying itself as if trying to purge more than breakfast. My ears rang with Shane's words: *Our kids will pay for this.*

I had to get home. Now.

I splashed water on my face and met my reflection in the mirror. The woman staring back wasn't the same one who'd walked in here twenty minutes ago.

This woman had three children to protect.

Shane was going to meet the real Katherine Valentine.

TEN
ISABELLA

"I'm here to see Shane Sutton."

My head throbbed. Tammi's comments and Davis's weird behavior cycled through my thoughts, mingling with memories of Katherine here with that man the other day. Not to mention, the Senate folder, and Jessica's business card sitting in my purse, either a lifeline or a lit stick of dynamite.

Can I go through with this?

The nurse behind the Plexiglass barrier didn't look at me, so I raised my voice. "Hi, I'm here to visit Shane Sutton."

Still, without looking. "Name?"

"Isabella Meyer."

She clicked on her computer. "Ah, you're on the list."

I'd known as much. Davis was the one who told me Shane had asked for me. Granted, Davis wasn't thrilled about it, but I was.

The smell hit me as soon as we entered the hallway, reminding me of endless nights watching monitors and praying to a God I didn't believe in. After Mom embraced conventional medicine, my tolerance never grew, even with Pop in and out of hospitals.

As if reading my mind, a text from my mom appeared. Despite how complicated our relationship had been, much of my heart stayed with them even when I wasn't there physically.

I glimpsed her message and felt the usual push-pull of family obligation versus self-preservation.

Miss you.

I sent back a quick message:

Miss you, too, see you tonight might be pretty late <3)

I tucked my phone away, pushing down the image of the mother I grew up with—the paranoid woman who made us drink boiled creek water because she thought the fluoride in tap water was government poison.

Instead, I tried to picture the mother she'd been the past few years. The one who had changed her ways and promised to love me and Pop no matter what. The one who was trying, in her imperfect way, to make amends.

I trailed behind the nurse, my heart pounding in my ears, before she shared, "He's had quite a few visitors today. His parents are here now."

Meeting the parents. *Yikes*. Not what I'd expected, not like this. My blood pressure spiked as we entered his suite, and his mom and dad met us at the door on their way out.

They matched the photos on Katherine's Facebook page, which I'd stalked for hours. I saw Shane in his dad's steely-blue eyes and his mom's cleft chin and toothy smile. Up close, Fred was frail, worn down. Nancy stood ramrod straight beside him, with her styled silver hair and designer outfit, like she'd dressed for an audience, not a hospital visit.

"Another visitor! Hello!" Fred extended his hand.

"Hi, I'm Isabella. I work with Shane." Fred's grip was weak. Shane's mother peered at me as if she were examining a handbag she was considering buying.

"You're prettier than the photos," she said.

What photos? Had Shane been showing his mommy pictures of me?

"Isabella, that's a lovely name. Shane has mentioned you quite a lot recently," Shane's father interjected.

"Oh?" I tried to keep my face neutral.

"He said you were very helpful during such a difficult time," Nancy said, her smile as sharp as a scalpel. "We're grateful to anyone who makes our son happy."

I wondered what version of our relationship Shane had told them. Assistant? Hotel Hussy? "I'm so glad to hear he's doing well. What a relief!"

"He's had quite a day, honey, but I'm sure he will enjoy having another woman around."

I gave a shallow giggle, unsure how to respond.

"Okay, well, bye! Nice to meet you." They waved and walked down the hallway, with Nancy's arm linked possessively through Fred's.

I glanced back at the nurse, who fiddled with Shane's IV bag while he slept. "Was that weird, or was it me?"

She lowered her voice. "You didn't hear this from me, but the wife ran out of here yesterday. Made a whole scene—screaming, crying, the works. They asked us to have security escort her out, but she'd already left. He told us she's like that. Dramatic."

Her eyes lingered on me a beat too long.

"Did she say anything else?" My voice squeaked.

"No, but maybe he will tell you something." She motioned to Shane, whose eyelids were fluttering. "I'll give you some privacy."

"Thanks." I moved to Shane's bedside. There was a whiteboard on the wall: last time he ate, four-thirty; blood pressure, 110/70; blood type, B. I sank into the seat beside him, wondering what I expected to find in the man who'd been the center of my life for months.

He turned his head toward me. The corners of his mouth lifted.

"Baby," he rasped. He reached for my hand, and his grip was firm—the same grip that had pinned me against walls and made me see stars. The warmth of his skin against mine sent an involuntary shiver down my spine, my body reacting to him even as my mind filled with questions.

"Shane, it's so great to see you." I squeezed back. Here it was, proof he still wanted me, not her. His attention was intoxicating.

"I'm glad you're here." He winced, and his eyes met mine. Those familiar blue eyes that could switch from warm to ice cold in a millisecond. "Katie and I are getting a divorce."

"Really?" I gasped. This was what I'd been waiting for. The path forward I'd been plotting since the day we met. So why did it feel like I was standing on the edge of a cliff?

"Yes." He squeezed my hand again. "I'm sorry it took me so long. I'd planned to do it when I got back from Whistler, but…" he trailed off, gesturing to his broken body with a self-deprecating half-smile.

Finally. *Finally*.

But I needed more intel.

"Shane, Jessica Banks confronted me yesterday."

"She's nuts. Completely unhinged. Stole money from the company." His words tumbled out, and a vein pulsed in his temple. "Jealous, I'm sure. Had a thing for me that I never returned."

I remembered Jessica's frightened eyes, her trembling hands. But she confronted me in a parking garage… Maybe that was unhinged behavior after all.

"What did she say to you?"

"Just nonsense," I lied. "Said you weren't a good person, and I should stay away from you."

He laughed bitterly. "Classic Jessica. Always the victim."

Shane's voice softened again, his hand tightening on mine. "I'm sorry that happened to you, honey. I wouldn't be surprised if Katherine put her up to it. They've been in contact, I'm sure, plotting. Katie came in here yesterday. She was hysterical."

He shifted from anger to tenderness and back in an instant. I felt myself pulled in, wanting to believe him. It would be so relieving to accept the simplest version of him, to stop analyzing his face like a crime scene. His soft smile and easy eyes. Handsome and sweet. And at times, it was easy to imagine being in love with him. That's why the lie came so easily.

"I saw her, Katie, with another man, and here of all places," I said. "They seemed… close."

"Yes." A dark satisfaction crossed his face. "Like father, like daughter."

I understood the reference. I had googled Katherine enough times to learn about her dad, including some less-than-flattering articles, but I still wanted to hear it from him—anything to make it clear in his mind that he wanted nothing to do with Katherine ever again.

"Her father used to fuck around with his college students. She's got Daddy issues a mile wide."

"That's crazy." I wondered if he considered his position fucking around with employees, but it wasn't the time. "I can't believe she'd do that while you were in the hospital."

A shadow passed over his face. "You don't know the half of it, Bells. She's capable of things you couldn't imagine. She must have been happy when I got into an accident." He pulled me closer. "You know what Davis told me? She was going through my phone while I was unconscious. Looking for dirt, for leverage. Can you believe it? While I was fighting for my life."

I pretended to be offended on his behalf, but all I wondered was…what did she find? And what did Davis gain by tattling on her? Was he trying to get Shane away from Katherine, too? What was Davis's angle?

"So, what did Katie say when you told her you were filing for divorce?"

He gave a humorless laugh. "That's the most fucked up part. She's filing. Can you believe that?"

I felt my ears get hot, like the admission had burned me. *Fuck.*

Fuck.

Fuck.

"Maybe she can get a punch card. Her second divorce. You know her ex was an ex-con?" Shane continued, as if convincing himself, not me.

This wasn't ideal. Not at all.

But it could still work. I could still make this work.

I gently kissed him, pushing my doubts aside. This was my chance to bring my plan to fruition. "I'm so sorry, Shane. I promise, I'm here for you."

"I'm happy to hear you say that." He interlaced his fingers with mine. "Because I'll need your help."

I squeezed back. "Okay, anything."

"I'm moving into the lake house. I need you to get into my home office in Magnolia and get my laptop before my father does."

His laptop. He guarded that thing with his life. Now? I had a free pass.

"I can do that," I said. "What else?"

"I want you to move in with me, Bells. We can start our life together. The two of us."

Behind Shane, the cardiac monitor tracked his heartbeat in jagged peaks and valleys. Up and down. Truth and lies. Jessica's warning, Tammi's cryptic advice, Davis's concern, and the campaign folder.

So many red flags, all waving frantically in my face. Every single one screaming: RUN, ISABELLA, RUN!

And yet, this was what I'd wanted all along, what I'd been working toward since the day we met. The payout that would change my family's life.

"Yes," I whispered, sealing my fate. "I'd love that."

ELEVEN

KATHERINE

"Are we in trouble?" Elliott tapped his fingers against the countertop.

"No! Of course not," I said, realizing my anxious behavior and solemn request for them to "sit down for a chat" might not have been the best approach. But my mind was fuzzy. I'd hardly slept. Last night, I had a dream about my father.

In the dream, I was thirteen again, crouched at the top of our stairs. But when I looked down, it wasn't my father I saw but Shane, his face contorted with the same cold rage I'd witnessed in the hospital.

"You think anyone will believe you?" Shane hissed in the dream. "You're nothing without me. Nothing."

My mother's face blurred, becoming my own. I saw myself nod, apologize, and promise to be better.

I woke, gasping, sheets twisted like restraints. I couldn't distinguish which life was real: the girl watching her family's façade crack, or the woman who'd recreated the same nightmare.

Both, I realized. Both were real.

His threat followed me the entire night, down into darkness: *Your kids will pay for this.*

"You're not in trouble. But I have something I need to tell you." I gathered my thoughts as the kids huddled around the kitchen island.

I'd planned this conversation every day for five whole days, and the words still felt like glass in my mouth, but I couldn't let fear control me anymore. I knew from experience that the best way to protect kids was to be honest with them. It's all I'd wanted from my parents when I was younger. Much of my childhood was at odds with reality, but my parents prioritized how others perceived us over who we truly were. My kids deserved the truth more than I deserved to look like some hero who had never screwed up. They didn't need a martyr; they needed a mom.

Emma clicked her tongue. "Mom. Bruh."

The words tumbled out. "Shane and I are getting a divorce."

I watched the three faces I knew best, studying Elliott's thick eyelashes, Ethan's smattering of freckles on the bridge of his nose, and Emma's full lips, the color of her pink nail polish. Emma shot Elliott a look. Ethan looked at the ground. The silence became the answer.

"You already knew."

They gawked blankly at me. Teenagers never talked on demand. Yet last night, after I tucked myself into bed and almost dozed off, Elliott asked for biology help, Ethan wanted screen time, and Emma dug through my bathroom for a tampon. Now? Speechless.

"When did he tell you?"

"A few days ago, Mom. It's not a big deal," Emma said. "I mean, we've been through this before. It's like, the circle of life or whatever."

"Guys." I pressed. "What did he say?"

Elliott shifted in his chair. "He said the accident was too much for you, and you couldn't handle the pressure, or whatever."

"He said maybe you…found someone else," Ethan mumbled.

My vision tunneled as I processed their words. Shane had gotten to them first, from his hospital bed no less. While I'd been agonizing over how to protect them, he'd been poisoning them against me. Painting me as the unstable, unfaithful villain.

My mind raced backward through the past few years, seeing his interactions with my children in a sickening new light. Elliott's front-row Mariners tickets, the expensive basketball shoes for Ethan, and all those arguments with Emma, where he positioned himself as the understanding parent, while I was the unreasonable one. They weren't acts of generosity; they were investments in an emotional bank account he could draw from. And that time was now.

I couldn't speak. The realization made me want to throw up.

"We have to get to school." Emma tossed her backpack over her shoulder. "I'm meeting with Mr. Carlisle, doing what you told me."

I nodded mechanically. "Good. That's good."

"Whatever you did, we still love you," Elliott said.

"Totally." Ethan mirrored his brother.

The words hit me like a wrecking ball as they walked out of the kitchen.

Whatever I did.

I became a statue, wanting to call them back and tell them all about the other women, about Seth, and about the threats. But what would that do except drag them deeper into this nightmare? The door slammed shut behind them, making me jump.

I'd told myself I wouldn't badmouth Shane or share all the salacious reasons behind the breakup. I'd let him spin the story if he wanted. I'd learned my lesson. Talking badly about Eric was toxic when we split up; even if he deserved it, I regretted it. I didn't want to make that same mistake twice.

But now? He was using his relationship with them against me.

My phone rang. Mom. Ugh.

I let the call go to voicemail, then listened to it.

"Oh, honey, Nancy told me. You kicked poor Shane out? What's going on with you? And why didn't you tell me?"

Shane's version had already reached her, too. Another strategic move.

I tried Shane's office one last time on the way out the door. Still locked. Fred likely had a key. Or the movers would have to break the lock. Either way, whatever I found, he'd deny.

I had to stay gone per Shane's lawyer's instructions, so I didn't "tamper" with anything. What a mess.

I turned to my dog. "Why did I get married again?"

Piper nudged my hand, her warm nose pressing insistently into my palm.

"We'll be okay, girl," I said, not entirely sure which of us I was trying to convince. "Somehow."

I arrived at the salon, longing for something familiar. Though finances would be tight for a while, a good cut and color was better than therapy in my book.

"Hi, my friend." My stylist, Kasey, swung her arms open for a hug. "Oh, honey, you've been through so much. Come here."

If it weren't for her infectious warmth and kindness, her impossibly long mermaid hair and perfect skin might have tinted even the most confident woman shades of green.

"So good to see you." I melted into her embrace, letting her soothe the worries I couldn't share.

"So, tell me, how is Shane doing? I haven't seen any updates!" Kasey's fingers worked through my hair, gentle but insistent, like her questions.

Ugh. How could I explain the divorce if I couldn't explain everything that led up to it? His threats loomed; she'd find out eventually.

"Improving, yep," I said, and let it drop.

"I had the loveliest conversation with him at the Christmas Bazaar. He was telling me about that anniversary trip he was planning for you."

I forced a smile, remembering the weekend perfectly. Shane spent the morning playing perfect dad and husband at

Puget Academy, then went out of town for business. That business ended up being MissPDX.

"Sounds like him," I managed.

Kasey continued, resuming her cutting.

"I told my boyfriend, 'Why can't you be more like Shane Sutton?' The man remembers every little detail, never misses an opportunity to make Katie feel special."

I could have choked on the irony.

I sat under the heater, processing, when I spotted an old issue of Seattle magazine. I smiled despite myself, knowing Kasey had planted it there on purpose. I opened it to a glossy spread of a campaign party at our home five months ago, lingering on the caption: Katherine Valentine, Sutton Stars Event Planner.

The woman in those photos was so confident, so poised, with a radiant smile, directing caterers and greeting guests. How official the title had sounded. How proud she'd been to see her name in print.

But it was another of Shane's manipulations. A title to appease me, with no salary. "It'll be great exposure," he'd said, and I believed him, pathetically grateful for the recognition he'd tossed my way. My favorite hobby and unpaid labor were another lever for him to use. He'd been using my talent and passion to boost his own public image, while privately dismantling my independence.

The heat from the dryer was suddenly suffocating.

I put Katie Valentine Events on hold again and again. And I told myself it was okay because I got to stay home with my babies. It was the best of both worlds: being a mom and planning parties on the side to express my creativity. I was grateful I didn't need a side job since Eric was the primary breadwinner, but I paid the price for that choice. By our tenth anniversary, our marriage had come to an end. You'd think I would have learned something, yet here I was, again, working for someone else's event company after leaving my dreams behind in a digital tomb. I fulfilled obligations while the men around me chased their own desires.

"Thank you, Kasey." I tossed my freshly cut and colored hair over my shoulder. "I needed this."

I passed her my credit card.

"Anytime, honey. That will be $220." Kasey tapped the screen of her square device and frowned. "It's saying declined. Do you have another one you want to run instead?"

My stomach did a small flip. "Weird. Here, try this one." I handed her the backup card I rarely used.

Another decline. She tried again. A third decline, and I was already fumbling with my phone, dialing the bank.

"The account you're calling about has been closed."

The words didn't compute.

"Katie, honey, is everything okay?"

"Yes," I said too brightly. "We had some cards frozen after Shane's wallet went missing in the accident. The bank is overly cautious."

"Sweetie, don't worry about it," Kasey offered. "I'll get you next time."

But I was already moving toward the door, mumbling apologies, promising to call her later.

In my car, I opened my banking app.

All I saw were zeroes.

"Wait a minute, what?" This couldn't be right; my

checking account and savings account were empty. All my credit card accounts, closed.

"No, no, no, no!"

I called customer service, hyperventilating. I took a deep breath through my nose and exhaled shakily through pursed lips, like I'd taught Emma to do.

I sat in the salon parking lot for twenty minutes, on hold with three different customer service representatives. Each one told me the same thing: Shane Sutton had authorization. Shane Sutton had moved the funds. Shane Sutton had power of attorney.

"When was this power of attorney document filed?"

"February 15th, 2022, ma'am."

The day after our wedding.

When we were still floating on newlywed bliss. When I trusted him completely.

A flash of memory: The stack of paperwork we signed with the notary. The prenup. Other financial documents.

"Oh." The word slipped from my lips like a stone.

"If you'd like, I'll submit a ticket, and one of our account support specialists will call you back."

"Okay," I said, flatly.

"Is there anything else I can do for you today?" Her voice was distant as the app refreshed to the same bold, round zeroes.

"I'm not sure…thank you, though."

I pressed my head back against the headrest to center myself.

My hands were shaking so badly I could barely hold the

phone. There had to be limits, protections. The kids' college accounts were separate, in my name alone. Those were safe.

Weren't they?

I opened the 529 website, my fingers moving automatically through the login process I'd done hundreds of times to check balances and make contributions.

`Emma: $0.00`

`Elliott: $0.00`

`Ethan: $0.00`

Shane's words echoed: *Your kids will pay for this.*

He meant it literally.

My body reacted before my mind could catch up. I flung open the car door and vomited onto the asphalt. Years of squirreling away money, building back up from nothing, to secure my children's futures—gone. The betrayal burned worse than my throat.

The affairs, money, and my self-respect. Shane could have those.

But I'd burn the world down before I let him hurt my children any further.

I wiped my mouth, then threw the car into reverse and accelerated out of the lot.

I needed help, and I knew where to find it.

TWELVE
ISABELLA

I passed Davis's desk before leaving the office. "Hey, Clark, I'm heading out for a bit. Do you need anything?"

He didn't bother to turn around. "Nope."

For days, Davis had avoided me. Cold and distant. I thought his stress level might ease once Shane woke up, but it spiked instead. Twice today, I'd caught him starting to say something, then stopping himself. Maybe my recent friendship with Tammi was causing a bit of jealousy, but I couldn't help my kinship with her. She was chill and easy to work with. If I asked her for help, she offered it without acting like she was doing me some favor, unlike so many of the dudes I'd worked with. And I never had to worry about her sending a dick pic.

"Okay, well, I'm meeting Fred in Magnolia to help move Shane out." I knew that tidbit would get him talking.

Davis fastened his eyes on his computer screen. "Yup, see ya."

What? How could he not take that bait? "Did I piss you off or something? What's with you?" I waited for him to face me.

He pushed his chair back and turned. "Shane told me you were moving in with him."

Oh.

I picked a hangnail while I processed what to say, but he spoke first.

"You're not the first, you know." He stared almost through me with a look I couldn't place. Was that guilt? Like he's watched this before and stayed silent.

"The first what?"

"The first one he made promises to." He held my gaze. "The first assistant he's done this with."

I forced my face into a grateful smile even as rage bubbled under my skin. His concern was five months too late and ten degrees too patronizing. "I get it, Davis, but it's not your place, okay? I'm fine." The words were more like reassurance for me. "Think of it this way: you wouldn't have to cover for us anymore."

Davis narrowed his eyes. "You think this is because I don't want to cover for you? Iz, he's taking advantage of you. How do you not see that?"

Oh, what peak irony. The contradiction of his loyalty and complaints annoyed the shit out of me. "You're one to talk. If Shane's so terrible, why don't you stand up for yourself?" Though I'd tried to keep my volume down, Neil and Tammi pushed back their chairs, watching like it was a show.

Davis clenched his jaw but said nothing.

"That's what I thought. Watch yourself. And maybe worry

about your own choices before you lecture me about mine, Clark." I walked away from his desk and stomped to the elevator.

When the doors opened on the garage level, my phone buzzed almost immediately with a text from Davis:

Sorry. I'm a dick. Stressed and worried about you. Happy Hour?

Goddamn it. I let out a sigh as I settled into my car.

Fs. I know you're just trying to help.

"Hey, you!" Fred greeted me as I entered the Magnolia house. With them split, I wasn't sure whether to call it Shane's house or Katherine's. Shane had said for so long it might be our house someday, Shane's and mine. Granted, it wasn't really my style, with too much marble and big pillars, like a chain restaurant trying too hard. I wasn't sure how I felt about a lake house, imagining a cabin or cottage, but no. Shane's modest second home was in Laurelhurst, one of the most expensive neighborhoods in Seattle, with each house more ornate than the next and sweeping Lake Washington views. Mom would rant about the "capitalist excess." Yet here I was, about to move right in. Was I betraying everything my parents taught me, or breaking free of their limitations? Maybe both. Either way, I doubted they'd say no to a free house.

The moving company gathered most of his things, but I offered to help Fred do a sweep for the smaller items the movers couldn't take. I certainly didn't volunteer for fun. I fucking hated moving. This was the perfect excuse to snoop.

Fred turned to me. "You mind helping me peruse Shane's office?"

Did I ever. After what I found at work? "You got it."

The door to Shane's office was wide open, revealing dark hardwood and heavy wainscoting. The room was colder than the rest of the house. Fred opened and closed drawers, and I did the same, each empty, except for a can of compressed air, a fifth of whiskey in a collector's box, a few pushpins, and loose change I tossed in a file box.

Fred huffed. "Shoot, I was hoping to find his laptop, but maybe the movers took it. I'm going to head out to the sports shed if you want to keep looking?"

"Sure."

His laptop.

I opened the middle top drawer where Shane had said the laptop would be, but it was empty. I reached farther back and felt something smooth and metal. At first, I thought it was part of the desk frame, but as I tugged, it snapped loose. A large rectangle of wood fell out, and behind it was his computer.

Whatever Shane was hiding, he'd gone to great lengths to keep it concealed. My mom would have a field day with this. If there was one thing both she and Shane understood, it was the power of fear.

I pushed the laptop's power button, but it wouldn't turn on. Instead of putting it in the box, I tucked it into my handbag. I had to know Shane's secrets before his dad did. And I had a curiosity that could kill multiple cats.

In the hallway, a gallery wall of photos caught my attention—family pictures with flowery captions, and several rectangles where Shane had clearly been removed. One of the largest frames held a photo of all three of Katherine's kids as toddlers on their dad's lap, with "Our Daddy" in swirling script below.

Holy shit. The same man I saw with Katherine at the hospital. Were Katherine and her ex-husband getting back together?

I paused at the threshold of Katherine's office, with its bright pink chair and dog bed underneath. It could have been on a Pinterest board called "Boss Babe Aesthetic." A wooden sign about wine and hustle would have completed it. I stepped inside, half-expecting alarms to sound, but nothing happened. Just like with Shane, boundaries that should have stopped me…didn't. I walked right through them. Maybe that's why Shane and I had a connection. We both took what we wanted.

I heard the back door close and jumped, scooting out of Katherine's office, as Fred padded into the room with his box of random things. "Anything else of Shane's that you found?"

Do I tell him? Not a chance. Sorry, Fred. "Nope, just a bunch of odds and ends."

"Well, then, I think that's the last of it. Shall we?"

We walked out of the house, probably for the last time, and set our boxes on the passenger seat of his Porsche. A small notebook sat on his dashboard, with three notes scribbled on it. "Nice car," I complimented, pretending to appreciate the vehicle while zeroing in on the handwriting that read:

Sutton4Senate!
SuttonforSenate
SuttonSenate

Was Fred workshopping slogans? Or was this some bizarre gratitude journal, manifesting thing? Did he know about Shane's plans?

"Oh, thanks." Fred put his hand on the hood. "Shane bought it for me. Not my style, but when a kid gives you a present, what do you do?" He gave a hollow chuckle and closed the door.

Rich people were weird. Fred had enough money to buy a Porsche, but Shane was the type to be showy. I always wondered whether Shane's love for toys and money came from his parents, but Fred was indifferent to it—like Shane was indifferent to Fred. Dismissive in a way I'd never understood. Fred was the reason Shane had anything at all. He should have been grateful. But Shane also had Nancy, who was a completely different story. There was something deeply off about her. Still, who was I to judge someone else's upbringing? Mine was as weird as they came.

"I'm heading to see him. It shouldn't be long before he's home." I said.

"Right." He put his hands in his pockets, looking uncomfortable. "Home."

Maybe I shouldn't have said that.

"Honey, you're a sweet girl, I know you've been so helpful since Katherine…you know."

I fiddled with my hair, nervously. "But?"

Fred glanced around. "Are you sure about moving in with him? Have you thought it through?"

"Um, yeah. I'm sure, but I appreciate the concern."

He rested his hands on his hips. "Be careful with my boy, that's all. And with yourself."

Then he patted my shoulder and walked away, leaving me with the impression he'd been about to say something else entirely.

"Thanks again for the help, honey." He called before sliding into his car and driving away.

Fred's genuine concern for me made Shane's dismissive comments about him seem even more callous. What kind of son mocks the man who gave him everything? The same type who builds secret compartments in his desk, I suppose.

I turned on my car, plugged the laptop into the charger, and waited for it to boot up. After a few moments, the screen lit up. Password protected.

Shit. But wait—the notebook in Fred's car. He'd come for the laptop after all.

Worth a shot.

I tried Sutton4Senate, SuttonforSenate. Nothing. Then SuttonSenate.

The desktop appeared. I was in.

I clicked on the Messenger icon and immediately realized the messages weren't Shane's but Katherine's. My heart raced with a voyeuristic thrill. I'd come to Magnolia to snoop, and this was a jackpot—intimate access to her private thoughts, her secrets, her life. Of course, Shane was spying on her, and shouldn't I know what he knew? To protect myself?

I went through the conversations: Emma, Elliott, Ethan,

and Eric. Christ, she was one of those alliteration moms. I suddenly wondered whether they would hate me, which stung more than it should have.

I opened a chat with Emma and read their exchanges. The girl seemed angry, combative, typical teenager stuff. But Katherine's responses were patient and loving:

I'll always be here for you, no matter what.

Thanks mom, love you.

I felt…jealousy? Longing? I never had a mother who said such things to me when I was younger.

I shook that thought away and tapped on the most recent conversation with her ex, Eric, scrolling back.

Need to see you.

Of course. See you after Bridge. 4 pm?

I'll be there, thank you.

Bridge? I made a mental note to Google what Bridge was. I checked the timestamp—the same time I saw her with him at the hospital. Relationship confirmed. No wonder Shane knew Katherine was cheating. Receipts!

I kept reading the most recent messages, sent within the last few minutes.

Got your voicemail, you sure this is what you want?

Yes, 100%. Don't trust anyone else with this. Can you reach out to your MOB buddies?

Of course, but if what you suspect is true...

The message cut off there. What did Katherine want from him? What did Katherine suspect? What else did she think Shane was up to? And who the hell were these *mob buddies*?

I tried to open a few other apps. Excel, locked. Word, locked. Every other application, document, and mail app, locked. None of the passwords worked. Then the screen went black. I plugged it back in and put it on the floor. I could snoop more tonight, dig deeper into whatever Katherine and Shane were hiding, and figure out who was hiding more.

A car pulled behind me in the driveway, blocking me in. A woman got out.

Katherine. *Shit.*

I'd been avoiding her for almost six weeks, trying to figure out which way was up. And here she was, about to blow my cover sky-high.

I thought I could trust her when she hired me last September.

My mind went back to that night—the campaign fundraiser held right here at this house. The night I went from server to asset.

The event was a masterclass in boring political shit. I'd been pouring overpriced champagne for hours, smiling until my face hurt, listening to blowhards debate tax loopholes. I needed a fucking break. I slipped into the master suite's walk-in closet and shut the door. I didn't know what I was looking for at the time, really, until I saw the table full of watches.

Expensive ones. A few big-ticket items to help chip away at Pop's medical bills. As soon as I stashed a heavy Rolex in my apron, his wife walked in. I expected security, police, and scandal. Instead, she quietly closed the door behind her and made me an offer that changed everything:

"All I need is for you to turn him against me and get him to divorce me. I'll pay you ten grand right now, in cash, and half of the divorce settlement when it's all over. We both walk away."

I'd been desperate then. I was still desperate now. The medical bills were piling up faster than Shane's lies. Katherine's offer seemed like divine intervention. My way out, and Pop's lifeline. So, I said yes. The $10,000 was enough to keep the lights on, to keep the collectors from knocking on our door, and to keep Pop alive another day.

But that was before I found out how much she was hiding, too.

Katherine approached my car with deliberate steps and knocked on the passenger-side window. When I unlocked the door, she slid in without invitation.

"We need to talk."

THIRTEEN

KATHERINE

Isabella's hands gripped the steering wheel so tightly her knuckles were white. She hadn't expected me here and certainly hadn't expected a confrontation.

"What do we need to talk about?"

She crossed her arms defensively, as she had back when I caught her stealing. Even when I offered her money, she maintained that stoic poker face.

The plan had been straightforward back then: to flirt and make herself the perfect candidate for Shane's assistant position. I had to give her credit; she pretty much nailed the role instantly. But then, things went off the rails. Somewhere along the way, the pretending stopped. He managed to win her over.

"Look." I softened my tone. "I don't know how or why you fell for him, but you can have him if you want him." I studied her profile. "But I don't think you will once you realize who he truly is."

She glared at me, a look deathlier than Emma had ever

given. "You think I fell for him? Girl, I'm just a better actor than you."

I relaxed slightly. "Good."

"Besides," she said. "You were the one who went against the plan, not me."

She was right. That was the whole point of bringing Isabella in: to make leaving me *his* idea. So we could split the money and run.

The problem was that Shane was more convincing than either of us had anticipated.

"Yes. I know," I said. "And even if I can't get this bullshit prenup overturned, I'm divorcing him no matter what. Especially since I found out about all the other women."

She scowled. "What other women?"

"There are others, Isabella. Lots of them."

She couldn't hide her shock, as if I'd spoken another language. This wasn't an act. She didn't know.

"Do you mean Jessica?" Her face contorted. "Jessica Banks, who used to work for him?"

"Yes, she was one of them. She was actually one of the first red flags." I cleared my throat, feeling the weight of saying it aloud. "Let me guess: Shane said she was crazy? That's what he told me."

"Yep, and how do you know she's not crazy? Maybe it's the truth?"

Oh Isabella. "Sure, maybe she is. But there's also Chelsea, Rhonda, Abby, Ruby, Molly, Mackenzie, Kim…and more. They can't all be crazy."

She turned away, the perfect sculpture of her face momentarily distorted by shock. "Are you serious? How do you even know about all this?"

"Positive. I found his dating profile on a website called OntheSide. For people looking for discreet hookups," I said. "All those trips and meetings out of town. He was even using a different name. Called himself 'Seth.'"

I passed her my phone, which she took from my hand, tentatively. She scrolled through the screenshots, the names, the profiles, then gave a bitter laugh. "God, I'm such an idiot."

"You're not." I fought the impulse to comfort her. "He's exceptionally good at this."

She turned back toward me, reclaiming her composure with visible effort. But I'd already seen it, the raw hurt of humiliation replaced by anger. "He convinced me you were the terrible one." She trailed off, then glared. "There were a lot of things you didn't tell me, Katherine."

"You could have asked me any time since we made our arrangement instead of ghosting me." We'd planned to meet the first Sunday of each month at a local park. No texts, no calls, nothing connecting us at all. Then, she stopped showing up.

She clicked her tongue, studying me. "You never told me he was planning on running for Senate."

My soul left my body.

"What?"

She straightened. "You…didn't know?"

My mouth fell open. "God no…I…what?"

"I figured you were part of it." She pulled out her phone

and showed me a photo. "The messaging is all family man stuff."

I squinted. "Saved a broken family? That asshole." He was using my kids and me for marketing.

"I think he's working to get McFadden elected, so McFadden will help him get elected. His messaging is…scary." Isabella bit her bottom lip. "Bruce was the tip of the iceberg. Apparently, running for office is Shane's endgame."

It all made sense. Shane's shifting political views. Backing candidates he'd mocked a few years ago.

He'd been radicalized into a world that could elect him.

Isabella peered at me, unwavering. "Also, I saw you with someone at the hospital—your ex, I think. You looked…more than friendly. Shane told me you were cheating on him from the beginning."

"Oh, for Christ's sake." I leaned my head back against the headrest. "Nope, Eric and I have been divorced for over a decade. We co-parent. He's one of my best friends. Nothing sexual whatsoever."

"So, Bridge, is…"

"Bridget. His girlfriend."

She pinched the bridge of her nose. "Oh, my God. Shane is such a fuck."

"That's putting it mildly." I felt equal parts sympathy and vindication. "And worse, he threatened me, threatened my kids. He stole money from us, drained the kids' college accounts, emptied our savings—"

"And he's reading your text messages," she interrupted.

"What?"

She pointed to the laptop at her feet, the one Shane always

kept locked up. She picked it up and cautiously typed in the password before handing it to me.

I scrolled through Messenger. Every conversation with Claudia about my suspicions, every message to my lawyer, every moment I believed was mine alone, right there for Shane to dissect and manipulate.

"Damn it." The violation made me want to scrub my skin raw. "That's how he knew. That's how he was always waiting with the perfect excuse."

He'd been inside my head this whole time.

I had the urge to throw up again, but couldn't move.

Then a small mercy occurred to me—Isabella and I had never texted about our arrangement, only met in person that night at the fundraiser and twice since.

"Can I ask you something else?"

"Anything."

"Your texts with Eric," Isabella continued. "He mentioned something about 'mob buddies'?" She raised an eyebrow.

I laughed out loud, realizing how our inside joke must look to others. "Our friends used to tease Eric about his work. Who the hell knows someone in digital forensics? It sounds like a made-up job." I almost told her how I'd fallen for him in rebellion, how my mother thought he was a punk, but I swallowed it back. "People would joke he was either in witness protection or had mob connections. It became this running gag."

"Shane said he was, like, an ex-con or whatever."

"Of course he did. He's thorough, I'll give him that."

Isabella sat still, as if waiting for an explanation.

I relaxed in my seat. "A dozen years ago, Eric partnered

with some guys who were mining crypto, back before anyone knew what crypto was. And, shocker, they weren't great guys. He was in jail for a month; it bankrupted us. We got divorced, not much else to say."

There was more to say, of course. About how I blamed Eric for our debt, because he was an easy target, even though much of it was debt from my three years of college at a private school with loans and no degree. Of the funds I insisted we borrow for IVF, or the house outside of our price range that put us in an upside-down mortgage. He'd tipped scales that were already unbalanced. But his crime was easy to point my finger toward.

She shook her head. "God. He made it sound like Eric was some hardcore criminal."

"Trust me, the most dangerous thing about Eric is his sarcasm," I said. "Shane's good at convincing people. No wonder he's so successful in his line of work."

"Do you think Eric can help us dig into that?" She pointed to the computer.

"Probably. I can ask him tonight."

"Good." She rubbed her temples. "I don't know what I'm going to do when he's discharged. I don't want him at home."

"Back up…Home?"

She let out a deep breath, as if bracing herself for my reaction. "I moved into the Laurelhurst house. He asked me to move in with him."

"Oh, boy." I sank back into the seat, processing this new development. "That's heavy."

I was torn. Thrilled he and I would no longer breathe the same air, but sad for her.

Then it struck me. I didn't understand what she truly wanted, apart from money. She clearly had other motives.

What if we could use this living situation to our advantage?

"How did you get into his laptop, by the way?"

"There were notes written on a notebook in Fred's car, and I tried them. Sutton4Senate."

"Fred knows about the Senate plans?"

"I don't know; he was dodgy. Like he was trying to figure out something but didn't have all the pieces yet." She shifted impatiently. "Shane was adamant that I get the laptop before his dad did."

The voicemail. "Fred called me. Last week. He left a cryptic message about financial concerns he wanted to talk about privately. It must be what he was looking for."

We were quiet for a minute or so; the only sound was the raindrops on the metal roof.

"I think there's still a way for us to both get what we want, if we work together."

She kept her green eyes on me. "How?"

"I'm not sure yet, but we need a plan. One we both stick to this time."

She nodded. "Okay. But we both need to be extremely mindful about how we communicate from now on."

"Right." I made a mental note to change my Apple ID and passwords immediately. "No digital communication at all. No texts, no emails, no social media."

"He monitors everything." Isabella glanced at the laptop.

"I need to work on getting this prenup overturned. My lawyer thinks we may have grounds if Shane hid assets."

"He definitely hid assets," she said. "I've been trying to dig into things at work. There's money moving somewhere."

"Good. I'll give that to my lawyer." I paused. "And I'll talk to Fred, somehow. Whatever he knows about the finances, I need to hear it before Shane shuts him down."

"And I'll reach out to Jessica." Isabella pulled a card from her bag. "She tried to warn me about something."

"You and me both." Why hadn't I talked to Jessica when she came to the house three years ago? Instead, I believed Shane's lies. I could have saved myself so much trouble. "Can you meet on Friday at noon?" I said.

"Same place as before?" Neither of us voiced it aloud in case, somehow, ears were listening.

"I'll be there." I opened the car door, then hesitated, a maternal instinct kicking in, knowing she was driving back to his…their house. He'd lied to her as much, if not more, than he'd lied to me. She was his pawn, too.

"Are you going to be okay, Isabella?"

Her face stiffened, reminding me she wasn't some naïve girl.

"I've survived worse." She gave a faint smile. "And I have something he doesn't."

"What's that?"

"An ally." Her eyes met mine with unflinching directness. "And call me Izzy."

I smiled back. "Call me Katie."

I closed the door, and she drove away. Either I'd found a partner, or I'd handed Shane the perfect weapon to destroy me.

FOURTEEN

ISABELLA

"I figured you guys would be happy to meet before work! Don't boomers like early mornings?" I teased, sliding a stack of account reports across the table. "Isn't that your natural habitat? Coffee at dawn, forwarding questionable Facebook articles by noon?"

Patrick and Neil looked painfully out of place in the hipster coffee shop, their golf polos and sensible watches a stark contrast to the sea of tattoos and thrift-store flannel. Meanwhile, I was running on four hours of sleep and my third espresso, survival these days, thanks to Shane.

"If it's a tee time, I'll jump out of bed. An 8 AM meeting? Not so much," Patrick grumbled.

The espresso machine hissed, and burnt sugar hung in the air. A milk pitcher screamed as the barista overshot the foam.

I'd asked for this meeting under the guise of helping Shane during his recovery, but what I really needed was access to financial records, something I could see before Shane got his hands on them and possibly manipulated or destroyed them.

"So. I was hoping you could help me with something." I kept my voice light and breezy. "Shane's been asking about the quarterly reports, and I want to get ahead of it before he's discharged. Can you give me access to the financial system? The basics, donor records, disbursements, that sort of thing?"

The temperature at the table dropped ten degrees.

They exchanged glances—the silent should-we-tell-her passing between men with secrets.

Patrick shifted in his seat, suddenly fascinated by his boring-ass coffee. "Honey, that's not something we can do."

"I'm just trying to help," I said. "I know you both want Shane to get better, too, so if I can have the reports ready, organize the data before he gets home—"

"Izzy, we want to help, but…" Neil trailed off, looking to Patrick for rescue.

Patrick cleared his throat, his charm evaporating. "We have families. We can't risk—"

I crossed my arms. "Risk what?"

They avoided eye contact. Neil wiped his palms on his khakis, while Patrick fiddled with the sugar packets.

"What the hell are you scared of?" I pushed. "I'm not asking for state secrets. I'm asking for access to the same financial software you use every day."

Silence.

Fucking men.

"We can't." Patrick's accent thickened. "I'm sorry, las. It's not personal."

But it absolutely was personal. They were terrified of

something, or someone, and I was pretty sure that someone was Shane.

Whatever he had on them was enough to make grown men sweat through an 8 AM coffee meeting and refuse a simple request from his assistant.

"Fine." I gathered my things. "Forget I asked."

"Izzy—" Neil started, but I was already sliding out of the booth.

"Did I miss a meeting?"

The three of us turned. Davis towered above our table. I slid a document beneath my notebook, but not before he caught the McFadden letterhead.

Patrick said, "No," and Neil said, "Yes," simultaneously. *Way to keep it cool, gentlemen. Real CIA material here.* Then, without another word, the two of them awkwardly walked out the door, leaving me to explain.

"Secret meetings now? What's going on, Iz?"

"It isn't a big deal. Just coffee." My breezy tone landed somewhere closer to frantic.

"Yeah. Looks real casual." Davis narrowed his eyes. "What are you doing?"

"Nothing, Davis, I had some questions and didn't need you to—" I searched my mind for a way to say, *You're a tattle-tale*, without saying it. "Look, anytime we all meet, you report back to Shane."

"Shane's the president of the company, Iz. That's what I'm supposed to do."

"Not while he's recuperating. He needs to focus on his health, not on day-to-day logistics."

He stepped closer, his voice dropping. "Speaking of that,

shouldn't you be playing nursemaid? Or did you finally realize what you've gotten yourself into?"

The question hit too close to home. I slid past him and pushed through the door, the cool, damp air a welcome shock. He followed me onto the sidewalk.

"Iz, hold up."

I kept walking. What could I say? *You were right; I'm in over my head.* Not an option.

He jogged to catch up, his hand closing gently around my arm, turning me to face him.

"Hey, I'm sorry. That came out wrong. I just… I hate this for you."

His grip softened, but he didn't let go. His thumb brushed over my forearm, sending a jolt through me that had nothing to do with the cold. "I hate watching you do this. Playing the happy girlfriend, fetching his water, pretending he's not… him."

"It's fine, Davis."

"No, it's not." He took another half-step, forcing me to look up at him. The space between us crackled. "Don't you remember that night? Before all this? Before *him*?"

The memory of that drunken, stupidly wonderful kiss slammed into view. His lips on mine, the smell of his cologne, the same one he was wearing now. For one idiotic second, I wanted things to be simple.

"It was a mistake," I said. A lie so thin it was transparent.

"Was it?" He reached out, his fingers brushing a damp strand of hair from my cheek. His touch was hesitant, but it left a trail of heat on my skin. The world narrowed to the few inches between our faces. He was going to kiss me. I was going to let him.

A city bus roared past, spraying a sheet of grimy water onto the sidewalk near our feet. The spell shattered. I stumbled back, yanking my arm away like it had been burned.

"I can't do this." A fresh wave of panic hit me. What had I almost done? How could I have been so reckless? "I have to go."

I swiveled around and raced to my car, hoping he wouldn't follow. Everything was unraveling—my work, my relationship with Shane, my confidence in who I could trust. Davis's words hung in the air, but it was the way he looked at me, as if he saw right through the cracks in my façade, that terrified me most. He could see the desperation I worked overtime to cover with bravado, and it was disarming as hell.

My phone pinged on the passenger seat with a text from Shane:

Where are you?

Three words felt like a collar tightening around my neck. He expected an immediate answer, a location, an ETA. I was ready to tap out a placating lie about traffic, but some new rebellious instinct took over. *No.* Not this time. Instead, I pressed the power button until the screen went black, started the car, and raced out of the lot.

I had to choose a side. For now, it would be my own.

I found her at a back table at Metro Coffee, where we'd agreed to meet, even though I absolutely didn't need more caffeine. Her head was bent over a book, and she'd swapped her floral tradwife outfit for jeans and a white T-shirt, looking nothing like the femme fatale Shane had painted her as—yet neither did I, and here we were. Her long strawberry hair was in a casual topknot, with tiny, shimmering, round raindrops on it.

"Jessica?"

She looked up, her doe-like eyes widening before recognition settled in. "Hi, Isabella. It's great to see you again."

"Call me Izzy." I sat across from her. "I'm sorry I'm late, things have been...well, you can probably imagine."

"It's absolutely fine. I'm pleased you reached out." She gestured to the chair opposite her. "Should I start at the beginning?"

"Please." I took off my jacket and hung it on the back of my chair.

"It started normally enough. Shane hired me in early 2020 and kept me on during the pandemic. I thought I was incredibly fortunate; all my friends were getting laid off." She wrapped her hands tightly around her mug, a cinnamon leaf floating on the foam. "After a few weeks, he made his interest...clear."

"Right," I said.

"We only ever stayed in hotels, because I had roommates, and he said he didn't want media following us, which I didn't question." She relaxed her shoulders slightly. "I didn't realize it was because he had a girlfriend living with him."

"Katherine?"

"One and the same. I didn't know that, obviously," Jessica said.

"Obviously."

"Then one night, he left his phone unlocked and open to the camera app. I realized he'd been recording us." She swallowed hard. "And I don't care if people are into that, but I'm not. I'm private, not a voyeur, so I told him it was over. That was a deal-breaker for me."

"Good for you," I said.

"And he was fine at first. But then, the next week, emails started appearing in Patrick's and my inboxes, with photos and videos of me, along with some conversations with Patrick, making it seem like he and I were messing around. He cropped innocent things—group photos, a hug—until they looked incriminating. We could have explained it away, but Shane told us he would send it to the entire office. Can you imagine?"

I leaned toward her. "So, you quit?"

"When I came to the office for work one day, I wasn't allowed in the building. I'd been fired with no warning." She tapped on her mug.

"And Patrick got to keep his job like nothing happened," I said. "Let me guess, Shane might have told his wife?"

I sank back in my chair—Shane's comment about Jessica being crazy.

"I'm sorry, Jessica. That it happened, and that I believed Shane's bullshit. I should have known better. The guy lies as easily as he breathes."

"Well, why wouldn't you believe him?" Jessica shrugged.

"And, honestly, there were rumors before I came along, too. I wish I had believed them."

"Like what?"

"The Sutton Stars program. Before the pandemic, some scholarship winners had the opportunity to intern with him. They received a stipend to cover room, board, and other expenses while gaining experience. But ninety percent of them were female."

"Oh, right." My stomach twisted.

"There was some talk about how he was, you know… grooming them. The internships stopped when the pandemic hit, and then the questions faded away. Somehow, he swept it all under the rug."

I wasn't surprised, just sickened. "So much for *Save the Children*."

"Shane Sutton destroys people, Izzy. And he never pays the price. Never."

Maybe it's time he did. "Can I ask you something else?"

"Sure." She took a drink of her perfect latte. It left behind a little milk mustache.

"You told me you knew I wasn't just an employee. How did you know about Shane and me?"

"I didn't at first. When I heard about Shane's accident, I realized he couldn't send the collateral from a coma." She wiped her mouth with the back of her napkin. "So, I went to the building to see if I could talk to Patrick, and they still wouldn't let me in. But that's when I saw you. And…I don't know. You reminded me of myself. We're his type, I suppose."

His type. *Ouch.* The newest model in a long line of young women who could be manipulated, used, and discarded. And

I'd been careless enough to think I was the one pulling the string.

"Tits and a heartbeat?" I offered.

Jessica laughed. "Basically."

I let out a sigh. "So, if Shane has leverage on everyone, how could any of us stop him?"

Jessica took a card out of her purse. "That's what I was hoping you could help me with."

She handed the card to me:

ALEXANDRA COLLINS
ASSISTANT DISTRICT ATTORNEY
KING COUNTY PROSECUTOR'S OFFICE

"She's been investigating Shane for years, but she's stuck."

I slid the card in my purse, next to Jessica's, like I was collecting fucking Pokémon cards. "Stuck how?"

Jessica's expression darkened. "She says she doesn't have enough evidence."

"Then how is she supposed to help us?"

She shifted in her seat. "Numbers, maybe. I'm in touch with a dozen former interns and employees. But everyone is scared of retaliation. We need more. More people, more proof."

I turned my phone on and looked at the time. fifteen minutes to noon. "Shit. I have to go, Jessica, but I'll be in touch."

We said our goodbyes, and I stepped back out into the persistent drizzle, while my phone continued to rattle like a snake. Seven missed calls from Shane. The screen lit up with his latest text:

> You have thirty minutes to get to the hospital, or I'm going to send someone to look for you.

Fuck. I turned the phone off again. One last meeting he couldn't know about.

After another 20 minutes in traffic, I parked like a true optimist: half a block from Olympic Sculpture Park, after doing a tight-lipped, "don't make eye contact, I saw it first" dance with a dude in a BMW. The curbside slot looked legal enough to pass a casual glance and sketchy enough to get me towed if the universe felt petty.

Katie had initially suggested this as our meeting spot, and at first, it struck me as...odd. Who picks public art as a rendezvous point when you're trading contraband? It had a very *Tony Soprano* vibe.

But I'd come to love it, with all its clean lines and salt air, a curated strip of quiet pinned between the city and the Sound. Here, we could be visible without being memorable, and move around without looking like we were fleeing. And if you needed to disappear, you just keep walking—down a path, around a bend, behind a piece of hammered steel the size of a small house.

The rain had stopped, but everything still gleamed: pavement dark as ink, leaves lacquered, the city lights smeared into the wet like someone had dragged a thumb through them. The water beyond was a sheet of pewter.

I spotted Katie near the entrance path, trying very hard to act like a normal woman who enjoyed culture and oxygen, but

I could see the dark circles under her eyes, which even expensive concealer couldn't negotiate away.

"Hey," I said when I got close.

"Hey, yourself."

We walked along the path. To our left, a massive black sculpture rose up, all severe angles and sharp edges. Farther along, a bright red structure cut into the gray like a warning sign. I never remembered the names of the art pieces, only the feelings they gave me, as if I was being watched.

Katie angled us toward a bench set back from the main path, where a twisting piece of metal arched overhead, framing the skyline in jagged slices.

"Eric finished the clone this morning," she said, reaching into her handbag and pulling out the laptop. "He copied everything onto his hard drive. Shane shouldn't be able to tell."

I unzipped the case, and I examined it as she passed it to me. Same scratches on the corner, same stickers, same dent he'd blamed on TSA. "When will Eric be able to dig into the files?"

"He said it could take a bit. Apparently, Shane's security is...impressive."

"Of course it is." I zipped the case and hugged it to my chest.

"Any headway with his coworkers or Jessica?"

I shook my head. "No smoking gun, but a few breadcrumbs to follow, I guess." I looked around, convinced we were being watched, but we were the only ones in the park. "I'd better go. Shane's waiting."

"Be careful," Katie said.

"I will. I've gotten pretty good at playing his devoted girlfriend."

Katie flinched. "I'm sorry. I know this isn't easy."

"I'll be fine," I lied. "We're almost there."

Katie walked back toward the entrance with tight shoulders and brisk steps, and I went the opposite direction, cutting down the path through the remaining art, until I eventually ended back at my car, no parking ticket in sight.

FIFTEEN

KATHERINE

The bathroom scale's digital display blinked twice as if questioning its own reading. I stepped off and back on. Still 119. My reflection in the full-length mirror confirmed what the scale had been telling me: my clothes hung off my frame as if they belonged to someone else. I pinched the fabric of my sweater, pulling it taut against my ribs, then let it fall loose.

My subconscious handled the one thing Shane couldn't: my appetite. Claudia called me a skeleton yesterday, and while my instinct might be to see that as a compliment, I knew it wasn't healthy. It was another twisted legacy of my mother's constant monitoring of my weight growing up. Perhaps I could write a book called *The Divorce Diet* to target other forty-something women who still carry a touch of disordered eating from their teen years. If it became a bestseller, my financial worries would disappear—though at this rate, I might, too.

I tucked the scale away and followed the sound of laughter downstairs.

The media room was a teenage wasteland of sleeping bags, blankets, and empty donut boxes. Claudia and Chris's kids stayed over, all six kids snug in their sleeping bags watching a movie, and for a moment, life was normal.

It was a rare weekend free from sports and activities, a gift of two days with no obligations. Back when they were small, days like these were endless and dull, filled with unstructured hours I was too tired to enjoy.

Emma laughed at the screen, her head thrown back in an unguarded way, making her look so young despite her eyebrow ring and adult posturing. Elliott sat cross-legged, quietly focused, his analytical mind likely dissecting the film's social dynamics. And Ethan, my baby, still gangly and growing into his limbs, made jokes, utterly unaware of the danger lurking in our lives.

The danger that had already tried to poison them against me.

These were the moments I was fighting for. I leaned against the doorframe, memorizing the scene as fuel for the difficult days ahead.

"Morning, Ms. Valentine." Jackson's words carried the faint odor of morning breath that came with six teenagers in one room. A colorful movie played on the giant TV, accompanied by catchy music.

"Whatcha watchin'?"

"*Mean Girls*," Ethan said dramatically as if forced to watch, though he was completely absorbed.

"Where's Lindsay Lohan?"

The kids laughed at me in unison.

"Girl," Josie teased. "This is the remake. Lindsay's in the old-fashioned one."

Ooof. *Girl? Old-Fashioned?* I laughed as the actors sang and danced in the hallways of a high school about a revenge party.

A revenge party? It may be time to plan a similar event for Shane. I'd write the guest list. What a celebration of pure satisfaction it would be to see Shane face consequences, while all the women he fucked over lined up to watch.

As the song played, Emma and Josie sang along with an enthusiasm that made my chest ache. How had I ended up here? I'd spent my entire adult life trying to avoid becoming my mother, only to end up where she had: with a husband who was "just the nicest"—the secret predatory behavior, the lies, the multiple women.

I had married my father.

But unlike my mother, I wouldn't stay, smile, and pretend anymore.

I checked the time and went upstairs. Eric was on his way to show me some things he found on Shane's laptop. We couldn't text anymore, so we chose to handle things in person since Shane might be watching.

I passed through the kitchen by the counter with the growing pile of unopened bills. The home was in Shane's name, yet a $250,000 renovation loan we took out was rolled into a line of credit in *my* name. I wondered why he hadn't paid it off completely, but he always brushed me off and told me it was "good debt." I kicked myself for never questioning why the debt was always in my name, and the properties were in his. Since I'd had a prior bankruptcy, he explained that it was better for my credit to pay back the loans monthly in my name. Back then, it sounded plausible, but now, it meant I carried the debt while he kept the assets.

My phone pinged with a text from Chris:

Preliminary hearing set for Friday!

Less than a week! Too soon, yet not soon enough.

I'd spent days on the phone with the bank and, sadly, discovered there was no crime. After speaking with the bank's accounting specialist and reviewing all the paperwork, it was clear that Shane had legal access to all the bank accounts. My signature was right there. I didn't remember signing over power of attorney, but I had. Without realizing it, I'd handed him my kids' futures.

Chris assured me that shielding funds during a divorce was illegal, but the power of attorney ate that boundary alive. It would be my word against his. The kids and I might never see the money again. Still, Chris said we could petition the court to recover the money, even temporarily, until we finalized the divorce.

I plopped down on the couch while Piper pressed her warm body against me, oblivious to personal space. I scratched behind her ears, and she licked my wrist, her tail thumping steadily against the throw pillow.

"At least you still love me, huh, girl?"

Another text:

Can't wait for Tuesday night.

I bit my bottom lip, heat curling through me. Hot Toddy and I were getting together this week, the one bright spot in my color-coded calendar. My mother used to say, *Idle hands are the devil's playground*, and oh, I hoped that was true. We'd been texting and sexting all week. Neither of us wanted anything serious; we were both recently out of relationships and did not want to make anything awkward for our kids at school. I told him my kids would be at their dad's, and he should plan to sleep over, which was not exactly subtle. There was no room for misinterpretation. As the youngsters would say, I was *DTF*, a phrase I'd learned from an awkward internet search while trying to decode teen slang. Claudia will be so proud.

I returned a text:

See you at 7. Don't expect conversation 

The response was immediate.

Yes, Ma'am.

How could I possibly wait three days?

I opened Facebook and continued the work I'd started yesterday: removing Shane from my timeline.

I deleted photos methodically, erasing every staged memory of our marriage. The wedding portraits when he was probably thinking of someone else. Pandemic puzzles with the family when he pretended he was an upstanding stepfather.

Sunset images from a romantic trip to Fiji, where he'd been texting other women while I slept. After half an hour of digital excision, I'd restored my timeline to photos of my kids and my dog. Clean and authentic, the way my life was meant to be all along.

Piper whined at the door when Eric arrived.

"Come in," I called.

"Hey, Katie." Eric walked in, and Bridget followed behind him.

"Hey, Bridge! What a nice surprise." I hugged her. I couldn't ask for a better bonus mom for my kids. Instead of jealousy, I was grateful. The woman who occupied my ex-husband's bed always had my back.

Eric closed the door and greeted Piper, then took off his shoes at the door, a rule he could never remember when we were married. Better late than never.

"I tagged along, but I'll stay out of your hair," Bridget said, scratching Piper's ears, sending her tail wagging like a helicopter. "I have to say I'm thrilled that absolute piece of shit is gone."

I laughed. Bridget wasn't only sharp-tongued, she was a medical examiner. She stared death in the face every day. If she thought Shane was a piece of shit, that was practically a professional diagnosis. "Thanks, Bridge. Me, too. Kids are downstairs watching *Mean Girls*…"

"Say no more!" She practically leaped down to the basement.

Eric surveyed the entryway, noticing the empty spots where Shane's coats and shoes had been.

"Feels different in here already."

"I put some coffee on if you'd like?" The one thing my stomach could always tolerate was coffee, my primary fuel these days. Even without the hospital couch, sleep hadn't returned.

He peeked at his watch. "I mean, I'm down. I can sleep when I'm dead."

I pulled two mugs from the cabinet, mismatched ones the kids had painted years ago at a pottery studio. Eric's had a lopsided baseball painted by Elliott; mine featured Emma's early attempt at our family portrait, stick figures with disproportionate smiles. The steam fogged my glasses as I took my first sip, and we made small talk.

"So, we agreed we would ground Ethan one more week, but I did promise he could go to Joshua's birthday party," I said. "Hopefully, that's okay."

"Yeah, that works." Eric stirred a dollop of cream into his cup. "Hey, when's the job start, by the way?"

"Next week." I tried to downplay how much it meant to me. "Part-time for now. It will still be chaotic, but…"

"But it's yours," he said. "Something he can't take away. Forward, not backward, remember?"

I laughed; it was our former well-meaning but out-of-her-depth therapist's mantra. "God, I wonder if she's still charging $200 an hour to tell people to breathe deeply."

"$300 now, according to Bridget."

I resisted my usual urge to prod about him, 'making an honest woman out of her' for once. Because who was I to give relationship advice? Eric drained our savings a decade ago, and I'd punished him for years. But I'd done something worse. I married a predator.

The thought brought me to tears.

"Katie, what…"

"I shouldn't have signed that prenup. I shouldn't have…" My voice broke.

"Hey." Eric reached across the counter, his hand covering mine. "This isn't on you. This is on him."

"But I chose him. I brought him into our kids' lives. I—"

"Katie, stop blaming yourself for someone else being a complete asshole."

I remembered Eric's face when we moved into Shane's house. He had said little. But later, when Shane wasn't around, he was more direct: "Katie, this is rushed. You barely know him."

I'd accused him of being jealous, furious at the suggestion that my feelings for Shane weren't real. But Eric had seen the truth all along. I fell in love with an illusion that I'd been so desperate to believe in, I ignored every warning sign along the way. He could say, "I told you so," but he never would.

"I'm responsible, too, you know," Eric said. "You wouldn't have needed his money if I hadn't fucked up our finances in the first place."

"Eric, that's water under the bridge. This is on me." Our bankruptcy was a decade ago. I couldn't use it as an excuse anymore, even if I wanted to.

"Well, on that note." He tapped the stack of papers in front of him. "I still haven't scratched the surface on the hard drive, but let me show you what I've found so far."

Eric's finger moved between two columns on a spreadsheet. "Look at this."

I wiped my eyes, and the columns blurred. "It looks like a nightmare; what am I looking for?"

"Same transaction, two different amounts." He pointed to one cell in the spreadsheet and traced his finger to the other side. "These numbers should match, but can you see how each is transposed? It's easy for an accountant to miss these small errors adding up to hundreds of thousands of dollars, sometimes millions."

I squinted to understand what he meant. The numbers were changed slightly, from a zero to an eight or a three to a nine, so it wouldn't be obvious to someone scanning quickly.

"It's not unusual to see one or two of these. Everyone makes math and transposition errors; most of the time, they're legitimate mistakes. But when there's a pattern over multiple documents and years, it suggests fraud." He pointed to another row. "Here, look at this specific entry from last June. $85,000 allocated for 'administrative expenses.' But in the quarterly filing, it shows as $58,000. So where is that other $27,000?"

I shrugged. "Is this a riddle? I don't know, where?"

He pulled out another sheet. "See these?"

A row of numbers, ten thousand here, five thousand there, another ten thousand, two thousand. I nodded. "Okay." I followed along,

"Withdrawals, cash. Totaling $27,000. And this is for one quarterly tax return."

I tapped my fingers on the table. "So, where's the money going?"

Eric sat back, satisfied yet surprisingly not smug. "Cash is used when people don't want a trace. My guess would be bribes, typical in politics. But no matter what it's being used for, it appears Sutton Stars is a front to embezzle funds, not to help students."

The organization Shane paraded at every social function to burnish his reputation as Seattle's most generous businessman. The foundation that politicians from both parties praised in their speeches had given Davis his start. Shane was stealing from it?

"What if he's already deleted everything? What if there's no digital trace?"

"Deleting a file doesn't make it gone. Everything leaves a digital fingerprint," Eric said. "He can't hide from that."

"So that's a smoking gun, right?" My voice was tight. "We can use this to prove he has hidden assets, even get the prenup thrown out?"

"Theoretically, yes, but the signature file is encrypted, so I'll keep working on it." Eric's bad-news face returned. He slid an envelope toward me. "In the meantime…"

"What's this?"

"Open it later. It's…private." He eyed me up and down in a secret translation I understood.

"Naked…pictures?"

He grimaced. "I'm sorry."

"Ugh, gross. Nothing you haven't seen before, I suppose."

"It's…not just you. That's why I—you should look at them, not me."

"Oh, God." Shane continued to disgust me more and more.

"Yeah. And like I said, I'll keep looking."

"Okay, thank you, Eric." I reached out my arms for a hug,

and he wrapped me in his. These moments were bittersweet. In many ways, he was my person, and here he was, playing hero for me while still being a partner to someone else. Sometimes, I still saw that flannel-wearing grunge hacker behind his grown-up façade, and it made my heart ache in the strangest, sweetest way.

My phone rang again in my hand, and Eric glanced down.

"Who's Hot Toddy?"

SIXTEEN

ISABELLA

I stared at the lake house, its sleek glass and modern angles against the gray February sky. A few weeks ago, this place seemed like a perk of doing business. Now, it felt like a prison with better landscaping.

Shane was out of the hospital and home, in OUR home—though that word had gone to shit. Medical equipment cluttered the living room like uninvited guests.

Overwhelmed? Try completely freaking the fuck out. My anxiety had anxiety.

After only a few days, I'd morphed from girlfriend to nurse, from assistant to possession—just another asset.

I stayed gone as long as I possibly could today, rehearsing my excuses on a loop: *Sorry, crazy day at work. The traffic was insane. My phone died.* Each lie sounded faker than the last, but whatever. I took three deep breaths, slapped on another coat of lip gloss, and braced myself for Hurricane Nancy.

"There you are, dear! Fred, Isabella is here!" Nancy's voice reminded me of a stepmother from a Disney movie, and I was neither living, laughing, nor loving it. She'd taken the news way too easily that Shane was with me instead of Katie. She barely questioned it. Even my moving in with him didn't faze her, like she had plucked Katie out and dropped me into their family dollhouse.

"Oh, hi, sweetie." Fred checked his watch. "Goodness, Shane told us to expect you at dinnertime! But I'm glad you're here now!"

"Sorry, yeah, I had a lot of work to catch up on." I tried to sound chill while my brain screamed at me to run.

Fred chuckled, his eyes wrinkling at the corners. "Oh, we've heard that story before. Shane was always 'caught up at work,' too."

"Fred," Nancy chided from across the room, "don't embarrass the poor girl."

"Not embarrassing. Observing." Fred winked at me.

"We're…different in a lot of ways, actually," I said, feeling the need to distance myself. "I'm going to check on him."

I walked through the kitchen to the bedroom where Shane lay awake in his fancy clinical bed, watching a draft of an ad on his tablet—Bruce McFadden in front of a public school, promising to put parents back in charge, while Shane nodded along.

"Hi, Bells," Shane mumbled.

"Hi! Can I get you anything?"

"Water."

I held the straw from his water bottle to his mouth, like a

babysitter in hell. My skin crawled as his lips puckered around the straw, making a wet sucking sound. Thank God he'd have visiting nurses starting tomorrow, though I questioned if he needed them or wanted the eye candy. Probably the latter.

"Thank you." He took a few gulps. "Where have you been?"

"The office, errands," I lied.

"It's seven-thirty. Pretty long errands." His eyes tracked my movement across the room. "Davis said you left around four, and then you didn't show up here until hours later?"

"Okay?" I folded my arms. "So, who's watching who?"

"What's with you?" His jaw tightened.

"Sorry, I'm…overwhelmed, I guess." I squared my shoulders. Truth: I'd left my phone at home so he couldn't track me. Digital detox, survival edition.

He softened, opening his arms. "Come here."

His tenderness made my body respond like a well-trained pet, a familiar warmth spreading through me despite what I knew. He gently rubbed my back. It scared me how easily he could still flip the switch. The worst part? My body still wanted to believe him.

I sat up and moved to leave the room when he saw inside my handbag. His head snapped toward me. "Wait, is that my computer?"

"Oh, yes! I totally forgot!" My voice went all squeaky-mouse as I passed it to him.

"Where'd you find it?" Shane's face was flat and emotionless.

Don't look suspicious, don't look suspicious. "Oh, when I helped move stuff out of the house with your dad, I threw it in my bag."

"Dad said it wasn't there." He opened the device and clicked through, each second stretching painfully as I waited for him to notice something was off. When he zoned out on his screen again, his shoulders relaxed, and I returned to the living room on shaky legs, like I'd run the mile in gym class.

I joined Nancy on the couch where she was unpacking boxes at a pace that was giving me literal anxiety. I side-eyed her, wondering how well she knew her son. Did she know about all the women before me? About the real Shane and Katie drama?

"You don't have many things, honey. You hardly had any boxes." She gestured around the room with her manicured hand.

Weird. She shouldn't have seen me with boxes. I'd moved things in myself. Was she watching me through the blinds? Maybe stalker vibes ran in the family. "I'm a minimalist."

"So, tell me about your family, Isabella. Do they live close?" She leaned in, elbows on her knees, invading my space.

Damn. The family questions I'd been dodging roundhouse kicked me in the face. I'd spent my life trying to escape my parents' paranoia, only to find myself constantly looking over my shoulder, wondering who knew what about Shane, about me, about Katie, about all of us. What comes around goes around, or some shit.

"Uh, yeah, they live about an hour away. I go back to see them when I can."

She plastered on a fake smile, but something about her tone made me look closer. Beneath her perfect hair and makeup, Nancy seemed…brittle. I threw her the most basic small talk I could think of, hoping it would head off an interrogation.

"How about you? Have you and Fred always lived in Seattle?" Thankfully, she took the bait and ran with it.

"Yes. Fred and I married right out of high school. We had to," she added with a laugh. "I was pregnant, and in those days, you didn't have choices. You did the proper thing. And I made sure we did it right. I always believed if you managed the details, the rest would follow."

Her voice softened as she smoothed a photo of Shane as a teen. "That's why I hated seeing Shane in the hospital so much. All those doctors acted as if they knew him better than I did. Telling me how strong his recovery was, how perfect his vitals were. It wasn't their medicine or machines."

I took a moment before speaking. "What was it?"

"Oh, Shane takes such good care of himself. I keep telling Fred the same thing, but he never listens. Stubborn man. If he followed my smart boy's advice instead of taking the poison the cardiologist prescribes…"

I froze. Her words hit too close. Herbs instead of medicine, faith instead of science.

She wiped her eyes suddenly, shifting gears so fast it made me dizzy. "Anyway, families always have their troubles. But I know what's best for Shane. Always have."

Raised voices distracted us. Shane and Fred's words carried right through the wall.

"You swore to me, Shane," Fred yelled. "After what happened last time—"

"Keep it down!" Shane hissed.

I strained to hear more, while Nancy waved a hand as if to say, "Don't pay attention to that."

"Fred's been difficult lately," she shouted, clearly trying to drown out the argument. "Questioning everything, interfering with Shane's business."

Her fingers twisted at the cross around her neck, but her eyes remained cold, calculating—the exact opposite of the grieving act she'd put on seconds before. No wonder Shane had mastered switching emotions on command.

"He's probably concerned." I tilted my head slightly to listen, catching fragments:

"—this isn't what I taught you—"

"—what we fought against—"

"—your fault when it all falls apart—"

"Men think they know everything," Nancy rasped. "But mothers understand what's best for their children. We always have."

I struggled to listen to the men yelling, but Nancy wouldn't stop yapping.

"Fred has never understood Shane the way I have. The way you understand him."

Shut up, Nancy!

Fred returned to the living room with a sheen of sweat on his forehead. He set down a box with a loud thud, like it had taken more out of him than it should.

"How are we doing, ladies? What can I help with?" He

pretended he hadn't been screaming at his son thirty feet away.

"Look at these pictures, Fred. Little Shane. Oh, my little darling." Nancy motioned Fred to sit beside her.

She didn't ask why they were fighting, what was wrong—she brushed right past it.

"Oh, Nancy, Isabella could use help with all of this." He ignored the photos, gesturing to the sea of boxes before us, then picked up one filled with books. "Where can I shelve these, Isabella?"

The distraction was a blessing. I didn't need either of them looking too closely at me or my life.

As creepily codependent as Nancy was, it wouldn't be long until she figured out I wasn't there to be the next senator's wife.

"Right over there's fine." I pointed at a random bookshelf. As if I cared where Shane's shit ended up. I trailed him while Nancy slipped back toward Shane's room. I wanted to eavesdrop, but couldn't be in two places at once.

"Here you go." He looked behind him to make sure Nancy was out of sight. "I see Shane has his laptop. Do you know how he got it?"

Shit. If I tell him the truth, he'll know I lied, but if I lie, he won't think I lied. Classic riddle.

"No, maybe Davis gave it to him."

"Right." Fred ran his hand over his bald head, eyes darting toward the doorway where Nancy had disappeared.

"Hey, listen—" He cut himself off, glancing over his shoulder again. "I need to tell you something, but not here."

"Um, okay. About what?" I said, but his face glazed over as soon as Nancy walked in.

"Welp, I'll grab some more boxes," Fred said, awkwardly. "Want these by the bookshelf, too?"

"Sure."

The whole exchange screamed *sketchy*. I climbed the staircase to the master bedroom, my refuge. Shane couldn't make it upstairs yet, which meant I had one sliver of space to breathe without his eyes on me.

But I couldn't shake Fred's concern. What did he want to talk about? The same thing he'd tried to warn Katie about? Money? Girlfriends? An evil twin? How bad could it get at this point?

I flopped on the bed and turned my phone back on. Notifications flooded in.

A text from Mom with her and Pop's goofy grins too close to the camera:

Missing you!

Since I'd moved into the lake house, at least I wasn't spending two hours commuting every day. But I felt empty without them.

I replied:

Miss you, too!

Then I scrolled. Multiple texts and calls from Shane. More from Davis. A few from Tammi. Shane's messages were the worst:

Where are you?

Answer your phone.

Davis says you left the office hours ago.

I called Tammi. She hasn't seen you either.

Isabella, I need you to respond NOW.

I'm having my mother drive me to the police station if I don't hear from you by 5.

Jesus. He'd basically built a whole-ass surveillance network from his sickbed.

I ignored his messages and opened Davis's thread, then stopped mid-thumb.

What if Shane was also looking at my messages? Wouldn't put it past him to have some creepy spyware on my phone.

Davis's last message blinked back at me:

Iz, let me know you're safe. If you need an out, say the word. No questions asked.

I wanted to answer. But I couldn't risk it, not yet.

I opened my hidden photo folder on my phone, the vault of pictures I couldn't share with anyone, especially Shane, and scrolled to an image, pixelated and overexposed, but still my favorite—me, Mom, Pop, and Misha, my beautiful sister. A moment frozen in time.

"What would you think of me now?" I whispered to the forever nineteen-year-old girl in the photo. Would she see me as strong, or as lost as she'd been? I closed the photo folder, but not the memory of her. My family was keeping me going, which was the reason I had to survive this. I just had to survive.

Then—a sound.

A gasp.

A scuffle.

The sickening *thud* of a body hitting the ground.

Then a hollow silence, as if the house held its breath with me.

Then Nancy's scream pierced the air, raw and horrified. "Isabella! Call 911! Oh, God, no!"

SEVENTEEN

KATHERINE

I checked the time: 6:45 PM. Todd would be here in fifteen minutes.

Wine glasses filled, I paced the living room, tapping my fingers against my exposed thighs. Not nervous. Hungry.

I tossed the empty wine bottle into the bin, along with junk mail, including Shane's latest campaign mailer about traditional family values, which featured a photo of our family. Still using us for his image. He'd built his reputation for virtue as a performance while living immorally. I'd spent my life trying to be a good girl: the perfect daughter, the perfect wife, the perfect mother. But Shane had destroyed that good girl, and that wasn't entirely bad.

Because I had a need, and it was primal.

I was going to fuck Todd Anderson's brains out.

I unbuttoned my sweater dress to check myself out in the mirror once more and hype myself up. Though I felt a little exposed, I had to admit I looked damn good. I was downright hot. I'd do me. The new bra-and-panty set, with too many straps and lace for comfort, was made for looks, not utility. Add thigh-high black suede boots, and I could be someone else, in the best way.

The doorbell rang. I buttoned up the sweater dress again and ran my fingers through my hair before opening the door. Todd wore a black T-shirt and jeans that fit perfectly.

"Hey, Katie." He walked in and kissed me on the cheek. The hair on the back of my neck prickled. God, his cologne smelled so good. Without thinking, I kissed him. One of his hands gripped the small of my back and pulled me closer, while the other went behind my head, into my hair, gently tugging. We both knew what this was.

I stepped back, guiding him to the couch. "Wine?"

"Not thirsty." He sat, leaning forward eagerly as I stood before him.

I unbuttoned my dress, and with each button, his mouth opened wider, like a man unwrapping fire.

"Holy hell. Yes." He ran his hands up the back of my boots, then my thighs, kissing between them. I flinched. He pulled me toward him, and I straddled his lap on the couch, mouth on his. He lowered his hand down my face, neck, and chest and freed my breasts from the fragile fabric. His mouth followed, drawing circles around my nipple with his tongue while the other hand slid down to my hips, pulling me even closer. He met my eyes and pushed my hair off my face.

"I don't want to be too forward, but can we go to your bedroom? I want to take my time with you."

"Yes, please."

He lifted me with him, with my legs wrapped around his

waist as he navigated the hallway past the wineglasses neither of us had touched.

We collided with the wall once, twice, before he set me down at the edge of the bed and stepped back, fumbling with his belt.

"You're fucking gorgeous."

He shed his jeans and shirt while I peeled off my boots. The rest of the lingerie came next.

When we were both naked, he hovered over me, cupping my face. "You sure?"

"Todd." I pulled him down. "Stop talking."

He laughed against my mouth as his hands explored, deliberate and attentive. His mouth traveled down me, my hands tangling in his hair. We found an effortless rhythm, all sensation and relief.

After, we lay enmeshed in sheets, both breathless.

"Christ." Todd kissed my shoulder. "Best first date ever."

I smiled. "Definitely."

We drifted in and out of conversation, wrapped in each other, until sleep pulled us under.

The next morning, dawn crept across the ceiling, and Todd's arm tightened around my waist as consciousness returned.

"So weird being back in the dating world at our age," he mumbled, thick with sleep.

"Tell me about it."

He propped himself on one elbow while his fingers grazed my hip. "Divorce is brutal, huh? I knew it would suck, but damn."

"The worst." I rolled to face him. "Though I have to say, last night made up for a lot."

His smile was crooked, boyish. "Happy to help."

We bantered back and forth about our exes, both clearly still working through the bitterness.

"She went full red pill during the pandemic. I could barely recognize who I married." He rubbed his face with both hands, the scruff of his beard catching against his palms.

"Shane too," I said. "I don't understand how it happened so fast. I remember him getting sick of wearing masks to restaurants, then being wary of the vaccines. It was one thing after another."

"We should set them up." Todd laughed.

"Shane and Melania…I mean…Melanie?" I winced. "Sorry."

He laughed louder this time. "The nickname fits. That's part of why we split. She became this different person, and her business consumed her."

"The wellness business, right? Pretty sure she tried to recruit me to be on her team at one point."

"Probably." He traced a finger along my collarbone. "Vitality & Grace. Sounded harmless when she joined. A bunch of women selling vitamins. Until it became her whole identity."

"She makes actual money doing that, though?"

"She makes bank." He leaned closer. "I know she was hiding money in the divorce. I tried to dig into it all; her finances were shady as hell. But my lawyer said it would cost more to fight, so I just…let it go."

His hand slid up my thigh, completely derailing our conversation.

We drifted back into each other, morning light exposing every inch, and for a few stolen moments, I let myself forget about everything else waiting outside the room.

Todd gathered his clothes while I brushed my teeth and put on makeup, and it struck me how different this was from the choreography of marriage. Not timing sex to get pregnant or not get pregnant, or checking off a list to appease someone. No fake moans to keep the peace. Pleasure for pleasure's sake.

He delayed his departure by planting kisses around my neck, gently avoiding my styled hair and makeup. His stubble left a pleasant burn against my skin. "Happy Valentine's Day, by the way."

"Is it?" I straightened.

Valentine's Day. I completely spaced on the Hallmark holiday. Though I hadn't planned it that way, I woke up in the arms of another man on my second wedding anniversary. A coincidence with a sense of humor.

"You should go before Eric gets here," I said, reluctant to end this moment but aware of the clock ticking down.

"I think he'd be fine with it. Eric's a good dude," Todd grazed my earlobe with his teeth.

"He'd be more than fine, but he'd tease me relentlessly."

"I might be okay with that."

I walked with him to the door, fighting the wild urge to drag him back to my bed.

He put his hand on the small of my back, and his mesmerizing gold-flecked hazel eyes swept over me. "This was…"

"Yes, it was," I said. "Let's do it again soon."

I opened the door. Eric was on the doorstep.

"Busted!"

Damnit. Todd sucked his teeth and gave me an apologetic glance. "Sorry!"

They shook hands and slapped backs in the easy, suburban-dad way, and I invited Eric in.

"I haven't seen your cheeks that red in a long time." Eric chuckled, waving goodbye to Todd as he drove away.

"Shut it."

Eric grinned wider. "Good for you, Valentine. So that's what Hot Toddy meant."

"Oh, my God, stop." I slapped his arm, grateful for the moment of levity, even though my cheeks burned.

Eric dropped into a chair at the table, still smirking. "Had a good chat with Ethan last night."

"Yeah? He's been giving me the teenage silent treatment." My youngest icing me out felt like one more insult on top of everything.

"There's a girl he's into. Trying to impress her."

"Oh, boy. He thinks getting stoned is the way to a woman's heart?" I turned to face him.

Eric's expression sobered. "It's not just that. He's been listening to…those podcasts."

"The ones—"

"Ethan said Shane introduced him to them. Yeah."

"Fuck."

"Yeah." Eric rubbed the back of his neck. "But we talked about it. He's bored, still upset about getting benched for the season. Maybe it's a phase."

I wanted to believe him, but the thought of Shane's poison

dripping into my son's ears made me nauseous. Ethan wasn't Elliott, mathematical and pragmatic. He was more easily swayed, still desperate to fit in.

"Thanks for talking to him. I appreciate all your help lately." I slid into the chair across from him. On top of hacking drives, he'd been carrying the parenting load. Field trip form? Handled. Paperwork? Signed. He was stepping up in ways he never had when the kids were little, when I'd been the martyr doing it all.

"Of course." He cracked his knuckles. "Unfortunately, there's more bad news." He flipped open his screen to face me.

I scanned the files, pulse racing. "What is it?"

"Look at the signature."

I read the final line. Every document bore the same name in crisp script.

Davis Clark.

"Oh, no." The betrayal hit me harder than I expected. I knew he covered for Shane's cheating, but financial crimes? "Are you sure? This can't be right."

"Katie, the signature is on multiple documents."

I chewed the inside of my cheek, pieces falling into place. "No wonder he's been so loyal. He's in on it."

I remembered Izzy's confusion about why Davis would warn her about Shane but never stand up to him directly. Davis was his accomplice.

"So is there anything in there we can use against Shane?"

Eric shook his head. "Not yet. But I'll keep looking."

"Thanks, Eric."

He tapped his fingers on the table. "Oh, there's a PAC that

keeps coming up, wondering if Shane ever talked about it." He flipped through a few spreadsheets. "Puget Coalition, did he ever mention that name?"

I gave a half-shrug. "No, I don't really understand how those things work."

"Most people don't. That's kind of the point." His eyes fixed on the screen. "Anyway, his firewall is no joke, and I have another encrypted partition to get through—"

"Eric, English."

He looked up, catching himself. "Sorry. I'll keep digging."

Before I could come up with a plan to warn Izzy, my phone rang. Chris. I answered on the second ring.

"Katie. The hearing's canceled."

"What? Why?"

"The judge made a bench decision. The prenup stands."

My legs nearly gave out. "Wait, we don't even get to argue?"

"I'm sorry. We knew it was a long shot. But—"

"What changed?" Panic rose in my throat. The hearing was necessary to protect my kids' college money.

Chris exhaled heavily on the other end. "Katie…Fred Sutton died last night."

The words gutted me. Fred, who'd baited hooks with Ethan. Who'd sat through school plays with his camera around his neck. Who'd told me more than once I was too good for Shane. Why hadn't I listened?

"Oh, my God. How?"

"Collapsed. I don't know the details yet. I'm sorry, I know you were fond of him."

Grief crashed into suspicion. Claudia's comment about

supplements instead of prescriptions. Fred's financial concerns. And now, as soon as I was prepared to challenge him, Fred was gone.

"So…can we appeal?"

Chris hesitated. "Well, appeals take time, and with Shane positioned as the grieving son, any move looks…"

"Opportunistic," I finished.

"The optics are terrible. We need to regroup."

"Optics, huh?" The word rang like a weapon. Fred's death was devastating, but the timing was too neat. My silence must have sounded damning because Chris interjected.

"Katie. Don't. Be cautious about accusations you can't back up. Men like Shane are most lethal when cornered."

"I know exactly who Shane is. And I'm done letting him take things from me."

I hung up the phone.

Eric looked at me, wide-eyed. "Katie, what's happening?"

"Fred died."

That morning, I'd woken in a man's arms, but I was still under another's thumb.

I scrolled through my contacts and found Nancy's name.

Eric's mouth hung open. "What are you doing?"

"Getting a message to Izzy."

I pressed dial before I could second-guess myself.

EIGHTEEN

ISABELLA

The numbers on the expense report melted together. Blink. Refocus. Nope. Still, Fred's empty eyes, body crumpled on the floor—another trauma for the stack.

"You okay, Iz?" Tammi said from the doorway.

I sat silent, the memory playing on a loop: paramedics rushing in, their urgent movements turning mechanical and slow. And Shane's face when they covered Fred with a sheet.

"Unfortunate," he'd said, like his father was a quarterly projection that hadn't met expectations.

Nancy had remained frozen, her face blank. No tears, no collapse. Nothing. She locked her grief away somewhere, if she had any.

Meanwhile, guilt sat in my throat like a brick. Fred was hauling boxes all over the house when he collapsed. Work I should've been doing. Work of the devoted girlfriend I pretended to be.

"It wasn't your fault," Tammi said, somehow reading my thoughts.

"I know," I lied, picking at my cuticles. Fred was the latest casualty in a plan spiraling beyond my control.

But maybe it wasn't fate. I kept thinking about Fred dying on the floor after Nancy preached about quack doctors and natural cures. It was a flashback from hell, dragging me back three years.

My dad's face, gray as concrete, lips cracked and bleeding. The fever burned for six days. My mom hovered over him with her tinctures and teas, elderberry syrup, goldenseal, anything but what he needed.

"The hospital will kill him," she'd insisted. "They'll pump him full of chemicals, put him on a ventilator—"

"Mom, he can't breathe—"

"This is what they want, Isabella. They want us dependent, scared, begging for their poison."

I'd watched him deteriorate hour by hour, while his chest rattled with fluid, and my mom muttered about natural immunity.

I swore I'd never let fear kill someone I loved.

I shook away the memory and moved across the room to Tammi's desk. "Hey, can I talk to you for a second? Privately?"

Tammi's eyes flicked to the foyer, then back to me, and I followed her out of the office.

"What's up?" Concern creased her forehead.

I pulled a sticky note from my bag, with three passwords written on it, the ones from Fred's notebook. "Fred was looking for something. Financial records, I think. Before he…

before it happened."

Tammi's expression shifted. "Iz…"

"I need you to try these passwords." I passed her the note. "On Neil's financial system. When he's in the meeting with the McFadden team, see if you can access anything Fred might have been looking into."

She stepped back. "That's basically hacking our own company."

"For Fred, Tammi," I said. "Please."

"Iz, if Shane finds out…" Tammi bit her lip. "He has dirt on me, too, you know."

My heart sank. Of course he did. "Tammi…"

"Don't, I know, okay…" She glanced at the door again. "Look, it was one thing giving you that key and looking the other way, but this? It's too risky."

"I'll take responsibility if anything goes wrong." I pressed the note into her hands. "Neil is watching me like a hawk; it has to be you. He trusts you."

She stared at the passwords for a long moment, then tucked the note into her pocket. "Okay. But you owe me."

"I know I do," I breathed. "Thank you."

I returned to my desk and slumped into my seat. All I was supposed to do was get a man to divorce his wife. That's it. Instead, he almost died, his father *did* die, and I was staring down at the possibility of going home empty-handed.

I was back in a hole with no ladder.

I closed my eyes, taking myself back to September's fundraiser, when Katie cornered me and offered the deal of a lifetime. Me in a borrowed black dress, screaming wannabe rich girl, serving champagne to Seattle's elite. I'd stationed myself near Shane deliberately, waiting for him to take the bait.

By the end of our "chance" conversation, he'd given me his card and suggested I apply for the assistant's position, as Katie had said he would. Back then, I thought I could handle danger. Now danger had its hands all over me.

On my desk, a new stack of McFadden campaign materials awaited my review. Even with Shane laid up in bed, the messaging was getting sneakier every day—**Make our food healthy again!** and **Say no to ultra-processed foods! Our kids deserve better!** Taglines my mom would have run with a decade ago. Bait for crunchy moms and rural dads in one serving. Word salad, Shane's favorite dish. Fred would roll in his grave, but he wasn't even in one yet.

The clock ticked closer to quitting time. Back to my cage. Back to the man I was supposed to outmaneuver.

One thing was for sure. If I wanted more intel, there was one person left I had to stop lying to: Davis.

I arrived at the lake house to find Nancy fluttering around in a frenzy of busywork. She unpacked boxes of picture frames, lining every surface with glossy photos of her and Shane: Her and Shane at little league, her and Shane at graduation, her next to Shane shaking hands with a politician. Not a single one of Fred.

"Can I get you tea, dear?"

Bleh. Tea. My mom's medicinal brews had left me with an aversion to anything steeped in hot water—another delightful childhood memory.

"No, Nancy, please. Sit. I'll get it." I gestured to the couch. Why was she here? Surrounding herself with Shane's greatest hits, in the house where her husband literally died?

I stepped into the kitchen, and that's when I saw them up close, a lineup of tan bottles: with Vitality & Grace on the label. The full-on wellness bro starter pack.

"Thank you for helping set up the wake," Nancy said. "I admit I wasn't crazy about having it at *her* house." The way she emphasized "her" made it sound like Katie was some homewrecking villain rather than her daughter-in-law of two years.

"Of course," I said." Shane had mentioned it dismissively earlier with sarcasm dripping from every word. He probably agreed because it was perfect stagecraft. Grieving son, recovering from a near-death experience, the ultimate power play. But I knew the truth—Katie had offered the Magnolia house to create a way for us to meet.

"I hope you don't mind me putting a few photos up of Shane." Her eyes bounced around the room. "You hadn't hung anything yet, so…"

"It's fine." She didn't need to know I was just a temporary guest. "How was Shane today? He was asleep when I left this morning."

"I'm not sure. He gets annoyed with me every time I go in there," she grumbled. "He's always been like that with me, even when he was a little boy."

"Oh?" My interest piqued.

"Oh, yes. He'd get so mad at me, such a stubborn little thing. If you told him he couldn't have something, he'd do everything possible to get it. And then when he got it, he would move on to the next thing." She tilted her head and glared at me, almost hypnotically.

"What kind of things?" I couldn't resist fishing for anything useful.

Nancy turned her face toward the window, as if looking into the past. "Oh, anything. If his father said no to something, I'd get it for him. A bike. A toy. A girl he liked." Her smile collapsed. "And he never appreciated it. Or me. I keep thinking something will bring us closer, Shane and me. Buying him things. Giving him money. Introducing him to a wife. Not even his father's death."

I wanted to run out of the house and swan dive into Lake Washington.

Nancy's eyes shimmered. "I've never been anyone's favorite. Not Fred's, not Shane's. What do I need to do to be someone's first choice?"

She turned to look directly at me. "With Fred gone, it's just us taking care of Shane now, dear."

What the hell? What was Nancy grieving? Fred, or the son who never picked her? I glanced away with second-hand embarrassment, and that's when I saw it: a photo she'd placed proudly on the mantel with a thick, gaudy plastic frame. A teenage Nancy, tiara digging into a shellacked updo, one hand gripping roses, the other on her hip. The banner across her chest read MISS KING COUNTY—RUNNER-UP.

She'd framed her second-place beauty queen photo. Here?

Suddenly, her words clicked into place: the endless buying, the desperate giving. Maybe Shane wasn't her only obsession. She'd been rehearsing for this role all her life. Always almost.

Instead of dissecting her weird Oedipus vibes, I excused myself. Avoiding was more my speed.

"I'm going to check on Shane."

I peeked into his room, where Shane sat in his fancy medical chair as usual, like a king holding court. He had a cane for show and a wheelchair for sympathy. His recovery was a miracle by all standards, though I wasn't sure all miracles were blessings.

"Hi." I knocked, trying to ignore how the air between us had changed, as if my capacity to pretend died with Fred. "You need anything?"

He didn't look up from his laptop. "I'm good. Is my mom driving you crazy yet?" He acted as if she were an inconvenient insect, not his own mother.

I stepped in and caught the glow of his phone on the table. Was that…a live feed? He snatched it up, but not before I caught sight of it: security camera footage from inside our office building. The angle showed Tammi's desk, and Davis walking past.

I held my breath. Had he seen me with Davis? The convos with Tammi? The coffee runs that lasted too long?

I tried to act normal, pretending that I hadn't seen anything.

"Nancy's fine. And she's grieving. Give her a break."

I wanted to believe the trope that *hurt people hurt people,* but it felt like a bullshit excuse to make monsters sympathetic. And the more I learned about Nancy, the less I believed she deserved sympathy.

Shane was already pounding at the keys again, with his attention locked on the screen.

"What are you doing on there, anyway?" I pretended I wasn't in the middle of a quiet panic.

He angled it away. "You know me, browsing, reading, world domination."

"Remember what the doctor told you about brain breaks? Too much screen time is bad for your recovery." I channeled my inner kindergarten teacher, which was disgustingly effective.

He smirked. "You're right. Okay. You talk to all the clients, hot stuff. I'll watch Netflix or something."

Netflix. Sure. More like his personal Big Brother channel.

"Let me do what I'm supposed to do. I have meetings with all our clients next week. If I hear you've reached out, I'm gonna be cross."

I folded my arms across my chest, faux scolding. He loved it when I played the defiant child. *Creep.*

He put the laptop aside and placed his hand on my thigh, fingers sliding under my skirt. "You're so good at handling things," he said in the throaty voice that used to make my knees weak.

I fought the urge to flinch and slap his hand away. Instead, I gently wrapped my fingers around his wrist. "Remember, again, what the doctor said."

"I know." His head flopped back dramatically. "Soon, though. I can't wait to get my hands on you again, Bells."

I plastered on a fake smile, then returned to the kitchen. Before the accident, I would have climbed him like a tree after a line like that. Lately, my body physically rejected the thought of his hands on me.

When did it happen? When did I lose the ability to

pretend? Shane came packaged as a hot zaddy, with a razor-sharp jawline and a body that looked just as good in a knit sweater as it did without one. I'd never had a strong man in my life. But I'd seen too much. And I saw how other people, like Davis, treated me. Like a person, not inventory.

Davis, who asked questions instead of giving orders. Davis, with those eyes—so deep brown I just wanted to fall inside them, and never leave.

I rested my elbows on the kitchen counter, avoiding Shane and Nancy in the rooms on either side of me, and scanned Instagram mindlessly. The algorithm knew me too well, serving up videos of people escaping toxic relationships and starting over. If only it were that simple. A text chimed from Mom.

We miss you! When are you coming home?

My heart melted. She was finally the mom I never thought I'd have. The one my sister and I always wanted. I'd sent Mom my last paycheck—a Band-Aid on a bullet wound. If she knew what I was doing to get this money, she'd call it brainwashing. Different church, same hymn. But what choice did I have? Some things were worth selling your soul for, temporarily.

Miss you too!

Then I texted Davis. I shouldn't. I knew I shouldn't since Shane could be watching, but he had become my lifeline in a home that felt like a cage.

Hey.

Hey you.

Looking forward to seeing you tomorrow, even if it's at a death party. 💀

Xo

Two letters, and my heart sprinted harder than Shane ever made it. I was such a walking disaster—crushing on Davis, living with Shane, scheming with Katie. Not a love triangle. A Bermuda triangle, and I was steering straight into the storm.

If I wanted to come clean to Davis, I had to get Katie on board and figure out who Shane was watching before he caught me watching back.

NINETEEN

KATHERINE

It's a surreal thing, hosting a wake for the dead father of the toxic ex who threatened your children the last time you spoke. Even more surreal: this wasn't charity or reconciliation. It was my job. Evergreen Events had the contract, which meant I was being compensated to curate sorrow.

The great room of our home (Shane's home? My home?) was staged for grief. Crystal glasses caught the afternoon light, scattering prisms across the table where family photos had spun the perfect Sutton family narrative. A narrative as substantial as smoke.

As I arranged another tray of bite-sized food, I noticed how many people kept glancing my way, with looks of pity and speculation. I'd let them, because that was the whole point. Without saying a word, this event announced to everyone that I wasn't Shane's property anymore. When he arrived with someone younger, I'd let them fill in the blanks.

I caught snippets of conversation as I moved through the room—McFadden staffers dissecting polling, lobbyists whispering about gun rights, private school vouchers, and emissions loopholes. A donor I recognized from the fundraiser circuit was cornering a city council member by the hors d'oeuvres table.

They were treating Fred's wake as a mixer for the same forces he'd once opposed. If the heart attack hadn't killed him, this would have.

Fred's death was a blow my kids didn't need. Breakup with Shane, gossip at school, dwindling money, and the death of a grandparent to top it all off. The kids hated the idea of the wake, not because they didn't love Fred, but because they thought it was morbid. "Someone dies, and you have a party? Creepy!" Emma had said. She was right. They attended the service but went home with Eric afterward. There was no reason for them to sit through this circus.

I still couldn't shake the urgency of Fred's voicemail: "Financial concerns…not in front of Shane." What had he uncovered, and why the secrecy? The timing of his death, less than two weeks later, plus Claudia's comments about the supplements, sat in my chest like a live wire. Heart attack, they said, plain and simple. But something about it all still didn't sit right. Perhaps I was being irrational. Or seeing things more clearly than ever.

I spotted Nancy sitting alone by the window in a pristine Chanel suit. She'd been curt on the phone when I offered to host this wake. The woman who once welcomed me as a daughter curled her lip as if I were a virus.

But she wasn't alone for long. A woman approached her. I squinted.

Melanie Anderson.

What in the world was she doing here?

I edged closer, pretending to adjust a flower arrangement.

"…so glad. Wellness is important while grieving."

Oh, brother. Was Melania seriously hustling her pyramid scheme at a wake? To the widow?

"Nancy."

I took the chair beside her, and Melanie drifted away with a tight smile.

"Katherine." The formality stung. From "Katie, dear" to "Katherine" as quickly as she'd once welcomed me into the family.

"I'm sorry, again, about Fred." My words were genuine. Fred had been kind to me, to my children. Nancy, on the other hand, had never been maternal. If anything, she was jealous when Shane gave my kids attention. "Fred was so wonderful with the children."

She gave a nearly imperceptible nod. I continued.

"I know we haven't spoken since—"

"Since you destroyed my son's life?"

I winced. "Nancy, I'm not the one who destroyed anything, Shane—"

"Oh, you naïve girl." Her laugh cracked like glass. "Do you think you've discovered some dark truth about Shane? You think you're the first wife whose husband has other needs?"

The words slapped me harder than any hand could.

"This isn't about me."

"Oh, but it is. You weren't strong enough." She shortened the gap between us, face collapsing into age, every line deepening. "I told Linda you weren't right for him. Too soft and needy."

My throat constricted. "Linda? My mother, Linda?"

"Yes, your mother," she scoffed. "You think Shane happened to show up at that school meeting? He needed a wife. The campaign demanded it. Family values."

The room tilted. The surrounding conversations became white noise.

"But you didn't understand the arrangement," she hissed, glare as sharp as a blade.

My hands went numb. "Arrangement?"

"A man like Shane needs…outlets. Successful men always do. Your job was to understand the cost of being chosen."

"You knew." I sprang to my feet, despite feeling faint. "About the other women?"

Nancy didn't blink. "I know about duty and sacrifice. What it takes to build a legacy." She gestured toward the room full of people. "Fred couldn't. But Shane can."

I walked away before she saw me break. I had to put distance between her and me.

The story of our chance meeting at Puget Academy crumbled like a sandcastle in the tide. Even our romantic origin story was a farce. The inspirational talk at my children's school delivered with so much care and compassion for education, the charming introduction, all staged. Like his meeting with Izzy.

I turned a corner and braced myself against a wall, out of her sight, out of anyone's sight.

The implications crashed over me. Shane required a wife and kids for his campaign. Nancy did Shane's bidding, and my mother thought I needed a man to save me. I was the bargaining chip. I wasn't chosen despite my vulnerabilities; I was chosen because of them.

The perfect wife who would pose for photos, make excuses for him, and never, ever cause a scene. My kids provided him with the ideal instant family and access to the network of donors and voters that would make his bid for the Senate more achievable. Being a bachelor was his biggest liability, and my children and I fixed all of that.

Now, I understood the truth.

It wasn't a love story.

It was a transaction.

This was worse than discovering the affairs. Those were about sex, about power. This was about my entire identity as his wife, deliberately manufactured for a senatorial run I just found out about.

Steps came toward me, and I tried to gain my composure.

My mother appeared around the corner.

Her eyes, so similar to mine, held that painful sheen of judgment I'd grown up with. She approached me with her usual church walk, shoulders back, and chin lifted, a woman secure in her righteousness. It was the same posture she'd adopted when defending my father's affairs, insisting appearances mattered more than truth. The perfect conspirator in Shane's gaslighting campaign.

I still hadn't confronted her about the conversation I found on Shane's phone. I'd barely spoken to her at all, using the excuse that I was too busy with lawyers and kids. But truthfully, I didn't know how to see her without figuratively ripping her face off, and perhaps literally ripping her face off.

"Hi, honey, how are you holding up?" She reached for my hand with the concern of someone who believes they're always helping, never harming.

What could I say? Thanks for offering me up for slaughter. Thanks for thinking I'm a failure who can't hold down a man. Oh, and super thanks for befriending my cheating husband and telling him I'm mentally unstable.

"Mom, not now." I pulled my hand back. Her face fell, but I didn't care about smoothing things over, about making everyone else comfortable at my expense. Not anymore.

The walls closed in around me. I choked for air, for space, to get away from all the suffocating lies.

But I couldn't, because Shane arrived. And it was pure theater, the wounded war hero supported by his devoted nurse. A ripple of whispers followed them as they entered, heads turning toward the spectacle. Forty-five minutes late, and he still got a pass. He always did. But hopefully not for too much longer.

Izzy settled him in, surrounded by sympathetic faces. She looked exhausted. The green dress that should have flattered her curves hung loose at the waist, and dark circles shadowed her eyes. I knew that look; I'd worn it.

As they moved toward me, Izzy snagged a glass of champagne from a passing tray and downed it in one swift motion.

"Katherine, Isabella; Isabella, Katherine." Shane introduced us as if we'd never met. Typical Shane, erasing history when it suited him. I wanted to wipe the smug smile off his face.

"The house looks lovely," Izzy complimented, in almost the exact location where I'd first met her, before she'd promised to help me escape this marriage. How things had changed since then.

"Thank you." I turned my attention to Shane, whom I hadn't spoken to since his venomous words in the hospital bed. *Your kids will pay for this.*

"I'm sorry about your dad. He was a great man."

I shot Izzy another look as I walked away. We had to talk privately, somehow, somewhere. She deserved to know what Eric found out about Davis.

Claudia materialized at my shoulder, whispering, "I can't believe she brought him. Are they…*together* together?"

"She's the assistant. Someone needs to take care of him."

"Does she?" Claudia uncapped a lip gloss and applied it aggressively. "God, we were idiots at that age. But hot idiots. Why didn't we appreciate it when we had it?"

I laughed, grateful for her sense of humor. She wasn't wrong. When had it happened? We'd gone from *hot damn* to *hey ma'am* at lightning speed in the harsh beam of the male gaze. In your twenties, you hate your body; in your forties, you hate the memory of hating it. A constant timeline of loathing and regret.

"Did you hear?" Claudia said. "About Mr. Carlisle?"

"The lit teacher? No, what happened?"

"The school put him on leave. Something about the banned books club?"

I stared at her. The parent coalition I dismissed as petty drama had metastasized. "He's Elliott's favorite teacher."

"I know—it's total bullshit."

A knot of dread formed in my gut, but over Claudia's shoulder, I caught Izzy's eye. She raised her chin slightly. One disaster at a time. "I'll be back, Claudia."

I slipped down the hallway toward the bathroom. As I turned the corner, I glimpsed Davis watching Izzy follow me. I quickened my pace, the thumb drive heavy in my pocket.

When she slipped into the bathroom a moment later, her face was flushed.

"I hate this," she said. "I hate everything about it."

"Me, too." I locked the door behind us. Even here, I felt watched. Privacy was an illusion now. "Listen, we don't have much time—"

"Nancy is a psycho," Izzy blurted.

"I know, I found that out myself. Apparently, marrying me was all part of Shane's election strategy."

"Fucker," she seethed.

"There's more." I pulled the thumb drive from my pocket with trembling fingers. "Eric found these. They're pictures of you."

Izzy stiffened. "What kind of pictures?"

I swallowed hard. "Ones you didn't know were being taken."

Her face drained of color. "You mean…"

"You and dozens of others. Some in lingerie, some naked, some…graphic. Even one of mine from a boudoir session I'd done as a gift for our first anniversary."

Izzy's hand flew to her mouth. "Jessica told me he did the same thing to her. Fucking pervert!"

For a moment, the silence stretched between us, two

women bound by the same violation, a sisterhood neither of us had asked to join.

"That woman out there," Izzy said suddenly. "I saw her leaving the Puget Coalition office the other day; she was acting sketchy as hell."

I took a step back. "Which woman?"

"Brown cunty bob, the one talking to Nancy by the window earlier."

"Wait, Melanie? She's the PTA president at my kids' school. Todd's ex-wife."

"Who's Todd?"

"Doesn't matter," I said. "You sure it was her?"

"Yes, I recognized her immediately. Bitchiest resting bitch face I've ever seen. The receptionist was whispering about a donation."

"Huh." I bit my lip. "She's a big McFadden fan, probably donating to his campaign. Anyway, that doesn't matter. There's something else."

"What?" Her face went flat.

"Davis. Eric found his signature all over the fraudulent documents. I'm sorry, Izzy, but whatever Shane is doing, Davis is in on it."

I pulled out my phone and zoomed in on the signature line. "Look. Signed and authorized by Davis. There are dozens of these going back years."

"That's impossible," she insisted. "Shane must have forged his signature or—"

"Izzy," I cut in, "don't let him fool you, too. Why do you think Davis stays? Why do you think he covers for Shane despite supposedly hating him? He's compromised. He's playing you, too!"

Tears welled in her eyes, whether from hurt, betrayal, or denial, I couldn't tell. Maybe all three.

"I don't believe you." Her voice cracked and she pulled the door open and stormed out.

I followed her, grabbing her wrist. "Izzy! We had a deal!"

She yanked her arm away. Her eyes flashed, wet and furious. "I'm done with this."

We both froze as a shadowy figure emerged around the corner backlit by the living room glow.

Davis.

"Tell me more about this…deal."

TWENTY

ISABELLA

"Davis." My voice pitched higher than I wanted. "It's nothing."

Katie stepped back. "Isabella promised to give Shane a ride home, but now she can't…I just…" She fluttered her hands, her usually composed demeanor shattering. "We were working out logistics."

"In the bathroom?" Davis's eyebrow arched. "In the middle of a wake?"

"Women things. Period stuff." *Smooth, Izzy. Nailed it.*

"Right," Davis said. "I don't know what's going on here, but it's not lost on me that the two of you are up to something…"

Across the room, Shane's head tilted, like a hawk sighting a mouse.

"I need to get out of here." I pivoted Katie's terrible excuse into an excuse of my own. "Can you take me home?"

"Uh, sure." He glanced uneasily toward his boss, and I followed him down the hallway.

"Izzy…" Katie protested, but we both brushed past her.

"I'll meet you at your car," I told Davis, as Shane's eyes hardened on me with each step I took toward him.

"What was that about?"

Phew. Only Davis heard what we were saying.

"She cornered me. About us." I let my voice sound desperate and shaky. "Called me a homewrecker."

Shane's features shifted to protective anger. Perfect. He fell for it.

I let the tears rise to the surface as I looked back where Davis was waiting. "I need to get out of here. Davis said he can take me. I don't want to be a bother, Shane."

He reached out and clasped my hand, stroking my wrist with his thumb. The first display of public affection between us. His way of staking a claim.

"Of course, my love." He kissed my hand, sealing my fate as his official conquest.

I turned and walked away, feeling eyes from every angle. Every glance of pity snapped into judgment. The faces I'd memorized from Katie's social media were animated with curled lips and whispers behind manicured hands. Big mean-girl cafeteria energy, grown up and dressed in couture.

The whispers chased me down the hall. "That's her…the one who…" and "So young…" I wasn't sure if I was hearing them or if my anxiety was creating a playlist of who I was. I was the other woman, the destroyer.

Everyone had a front-row seat to my walk of shame.

I wanted the polished marble floor to crack open and

swallow me. These people and their judgment could all go straight to hell. And I had to get out of here before someone started asking the right questions, before Shane's political instincts kicked in and he realized his wife and girlfriend were way too cozy.

I walked faster, desperate to escape before I either burst into tears or started flipping people off—equally likely at this point.

I was practically sprinting by the time I reached Davis's car.

I couldn't stop crying, and I couldn't tell Davis why, not the real reason. My perfect lie was imploding in real time. Months of tension, lies, and manipulation splintered apart.

Davis kept glancing over, helpless.

"Iz, please… Tell me what I can do," he said for probably the tenth time.

His kindness broke me further. I didn't deserve compassion. Not from him. My tears bled into the silk of my dress, stains spreading like guilt taking shape. "I can't go to that house. Please, can we go to your apartment?"

He turned on his blinker without answering.

A memory surfaced—I was five, maybe six, sitting with my little sister at our kitchen table while Mom paced, her eyes wild, her hands shaking as she peered through the curtains over and over.

"They're watching us," she said, though there was no one to hear but us. "Always watching. Tracking our movements."

The "who" didn't matter. The government. The shadow elite. Whomever she and Dad thought they were outsmarting.

"My smart girl," she'd say. "You'll never be fooled, will you?"

"Never," I promised, hungry for her rare approval.

Later that night, she made us drink a bitter concoction that turned our tongues black and left us in a daze. I was sick for days, and Misha was practically lifeless. But doubt never entered. My dad encouraged it. Their madness was our truth.

And here I was twenty years later, lying, manipulating, like I hadn't escaped after all. I'd just traded for a different poison.

At Davis's apartment, I collapsed into his arms, and he guided me to the couch.

I sank and let out a breath I'd been holding. "Sorry about…that." I gestured vaguely toward his car, where I'd ugly cried for twenty minutes. "Not the cool, collected vibe I was going for."

"It's okay. I'm not sure how you've held it together this long." He searched my face. "You and I aren't so different. Doing what we have to do to survive."

Surviving sounded right. We'd shared snippets of our childhoods with one another, more than I'd shared with most people, and I knew, like me, he'd worked harder than many to overcome circumstances. We grew up broke and bitter, both still clawing at the world.

I should have asked him about his signature, his involvement, all the things he was keeping from me. But sitting there, close enough to feel his warmth, I couldn't make myself do it. Katie could be wrong or lying. Tonight, I was desperate enough to believe someone wanted me for me, not for what I could give them. I leaned closer.

"Why do you stay with him? You could work anywhere."

"Same reason you do, I suspect. He knows things about me that could ruin me. Dumb shit I did when I was young, desperate for his approval. And he reminds me of it every time I step out of line."

His admission hung in the air, a shared understanding of what it meant to be caught in Shane Sutton's web. I wanted to ask more, but something in his voice warned me not to push.

"I hate that you live with him, Iz. It fucking kills me," he said through gritted teeth. "You deserve better than this. Better than him."

"I know." A betrayal and a relief. "It's been too much." I studied the curve of his mouth, the strong line of his jaw.

He turned toward me, brow furrowed. "What did Katie mean about a deal?"

The question sliced through the electricity.

"It's complicated. She…she already knew about us."

"Well, obviously, you live together, it's—"

"No, I mean, she's always known. From the beginning. She wanted to leave him and she…"

His head snapped up straight. "Wait, are you saying she *wanted* you to see him, so she'd have a reason to divorce him?"

"Basically." It wasn't the whole truth—not even close—but it was more than I'd told anyone.

"So, she was…what…pimping you out?" Davis went completely rigid.

"No." I said, "It's not like that—"

"Iz, you don't owe Katie shit. Shane doesn't deserve you. It's not too late to change your mind. You can always change your mind, you know?"

"That's not what I said, I don't..." I stumbled. "I can't explain everything right now, Davis."

"Try." He moved within inches of my face. "Tell me."

My eyes dropped to his lips, and my resolve disappeared. I'd been playing Shane's devoted girlfriend, the perfect assistant, the woman with a plan. But with Davis, I caught glimpses of who I could be if I were with him. The voice telling me to stop was nowhere to be found.

For one night, I wanted something real.

I pressed my lips against his, to show him what my words couldn't. He responded immediately, his surprise melting into desire before he pulled away.

"Iz...Shane's—"

"Shane's not here," I cut him off, breath ragged, too loud in the quiet room. I leaned in again.

"I can't." He stopped himself, even as his hands cupped my face. "Shane would—"

"Then we make sure he doesn't find out." I felt him tense beneath me. "I know you can keep secrets, and you know I can too. What's one more secret?"

Our mouths crashed again, and my hand slid higher. I felt him, hard underneath me.

"Fuck, Iz," he moaned while I fumbled with his belt.

"Show me what it's like when someone actually wants to make me feel good," I whispered into his ear. He shuddered, restraint snapping like a wire.

"You're killing me," he moaned.

"What a way to go."

His lips trailed down my neck, across my collarbone. His hands found the zipper at the back of my dress, sliding it down in one fluid motion. The cool air hit my bare skin, raising goosebumps along my spine.

"No underwear at a funeral?" he teased, exploring the newly exposed skin of my back.

I worked at his shirt buttons, pushing the fabric from his shoulders to reveal the body I'd imagined so many times. His skin was warm beneath my fingers, smooth over hard muscle.

It was raw and real, and scary as hell in the best way.

He pulled his pants from beneath his hips, and I straddled his lap. His hands circled my waist, pulling me down, and I gasped as I took him inside of me.

We were hungry, eyes open, because I needed to see him, to watch his face and know if this was real or if I was being fucked in more ways than one.

But his attention was fixed on me, more interested in my pleasure than his ego, which was so fucking hot.

My fingers dug into his biceps. "I'm close, don't stop," I begged, leaning back while he pressed his thumb right where it mattered.

I came fast and hard, barely able to take it, not wanting it to end. When it did, we collapsed on the couch, a tangle of arms and legs and sweat and satisfied breath.

"That was…" Davis said, breathless against my hair.

Life-changing? Earth-shattering? The best thing that had happened to me in months? "Yeah." I melted into his chest, listening to his heartbeat gradually slow beneath my ear. He kissed my bare shoulder, sending pleasant shivers down my spine.

I was…peaceful. No schemes, no lies, no constant calculation of what to say or how to act. Being seen and not studied.

He caressed my back, and I wanted to trust this. Trust him. I tilted my head to look at him. If he was lying, he was the best actor I'd ever met.

I clutched him closer, as if I could merge our bodies permanently, though we were already skin to skin.

I wanted to stay in this bubble forever, erase everything but this. Or fast forward to a future where this could be my reality. But I wasn't sure which parts of my life I would need to edit out to make this okay.

Davis's phone vibrated against the coffee table. Once. Twice. Three times in rapid succession.

He reached for it. "Shit."

"What?"

"Shane. He's asking where you are."

And the spell shattered.

All I could picture was the surveillance on Shane's phone. The office cameras. Was he watching us somehow? No, it wasn't possible. Was it?

"Fuck," I muttered to myself. "Fuckfuckfuckfuck."

"Iz, it's okay." Davis sat up, instantly alert.

"This is not okay." I gestured between us.

"Does he know I'm here?" My words came out too fast. "Right now, does he know I'm here?"

He blinked. "How would he?"

"Cameras? Surveillance?" I searched for my dress, panic rising in my body.

"Look at me," Davis said, steady. "He can't possibly know you're here."

I scrambled to my feet, aware of my nakedness in a way I hadn't been minutes before. "I just complicated everything. I had a plan. People are depending on me. And I blew it for—"

"For what?" Davis said. "For something you actually want?"

I didn't answer. "We can't… We shouldn't have. I'm an idiot."

I stepped back and tried to cover myself, Katie's warning about Davis echoing in my mind. Was he truly on Shane's side? Was this a trap?

Davis tried to steady me, but I pushed him away. He clenched his jaw and got dressed, mirroring my actions. The only sounds were our still-heavy breaths and the zippers, buttons, and fabric against our skin, until he broke the silence.

"How can you be with that guy, Iz?" Davis demanded, pulling his pants back on with jarring movements. "I don't get it. He's a snake!"

"Now you tell me?" I shot back.

"I've been warning you for months!"

He was right. He had warned me. But I couldn't explain why I was still stuck in Shane's web, even if I wanted to.

"That fucking guy," he muttered.

I came unglued. "That fucking guy? The man who owns your entire soul, but you're too scared to admit it?" The words poured out, toxic and unstoppable. "At least I know I'm being manipulated."

The words scorched as soon as they left me. *Low blow, Izzy.*

"I'm sorry, Davis. I just need you to trust me a little longer."

He stepped toward me and put his hand on my cheek. "Don't tell me this was a mistake."

I wanted to lean in closer, but I pulled away.

"I promise, Davis, when this is over—"

"When *what* is over, Iz? This game you're playing?" He stepped back. "I hope whatever you're after is worth it."

A chime from my phone this time. Shane.

Where the hell are you?

"Fuck."

"What?" Compassion returned to his face in an instant.

And I knew he was right. This game was not working. I needed him on my side. If I came clean, maybe he would too.

"We need to go. Now. I'll tell you everything."

TWENTY-ONE

KATHERINE

Every footstep reverberated in the empty house, reminding me how alone I was. I stacked the last dishes, wondering if I should start packing. The thought chilled me. Another home lost, another forced fresh start. Izzy had chosen Davis. I couldn't even blame her. What I'd hired her for had become darker than either of us imagined, with no end in sight. She deserved something for herself.

I ran my hand along the upright piano in the great room, the cool ivory keys smooth beneath my fingertips. I pressed one, the solitary note hanging in the room like a question with no answer. It wasn't fancy, a scraped-up old Baldwin I'd hauled from house to house. My attempts to teach my kids failed spectacularly, and the piano sat unused until Fred came into our lives.

Fred could play by ear, accompany any tune, his fingers dancing with effortless grace. He was the reason I started singing again. I was the only one in my family with any musical ability, but the last time I sang formally was in a church choir as a kid. I loved it but hated all those judging stares, like the ones today.

But next to Fred, I'd found strength. His gentle encouragement—"Come on, Katie, one more"—had coaxed songs from me I'd thought I'd forgotten. We'd sing for hours until someone shushed us. Now I wondered if the piano would ever be played again. I'd probably drag it with me anyway, another memory too heavy to leave behind.

I sank onto the couch with my feet up. Piper put her big floppy head in my lap. The house settled around us, creaking and sighing as if it knew changes were coming. I closed my eyes, allowing myself one moment of stillness.

Then, a loud knock jolted me, and Piper's ears shot up. Who would come here now? Shane? One of his lackeys?

I opened the door and lost my words. Davis and Izzy were side by side on my doorstep, with rumpled clothes and disheveled hair. Not subtle. Warning bells clanged in my head.

"He's on our side." Izzy's green eyes were pleading. "I told him everything."

Damn it, Izzy. I studied Davis's face for any sign of deception. His name was all over Shane's fraudulent documents. How could he talk his way out of that?

"Why should I believe either of you?" I blocked the doorway. "Last I checked, Davis, you were Shane's loyal lapdog."

"Please, Katie." Davis's voice cracked.

I weighed my options. If this was a trap, I was already cornered. If it wasn't, turning them away meant losing the only allies I had left.

"Okay, fine. Come in." I stepped aside but kept my distance.

They sat on the couch. Piper, oblivious, wedged between them, tail thumping. I remained upright, unwilling to surrender the higher ground, then lowered myself into the armchair across from them.

"Tell her what you told me," Izzy said.

Davis sucked in a breath. Lipstick smeared his collar, matching the shade Izzy wore.

"Shane's been blackmailing me for years." He clasped his hands together. "It's complicated."

I folded my arms. "Uncomplicate it for me." Trust had become a luxury I couldn't afford.

"It started when I was in high school. He was my mentor."

"Yeah, yeah, saved your life, we've all heard it." Shane bragged about Davis's scholarship every chance he got. "Be specific," I snapped.

Davis flinched. Izzy put her hand on his.

"My senior year, I had an SAT session with a private proctor. Shane pulled strings, and I didn't ask questions. Figured it was part of the scholarship." He looked down at the floor. "But when the scores came back, they were perfect. Couldn't believe it."

"Why?"

"I left the last page blank, Katie." He swallowed. "I even called the College Board. Told them there must be a mistake, but Shane stopped me. Showed me *my* test—except it wasn't mine. My name, someone else's handwriting. He paid the proctor. Bought me a perfect score, and acted like it was a favor."

"Why would he do that?"

"The scholarship money. I got a full-ride from the University. He said he'd invest the Sutton Stars scholarship funds for me. Told me I'd be set. I was eighteen, and my parents were proud. I didn't want to look like a fraud, even though I was."

"Davis, you were a kid." I thought of Emma, how easily she could be pressured to please, not to disappoint. "He found your soft spot and exploited it. That's what predators do."

"Yeah, but then it escalated," Davis said. "During my internship, it was padding expenses, shifting numbers. Each time, worse."

His voice dropped. "I never spent a cent of any of the money. But on paper? I know I look guilty of all of his crimes."

Years of signing what Shane told him to sign. I could see the weight of it crushing him.

"Every time I hesitated, he'd remind me: 'I made you. I can unmake you.' And when I saw what he did to Patrick and Jessica. That was my warning."

Izzy turned to him. "You knew about that?"

"Yeah." He shrank into himself.

"What about the other interns, the women—"

"Shane kept me on the campaign side, them on the admin side." He rubbed his face. "I thought he was being protective, keeping them focused on their studies. But he was isolating them. Making sure none of us talked to each other."

"So you had no idea what he was doing to them?" Izzy said.

"No. And by then, I was too deep in my own mess to help anyone else. Every transfer, every NDA, every bullshit consulting fee has my signature. He said if I ever turned on him, I'd go down first."

I relaxed slightly. "A decade of this, Davis? Why not tell someone?"

"Who'd believe a Black kid versus a polished white entrepreneur? And the paper trail kept growing."

I wanted to borrow Izzy's certainty and trust in Davis. But I'd been fooled before. Hope always came at a price.

"How do I know this isn't another one of Shane's games? That he didn't send you here to get information?"

"Because I'm turning myself in." His eyes hardened. "Tomorrow morning. Whatever happens, I'll face it." Izzy put her arm around him. "It's one thing if I get in trouble. But what about you two? Or your kids?"

The mention of my children jolted me, but none of us should be in danger. The only crime we'd committed was trusting the wrong man.

I drew a breath and made a choice I hoped I wouldn't regret.

"No. He did this. Not us." I leaned forward. "We need to understand the full picture. He's having documents forged because crimes are being committed. So we need to prove he's the one committing them."

"Jessica told me the DA has been investigating," Izzy offered. "I'll meet with her to see if we can figure out what she knows."

"I'll get whatever I can from Sutton Strategy," Davis said. "Emails, meeting notes, even if it's circumstantial."

I rubbed my temples. "Okay. Eric is still digging through

the hard drive. So lets regroup, and pool together what we find and see how it fits together."

Izzy threw her arms out. "Before we do what?"

That was the question. "I don't know. If we have enough information together, the authorities might do something. Shane's not untouchable."

But even as I said it, I wondered. Shane had spent years building his web of influence, collecting leverage on everyone who mattered.

Then again, there were three of us, and one of him.

"We need to be careful," Izzy warned. "If Shane suspects we're working together—"

Her phone dinged.

She glanced at the screen and her face drained. "Shane."

Fear hung thick in the air.

My body tensed. "What did you tell him? Where does he think you are?"

She typed quickly, her nails clicking against the glass.

Davis tapped his foot nervously. "Izzy, what?"

Her phone chimed, and her shoulders dropped again. "I told him you brought me back to get my car. He bought it."

"Good. But does he know about…" I gestured between them.

"I don't know how he would." Izzy frowned at the phone. "Doesn't seem like it."

"I'm worried about you going back to the lake house." Davis gripped her hand. "After tonight—"

"I'll be fine," Izzy cut in. "I have to finish what I started."

Davis looked back at me. "So, we're doing this?"

"We don't have a choice," I said. "Not anymore."

I watched their cars fade down Galer Street, brake lights flashing once at the corner before disappearing entirely in the darkness.

Fred once told me survival required compromise. I hadn't understood then. But now I did. To protect my kids, I'd align myself with his mistress and his accomplice. The people with nothing to lose, but everything to gain from his destruction.

Shane thought he'd isolated us, turned us against each other. Instead, he'd created the perfect alliance.

TWENTY-TWO

ISABELLA

By mid-morning, the office was its usual buzz of chaos, but my brain was miles away, plotting Shane's takedown while pretending to give a shit about quarterly reports. Less than a week since Fred's wake, and Shane was already acting like it never happened. No grieving, just spreadsheets and spin. The creepiest and most comforting part was how Shane hadn't shown a single sign he knew about what happened between Davis and me. In fact, he'd been warmer to Davis than usual, so he was either clueless or playing the longest con alive. Both scared the hell out of me. Meanwhile, Nancy still floated around the lake house like an old-timey ghost with no grief. Their codependent relationship was straight-up *Manchurian Candidate* energy.

I refilled my third cup of coffee of the morning because sleep was a distant memory, and headed toward Tammi's desk. One more favor.

"Tammi, any chance you could pull our client lists for the last five years? Since Shane took over for Fred?"

"Yep, I'll have them in your inbox by the end of the day!"

"You're a literal lifesaver. You should get paid triple for this, honestly."

"Maybe Shane's head injury knocked some generosity into him." Her words were pure snark.

I forced myself not to flinch at the idea of him strolling back in here. "I'm going to make sure you get what you deserve, Tammi. It's my entire mission statement." I mentally added her to my "rescue from this dumpster fire" list. Plan: cross-check every client, every number, and nail Shane's sneaky accounting. Receipts were everything.

"I'll be out the rest of the afternoon, Tammi. Thanks again." I appreciated her more than she knew. She'd used Shane's password and delivered the full download of every complaint from former employees and interns that Shane had buried. Their birthdates practically screamed from the pages next to their "reasons for termination" and NDAs: eighteen years old—inappropriate relationship. Twenty years old—inappropriate relationship. Shane blamed women for coming on to him, but I knew better. Absolute trash human.

Across the office, Patrick's accent carried through the air as he laughed into his phone. Neil shuffled past with his mug and gave me a thumbs up, blind to the takedown happening three feet away.

Let them stay oblivious. The less they knew, the safer we all were.

Before I left, I stopped by Davis's desk. He was hunched over his computer.

"Hey," I whispered, after checking for eavesdroppers. "We still on for later?"

"Yep, I'm downloading what I can, all my banking statements to prove I never spent a cent of client money." His eyes met mine.

"Be careful today, Iz, okay? No hero shit."

I touched his hand briefly, electricity buzzing through me. "I'm always careful."

"See you after. We'll compare notes." He bit his lip in that way that should be illegal.

My insides clenched like a fist as I left the office. The audacity. Truly. Another totally normal day pretending I wasn't feral for my coworker while plotting to take down my boyfriend.

I pushed into the trendy vegan café on Capitol Hill, already out of breath (cardio was so not my thing). The place was peak Seattle—Edison bulbs, reclaimed wood, and white people with dreadlocks taking selfies with overpriced cashew cheese.

I spotted Jessica at a corner table.

Next to her sat a woman in her fifties, with dark hair pulled back in a severe bun, sharp features, and eyes that tracked my approach as if I were a suspect.

"Isabella," Jessica gestured to the woman. "This is Alexandra Collins. Alex, this is Izzy."

Alex offered her hand. Her grip was firm, no warmth, all business. "Hello, Izzy."

"Thanks for…seeing me?" I sat, suddenly aware of how

young I must seem to her. "This feels very *Erin Brockovich* right now. Or *The Godfather*?"

The corner of Alex's mouth turned up. "Less glamorous than either, I promise."

A server appeared. I hadn't planned to eat—meat lover, veggie hater—but the food on other plates looked solid enough. Jessica ordered a beet salad. Alex got black coffee.

"Vegan mac and cheese," I said, because apparently I was on a quest to understand how that was even possible.

The server left, and a fog of silence settled over the table.

Alex broke it. "Jessica tells me you have information about Shane Sutton."

"And she tells me you've been investigating him for years." I refused to look away from her, even though I was intimidated as hell.

Her jaw tightened. "I have. But I'm stuck." She glanced at Jessica, then back to me. "Jessica says you might have something that helps?"

"I might."

Alex almost smiled. "Fair enough. Let me show you this." She pulled out a folder and slid it across the table. "Sutton Stars Scholarship program."

I picked up the glossy ad featuring bright-eyed co-eds holding giant novelty checks. "What about it?"

She opened the file and tapped on a spreadsheet. "Scholarship funds are funneled through PACs into McFadden's campaign. Donors think they're funding education, but they're bankrolling attack ads."

I frowned. "How are the students going to school if they don't receive the scholarship money?"

"Well, I can't divulge too much." She flipped to another page with names, dates, and dollar amounts. "These are some students listed as recipients. The ones we can't track down."

The comment floated over me. "Meaning?"

Alex sighed. "With any scholarship program, there are always a few students who drop out, change course. You expect to lose track of a couple. But this many?" She raised her brows.

"Are you saying…they don't exist?"

"Exactly. And yet the funds show as disbursed."

Jessica clicked her tongue. "Well, can't you ask the school for their records? See if they match up?"

"Because of privacy laws, we don't have that transparency. We cannot access university data without a subpoena. We can't get a subpoena without students complaining. And students won't complain if they don't exist." She let out a short, bitter chuckle. "You see our problem here."

"Well, isn't that strategic." I folded my arms.

Jessica chewed on her bottom lip. "But using charity money for political campaigns is illegal. That should give you power to dig deeper, shouldn't it?"

Alex pulled a pen from her jacket and started sketching on a napkin.

"Let me break this down simply. Shane creates fake applications, fake profiles, and fake transcripts. Cuts checks in their names."

Oh, good, crime napkin diagrams. She drew boxes and arrows:

Donors → Sutton Stars → Fake Students → Shane's Accounts

"The money goes to bank accounts he controls. Then he allegedly funnels that stolen money to a political group called Puget Coalition. Then those funds are to go to McFadden."

Another arrow:

Shane's Accounts → Puget Coalition → McFadden

I stared at it, the simple arrows making Shane's crime painfully clear.

"So, they're just…buying power?" I asked.

Alex's voice hardened. "Yes. That's likely how McFadden went from eight percent to thirty-two percent in the polls. Increasingly extreme ads, all funded by charity money that should help kids go to college."

Our food arrived at the absolutely worst time. I took a bite of the mac and cheese—actually not terrible, but my appetite had vanished.

Jessica pushed her plate away. "Okay, so Shane wants to run for office, and he wants to collect women. But what would McFadden have to gain from all this?"

"That's not clear." Alex gave a half-shrug. "His policies are…divisive to say the least, but as far as politicians and millionaires go, Bruce is a decent guy. No questionable audits, no harassment complaints—"

"That's the bar we are setting for 'decent guy' these days?" I said too loudly.

Alex glared. "I know. He wouldn't align with Shane and

let Shane run his campaign if he wasn't benefiting. But the benefit may simply be his surging numbers, and nothing more. So our focus is on Shane Sutton, not Bruce McFadden."

"Okay," I picked at my food, frustrated. "So, what can you do? About Shane?"

"Here's my problem." Alex pushed her untouched coffee aside. "His lawyers are too good, and his connections are deep. Every witness is either compromised or scared."

Jessica and I locked eyes. This was hopeless.

"So." She turned to me. "Might you have something for me, now?"

I fiddled with my handbag. I couldn't give her everything I had, not when she didn't seem serious about pursuing. I brushed past the list of NDAs, the paperwork that would implicate Davis, and his statement about his SAT scores and scholarship fraud. It was too risky. Instead, I pulled out the USB drive, intimate moments compressed into one small piece of plastic. "Blackmail photos of women. Dozens of them. Some are barely over eighteen."

"Revenge porn." She glanced at Jessica. "He's still doing that, I see."

Jessica wrapped her arms around herself. "Well, apparently, he can still get away with it."

Alex cleared her throat. "How did you get this?"

"Does it matter?"

"I suppose not." She scribbled a note. "It could get him arrested. Is that what you want?"

"At least, yes." I couldn't keep the irritation out of my voice.

"If he recorded without consent and threatened distribution for leverage, that's extortion." She glanced in Jessica's direction. "But, again, we've been through this before. With no record and a good lawyer, it's he-said-she-said. And that doesn't touch retaliation. Which Mr. Sutton is…known for."

"What if we all came forward. The dam would break," Jessica said. "Safety in numbers—there are dozens of us."

But Alex didn't even look up. "Ladies, I appreciate the enthusiasm, but I need you to let the legal process—"

"The legal process is broken," I snapped. "If you're stuck, if the victims are scared, and everyone's waiting for safety that might never come—" I stopped myself.

The server returned with our check, again at the worst time. Alex pulled out her wallet and slid cash onto the table. "I've got this."

"You don't have to—" Jessica started.

"I do." Alex left her seat, all business again. "Isabella, thank you for the information. I'll be in touch."

She left the restaurant without looking back.

Jessica and I sat in silence for a moment, watching through the windows as Alex climbed into a sedan and drove away.

"She still won't do anything."

Jessica nodded. "Probably not."

I rubbed my temples, headache building. "If the fucking DA won't help us, who can we trust?"

"I don't know." Jessica's voice was small. "That's what terrifies me. What if the whole system protects him because too many people have too much to lose?"

"By the way, Tammi got this off Neil's server." I pulled the list of former interns out of my bag. "Maybe you can do more for these women than Alex can…"

"This is great, thank you." She snapped a photo with her phone. Shane's trail of women. Complaints dating back to when Shane took over Sutton Stars. "I remember this one." She pointed to a name. "Shelly. Pretty sure she was the last intern."

"Oh, did you work with her?" I had to force the words out.

"No. She went home during the lockdowns. Guess Shane figured out a more legal way to exploit women." She rolled her eyes. "Employees instead of interns."

"Yeah." I folded the sheet and creased it.

"I'm sorry this wasn't more helpful, Izzy."

"Me too." My legs were wobbly beneath me as I stood.

We walked out together into the gray February afternoon. The cold air hit my face, sharp and clarifying. I got in my car and opened the complaint sheet again, reading the names.

Michelle "Shelly" Foster. Grover High School 2019 Graduate.

I traced my finger across our old address and phone number—the tiny apartment where I raised my little sister, where we'd been happy for five years before Shane Sutton destroyed her.

I folded the paper again and tucked it in my purse. For Misha's sake, I'd burn Shane Sutton's entire world to the ground.

TWENTY-THREE

KATHERINE

Street parking on Western avenue was scattered and inconvenient, the way it always is when you're running on fumes.

The sky couldn't decide whether to rain or threaten it forever. Same result either way, with everything damn, gray, and holding its breath. An ominously perfect backdrop.

I walked into the park, keeping my pace even, my shoulders down, like a person with nothing to hide.

I found a bench in front of my favorite sculpture—Calder's Eagle, bright as an open wound against the slate sky—while I rehearsed what I wished I could say to Izzy.

I'm sorry I dragged you into this. I'm sorry Shane's worse than either of us knew.

Izzy appeared on the main path with her hands stuffed into the pockets of her oversized flannel, and sat next to me.

"Hey."

"Hey, yourself."

Izzy took a deep breath, as if she had info, but wasn't quite sure where to start.

"So," I said, "Alex Collins."

Izzy's shoulders dropped. "Complete waste of time,"

"That bad?"

"Worse." She pulled a napkin out of her purse, arrows connecting words, and pointed. "She walked me through the whole scheme. Most of the scholarship recipients are fake. Federal fraud, which should be open and shut."

"But?"

"But she can't move forward." Izzy shoved the napkin back in her pocket. "Won't, actually. Said his lawyers are too good and his connections are too deep."

"What about the photos—"

"Useless. Her words, not mine."

I tapped my foot nervously against the cement. "So she knows he's guilty, has proof, and can't touch him."

"Won't touch him," Izzy said. "There's a difference."

We were on the same wavelength. "So, do you think..." The metal bench creaked beneath me. "She's compromised."

Izzy nodded without looking at me.

"If the DA is compromised, who isn't?"

"I wanted to give her more." Izzy picked at her nail polish. "But I couldn't risk it without knowing Davis would be safe."

"What about the NDAs and settlements?"

"Shows a pattern of abuse, but no fraud," she said.

"Fuck."

"Super Fuck."

I swallowed. A few people moved past us and we both looked opposite directions, as if we were strangers occupying the same bench. I glanced around for familiar faces. "Is Davis still coming to meet us?"

"Should be here soon."

Izzy's stomach growled audibly, and she put her hand on her belly. "God, I hate vegan food. I swore after growing up eating roots and herbs, that I'd never touch another meal without meat or preservatives. And here I am, duped by fake cheese."

I turned to look at her. "You don't read 'crunchy granola' to me."

She chuffed, "What, you expected hemp jewelry and patchouli oil?"

"Not that extreme. More…suburbs, cheerleader, club soccer?"

"God, no. We were practically off-grid. My mom grew weed and sold it way before it was legal. Made weird herbal tinctures and syrups. And at one point, she believed the earth was flat. So, yeah."

My mouth hung open. "You're kidding."

"Wish I was." She twisted a strand of hair around her finger. "Funny that I've landed in a real conspiracy."

"That's wild. Is your dad the same way?"

"Yeah. He followed her lead. Great guy, but…gullible, I guess. Honestly, Fred reminded me a lot of him in that way. Loyal to a fault." She cleared her throat. "But during COVID, he got super sick and...well, it changed things."

"Oh, well, that's good, I guess?" I offered.

She smiled. "And I make my mom sound terrible, but she isn't. Our relationship's strained, yeah. Still far from mainstream, but at least she's come a long way."

"I get it," I said. "I have a strained relationship with my mom too." I looked over my shoulder as if Linda could somehow hear me.

Izzy drummed her fingers on her thighs. "Shane mentioned some…issues with your dad."

"Wow, talk about the pot calling the kettle black." I sighed dramatically. "Yeah, he had alcoholism, but his addiction didn't stop at booze; it was women, too. His students. Technically adults, but they weren't much older than I was then." I pinched my eyes shut for a second before turning to her again.

She looked away. "God, men are pricks."

Out on the Sound, a container ship cut a slow line through the gray, steady, and indifferent. I thought about patterns and generations repeating themselves, no matter how hard you fight. Izzy and I had both sworn we'd never end up here, yet here we were, like our moms, rewriting reality to survive betrayal.

A text pinged from Eric:

Want me to pick you up or meet you at the school this afternoon?

I typed back:

Meet you there.

I dropped my phone into my bag. "Eric and I are getting called to the principal's office this afternoon. Something about Elliott and an altercation with another student. Just what I need."

"What happened with you two? I mean, beyond the crypto shit. You guys seem so compatible. So normal."

I smirked. "Depends on what normal means. We were young when we met. I was rebelling, and what better way than dropping out of college and dating some Y2K hacker? I thought he was so badass, and the complete opposite of a man my mom wanted for me. Had no clue what he did for work."

Izzy grinned. "The mob stuff."

"Right." I laughed. "Our marriage was good for a long time, not perfect, but typical, I guess. We did IVF for years. It was my sole focus." I swallowed back memories of that time, all the heartbreak, the loss, all the injections. "It was a bit of a blur. I went into survival mode when everything collapsed. Divorce, Bankruptcy. Foreclosed home."

"Jesus."

"Yeah, didn't think the kids and I would survive it, but we did."

I didn't tell her how long I punished myself after, sometimes still did, convinced I could have been more patient, more forgiving. Sometimes, I wondered if we'd have survived together. But if we hadn't split, I'd never have learned I could fight monsters like Shane.

Izzy tilted her head, waiting for me to continue.

"Anyway, Eric walked the walk. Made amends and rebuilt his career and his reputation. Most people wouldn't claw their way back the same way he did. He's a great dad, and a great guy."

"Okay, so maybe not all men are pricks," she said.

As if on cue, Davis appeared on the path, scanning over his shoulder before he came closer. He passed by, looped around one of the steel walls, then returned, as if he'd simply changed his mind about where to walk.

"Hey, how did the meeting go—"

"Terrible, she can't help us," Izzy interrupted.

He pressed back against the bench, jostling all of us. "Fuck."

"Yeah."

Izzy's phone chimed. "It's him."

She flipped the screen so we could read it.

> Doctor gave me clearance to resume activities. I'll be home at 5 pm. I want you waiting for me.

"Activities." Davis clenched his jaw.

Izzy swallowed hard. "We end this today."

"What? How?" My spine stiffened. "Alex is stuck, the press would give Shane a chance to spin it, and all the victims are too scared to come forward."

"We confront him ourselves."

Davis and I turned to stare at her.

"I mean it." Izzy's gaze didn't waver. "What if we let him think he's already won?"

I blinked. "What are you talking about? How?"

"I get him comfortable. Vulnerable." She ticked points off her fingers. "Tell him I know about Chelsea, Rhonda, all of them. That'll throw him off balance. Then I'll mention that I know he's been funneling money through Davis's name."

Davis leaned forward, elbows on his knees, "He'll deny everything."

Izzy bit the tip of her fingernail. "Not if I act impressed.

Like it's brilliant. Sexy, even. I'll stroke his ego. I've backed his every bullshit talking point at work. I know how to convince him his schemes are genius. I'll be on his side. And once he admits it, we've got him."

"I hate to say it," Davis cut in. "But that could actually work." I felt the slightest spark of hope. They were right. Shane's ego could easily be his downfall.

"He's expecting me, it's the perfect time to end it—"

"Now?" My voice pitched higher. "No, I have a meeting with the principal—"

Izzy cut in. "It's better if you're not there. He'd be too suspicious."

"You're not going without me." Davis left no room for argument.

A ferry horn blasted across the water, making us all jump. My coffee sloshed. I shifted in my seat, suddenly aware of how exposed we were and how close everything felt. "Guess we're all a little twitchy." I wiped my hands on my jeans.

"With good reason," Izzy said.

But as Izzy and Davis coordinated their details—what to say, what not to say—doubt bubbled up in me anyway. Because I wasn't the one walking into that house, and because I had children, and consequences, and a life that would still exist after this, no matter what.

"Are we sure this is our only choice?" The words escaped before I could stop them.

"Men like Shane operate above the law unless they're stopped." Izzy turned to face me. "We need to meet him where he is. Nothing else is working."

Davis squared his shoulders. “What other choice do we have, Katie?”

I remained still. Gripping the bench edge as if it could anchor me.

There was no other choice.

“We’ve got a few hours.” Davis checked his watch.

“I’ll meet you there at four.” Izzy’s voice was steady, resolved.

“And I’ll keep my phone on.” I looked between them. “If anything goes wrong, anything at all, Puget Academy is five minutes from the lake house. Call me immediately.”

We sat with the plan between us. Three hours to catch a predator who’d either free us or ruin us.

Izzy surprised me with a hug. “No matter what happens,” she whispered, “thank you for trusting me.”

She felt so small in my arms, like one of my children. Small, like Shane and men like him wanted us to be. But I could feel something else: our rage. We’d absorbed Shane’s damage and kept moving. Given the benefit of the doubt, we stayed beautiful and fuckable, and he’d built his empire on all of it. I still wasn’t sure why Izzy wanted revenge so badly, but I knew, like me, she was done waiting for justice to arrive.

TWENTY-FOUR

ISABELLA

I stared at myself in the bathroom mirror, trying out faces I'd never had to fake before. Surprise. Hurt. And the hardest performance of all, pretending I actually wanted Shane Sutton touching me.

"Wow…that's genius," I whispered to my reflection, practicing the breathy voice Shane loved. I widened my eyes like he'd just pulled a rabbit out of a hat to sell awe and stroke his ego.

The stairs creaked under Davis's weight as he climbed. He turned to me. "Last chance to back out, Iz."

"No backing out. Not after what he's done. Otherwise, he wins."

Davis crossed the room in three strides and pulled me close, his arms wrapping around me tightly. I buried my face in his shirt, memorizing the rhythm of his heartbeat like it might be the last time I heard it. "If you need help, you say the word and I'm coming out."

"Got it," I mumbled against the cotton.

"I mean it." He pulled me back to meet my gaze. "Your safety matters more than nailing this bastard."

"I know. But if we don't nail him, none of us will ever be safe. You know that."

Davis checked his phone one last time, then froze when I took off my robe and slid onto the bed. "Jesus, you look smoking hot."

I adjusted the lace on my thigh and let his eyes drag over me appreciatively. But this wasn't for him. This fragile outfit was bait for a monster to take one last bite.

I'd become a woman I'd sworn I'd never be. But this wasn't a necessity; this was a choice. A calculated, deliberate choice to use my body against a man who used his power against everyone. The distinction mattered. Using your sexuality as strategy isn't degrading if you're the one strategizing.

Davis walked back toward the door. "You scared?"

"No. I've basically been the sex decoy since day one—might as well finish the job."

Gravel crunched outside. My stomach plummeted, the free-fall sensation of a roller coaster dropping. I peeked through the curtains to see Nancy's car pulling up to the garage.

My brain stalled.

"He's early."

"Call for me if anything is off." The pleading edge in his voice made me want to cry as he raced back downstairs. I watched Shane through the window, getting out of the passenger seat.

He straightened, miraculously dropping his limp the

second he thought no one was watching. Even his injuries were fake. Nancy said something to him—a warning? A reminder to stay in character?—before driving off.

I settled on the bed, hyperaware of the silk against my skin. My heart was thumping so fast my fingertips were pulsing.

The front door creaked open downstairs. Footsteps in the foyer. Then the heavy, deliberate thump of his cane against each stair—thud, thud, thud—like a countdown.

"Baby," I called. I'd been sexting him all afternoon, dirty breadcrumbs to set the stage. He was always most honest when sex was currency. And I needed him honest, distracted. To say anything I could use against him. "I'm up here, my love."

The bedroom door swung open, and his eyes raked over me, like I was a toy he'd left on a shelf and was pleased to find it waiting for him. The cane clattered to the floor. A mere prop.

"God, I've missed this," Shane growled.

I reached for him. "Me, too," I lied.

How many times had I said those words and meant them?

His hand shot out, gripping my wrist. Hard. I felt my bones shift. "You know what I've been thinking about all this time?" His grip tightened, like handcuffs. My hand throbbed. "How well you've played your part. So devoted. So convincing."

I forced a neutral face. "I try."

"So devoted," he continued, "that you'd rearrange your entire schedule for me." He straddled me and caught my other wrist, trapping both above my head. "Postpone meetings. Cancel appointments. Drop everything the moment I texted."

I kept my smile steady through sheer force of will, even as my heart threatened to beat out of my chest.

He pressed his weight on me, springs creaking under us. His stubble scraped against my chest as he kissed my neck, then up to my ear, his breath warm and wet. "Davis has always had excellent taste."

My nerves shot down to hell. "What?"

"You know what I'd love, baby?" He halted, savoring. "Why don't you fuck me the same way you fucked Davis the day we buried my father?"

Everything inside me froze, then lurched like I'd been shoved off a cliff. How the hell did he know? Every possible question spiraled: Did Davis tell him? Was he watching us? His weight squeezed air from my lungs.

I kept my face loose, my body looser, fighting every instinct screaming at me to push him off and run.

"Shane, wait—stop!"

"You thought you could outsmart me?" He kissed down my body, feeding off my panic like oxygen. "So cute, playing detective. Trying to blackmail me."

This was turning him on.

"No, you're blackmailing Davis…stealing from Katie…the company…"

"Oh, Bells." His head lifted with fake admiration. "I should thank my wife, though. Hiring you to fuck me into leaving her, so you two could split my money? Extortion? Absolute genius."

Acid scorched my throat, hot and bitter. I forced it down.

He knew. We hadn't been playing him. He'd been playing us, watching us scramble like mice in a maze he'd designed.

"You two can bunk together in minimum security," he mocked. "Probation, if you're lucky. But Davis? Oh, Davis will do real-time. Commingling Sutton Stars funds with his own? Running it as his personal dating service, and winning you as a prize?"

He tilted his head back to laugh, and I shoved him off me and scrambled to my feet. My legs were weak. I needed to get out.

But Shane was between me and the door.

"Davis," I yelled, moving out of the room toward the staircase.

Shane laughed louder. "Wait, Davis is *here*?"

I screamed, louder this time. "Davis, help—"

The word died in my throat as Shane grabbed me by the back of my hair and pulled me against him. Pain exploded across my scalp. My neck snapped back.

I clawed at his hand, trying to pry his fingers loose, but he was so much stronger than I was. Davis appeared below on the landing, frozen.

"Let go of her!" Davis screamed.

Shane continued to laugh.

"Hell, Davis, let's cut a deal. I won't turn you in if we share her. Think what we could do together, the three of us."

He pressed his erection against me, hard and insistent, leaning in to my ear so only I heard. "Money or no money, Bells, you're still white trash. Like your sister."

My blood ran cold.

Misha.

Her image detonated in my mind with the force of a bomb. My sister, so beautiful it almost hurt to look at her. My revenge plan with Katie, the money—all of it—vanished, replaced with pure, molten rage. Every humiliation, every lie, every pathetic compromise I'd made for this manipulative bastard. Every time I'd smiled when I wanted to scream. Every time I'd fucked him when I wanted to strangle him.

Every woman he'd used and life he'd destroyed.

His fingers tightened in my hair, yanking my head back again until tears sprang to my eyes.

White-hot pain. I felt strands ripping free. But the pain burned away my fear, leaving only rage.

Pure, perfect rage.

Who the actual fuck did he think he was?

I didn't think. Didn't plan. There was no strategy left, just pure instinct.

My body moved before my brain caught up. I drove my elbow back into his stomach—hard. The air rushed out of him, and his grip loosened just enough. I spun around and shoved him away with everything I had, putting every ounce of fury and grief and betrayal behind it.

Then time slowed to a crawl, like a movie, as Shane stumbled backward, losing his footing. His arms windmilled, and his fingers found one of the thin metal slats of the modern staircase.

It wasn't enough.

He slammed against a panel, shattering it, and tumbled through the broken glass.

"Shane—" Davis lunged forward, his hand reaching out

like he could somehow stop what was happening. But Shane was already falling over the side.

His arrogant expression morphed into something I'd never seen on his face before: shock. His hands reached out into empty air, fingers grasping for anything to save him. But there was nothing there to catch him.

His shoulder slammed into the edge of one of the floating stairs on the way down—*crack*—and then he pinballed off the wall before hitting the marble floor.

The final impact shook the house.

Then—silence.

The most beautiful sound I'd ever heard.

I gaped at my hands, still outstretched and tingling from the push. The same hands that had poured his drinks, typed his emails, stroked his ego. They'd just pushed him down the stairs.

Holy. Fucking. Shit.

"Jesus Christ..." Davis's voice sounded miles away. "Izzy..."

I looked over the railing, legs trembling as I forced myself to move. Shane lay sprawled on his back, motionless. After every threat, every lie—

I'd finally shut him up.

TWENTY-FIVE

KATHERINE

I hurried down Puget Academy's polished hallways. My nerves split between whatever Izzy and Davis were doing with Shane at that exact moment and being summoned to the principal's office. My phone had been silent for twenty minutes. No updates from Davis, no panicked texts from Izzy. Which meant either everything was going according to plan, or it had gone so catastrophically wrong that no one could contact me.

When I reached Mr. Morris's door, Eric was already waiting outside.

"Ms. Valentine, Mr. Gray, please come in." Mr. Morris gestured us inside.

Even at forty-two, the principal's office still made me feel twelve years old and caught red-handed.

Eric and I sat on either side of Elliott, who avoided eye contact. Mr. Morris sat in front of us. His button-down gaped, revealing a T-shirt underneath, Jesus's face, and the words

Who's Your Daddy? The absurdity almost made me laugh. Almost.

"Elliott," Mr. Morris began, folding his hands on the desk. "Would you like to explain to your parents what happened today?"

Silence. Elliott kicked his faded blue Converse together.

I reached over and patted his knee. "It's okay, bud, whatever it is."

A tear fell from Elliott's face onto his jeans. I turned my head toward the principal to fill the silence.

When Elliott remained quiet, Mr. Morris sighed. "There was an altercation this morning. Elliott punched another student between classes."

"Elliott, what the hell, dude?" Eric earned a death glare from me for swearing in the principal's office.

"This isn't like you." I tried to catch Elliott's downcast eyes. My quiet, thoughtful middle child. The one who usually flew under the radar. "Punching someone? That's not who you are."

Elliott hunched deeper into himself, a wall of silence.

I turned to Mr. Morris. "Were they hurt?"

"Only his pride," Elliott mumbled.

"That doesn't make it okay," I said, silently exhaling relief. "What happened?"

"Nothing. It doesn't matter."

"It matters to me."

Elliott's head shot up. "Brock said you were a gold digger, Mom." His fists were tight against his thighs. "He said you married Shane for his money, and now you're fucking his dad."

The words sucked the air from the room. My throat constricted, tears threatening. Mr. Morris shifted uncomfortably in his chair, denim scraping against wood. "I've called Mrs. Anderson. She's not happy. Threatening to press charges about our school being a hostile environment."

Eric leaned forward. "Her punk son called Katie a whore, but sure, hostile environment."

"Eric." I glared again, then turned to Elliott. "And you thought throwing hands was worth a suspension?"

"I didn't punch him that hard," Elliott muttered. "Just enough to shut him up."

Eric coughed to hide what sounded suspiciously like a laugh.

I closed my eyes. This was exactly what I'd feared most about the divorce becoming public knowledge. Here was my son, fighting my battles for me because I hadn't been strong enough to end my marriage sooner.

"A three-day suspension is standard in physical altercations like these," Mr. Morris said. "And I'll deal with Mrs. Anderson."

Elliot hurried out, and Eric followed behind him. "Mrs. Valentine, before you go."

Mr. Morris passed me two stapled-together pages, and I skimmed the title:

`Following the Money: Who's Really`
`Funding Our Parents Coalition?`

"Emma's article," I said. "The one you killed."

"I caved. I'm not proud of it." His face reddened. "Look,

between you and me, this parent coalition is a nightmare. I promise I'm doing everything in my power to get Mr. Carlisle back and get our school paper up and running again."

"Thank you. For this. And for being honest." I shoved the article in my purse and left the office before tears spilled down my cheeks.

Walking that long hallway toward the parking lot, I was sixteen again. Listening to rumors. Whispers. My father's sins had bled into my life, and now, mine were staining my kids'. Elliott put in his earbuds and climbed into Eric's car without looking at either of us. Was this who he'd always been, or had Shane carved it into him?

"You cannot blame yourself. Kids are assholes, you know that," Eric said. "But aren't you the least bit proud of him for defending your honor?"

"No. I don't need defending. I hate that toxic masculine crap." I thought of Ethan, already parroting Shane's "alpha" garbage from those podcasts. I hated that it may have rubbed off on my kids.

"Okay, okay. I don't think it's that deep, Katie. He lost his cool. I'll talk to him, all right? But you can't blame yourself. Please?"

Easier said than done. My phone rang. Davis's name flashed on the screen. "One sec."

"We have a problem." All I heard was panic. "Get to the lake house, now."

"What happened?"

"Get here. Soon."

The line went dead.

Eric stared at me. "What is it this time?"

"Something's wrong." I gestured to our son in the back seat of his car. "Take him home and keep your phone on."

"Okay." Eric placed his hand on my arm before I got in the car. "Be careful, Katie."

Adrenaline surged through me as I pulled out of the lot. Whatever happened, there was no going back.

I parked beside Izzy's car, noticing Davis's was hidden around the side of the house. The wind whipped off the lake. I pulled my coat tighter and hurried to the door, which opened before I could knock.

Davis stood in the doorway with eyes too wide, chest heaving like he'd been running.

"Thank God." He pulled me inside. "We didn't know what to do."

Izzy sat at the base of the stairs, her face drained of color, staring at something on the floor. As Davis closed the door behind me, I saw what had happened. I didn't need to ask, and I didn't want to ask. I already knew.

I'd seen this sight in nightmares once. Lately, I'd dared to picture it as wish fulfillment. But nothing prepared me for the reality of it.

Shane's body was sprawled at the bottom of the stairs. His legs were splayed out like a broken doll. His eyes were closed. A calm settled over me, as if I were floating above the scene, detached. "How long ago did this happen?"

"Fifteen minutes ago?" Davis paced back and forth. "What the fuck do we do?"

Izzy hadn't moved from her spot, arms wrapped tightly

around her body as if she was holding herself together. "Are you okay?"

Stupid question. Of course, she wasn't okay. But I needed her present and functional.

"I'm thinking." She violently bit her cuticles. "He knew about…things he shouldn't. About Davis, about us… How?"

She looked up at me, finally. Her mascara smudged beneath her eyes.

"Maybe he read a text message or overheard something," Davis said.

"No, I never mentioned anything. But now…" Izzy pointed to the ground. "I guess it doesn't matter what he knew."

"Right." I kneeled to get a closer look without touching anything. "Look, he fell. He has a cane and was at the top of the stairs. As far as I can see, or anyone else will see, this isn't a crime."

Davis's ragged breath slowed along with his panic.

"You understand what I'm saying?" I rose to my feet. "And bonus. Life insurance."

It sounded coldly matter-of-fact, but Izzy lifted her head with a start.

Money. That's what this was about, wasn't it? The thing Shane had used to control us, the thing he'd dangled out of reach. A five-million-dollar policy that would save all of us.

Davis stopped pacing. The three of us realized at that exact moment that all our problems were solved.

"All right, should we call 911?" Davis reached for his phone.

I held up a hand to stop him. "Wait. We need a story first."

"Okay, he and I were…you know…" She gestured down her lingerie-clad body. "Davis stopped by for work. Shane got startled, fell down the stairs."

Davis frowned. "Okay, but why would Katie be here?"

"Because you called me, you idiot. Cops can look at phone records. Which is why we need to call them now."

"Oh, God." Davis picked up his phone and dialed. "Yes, 345 Lakeview Lane. My boss fell; he's not breathing. No, no pulse. Okay, yes, thank you." He hung up. "They are ten minutes away."

"Should we try to do CPR or something?" Izzy whispered.

"Right, good point." I crouched beside Shane's body again. My knees protested. His skin was still warm as I put my fingers on his wrist, searching for a pulse. Nothing.

I moved to Shane's neck, pressing my fingers against his carotid artery. The skin there was warmer, softer. I tried not to think about all the times I'd kissed that spot, back when I thought I loved him.

A faint but unmistakable pulse fluttered beneath my fingertips.

"Oh, no, oh, no oh, no oh, no oh, no." The words escaped in a horrified whisper.

"What?" Davis dropped to his knees beside me.

"He's still alive."

"You've got to be fucking kidding me," Izzy yelled.

"He saw me, saw you." Davis ran his hands over his face. "If he comes to, we're fucked."

"Wait," Izzy blurted. "My mom has some tinctures. They'll stop his heart eventually. Totally undetectable."

I tilted my head. "Now, you tell us!"

"Well, I didn't think we were going to fucking kill him, Katie!"

"Neither did I, but here we are."

"Oh, this is bad." Davis wrung his hands. "And of course the Black guy will go down for it."

"No. I'm not letting that happen. Let me think." My mind spun. All those nights wide awake, terrified of what Shane might do to my kids. Every threat. Elliott was in tears today, defending me against Shane's poison seeping into their school. If Shane survived this, he'd destroy us.

I breathed deep, clarity slicing through the panic. "Okay, we don't have time for your poison run, Izzy."

"No. No, we don't," she whispered.

"And you—" I pointed at Davis. "You're right. You'd be arrested, and Shane's paper trail isn't going to help."

"Yeah," Davis muttered.

"Who's the least likely to go down for this?" My tone was almost calm, as if I were explaining a catering order. "The rich white lady whose prenup is already shot, who's already got another boyfriend, who's already moved on in every sense of the word."

I examined Shane's face, the man who had threatened my children, stolen their money, and manipulated us all. The man I'd once believed was my salvation.

"Besides, he might not last much longer—"

But an unmistakable sound came from beneath us.

A gurgling, rattling breath. Then a faint, guttural laugh.

Shane's eyes, once closed, were straight on me. His lips curved into a smirk.

"You're…all…fucked…" Shane rasped, each word a labored victory.

Sirens screeched in the distance.

Time slowed. Izzy's horror, Davis's panic, Shane's smug certainty that he would win, even now.

In that moment, I understood that if Shane Sutton drew breath, none of us would ever be safe.

I put my face directly over his, meeting his gaze directly for perhaps the first time in our marriage. No more flinching. No more looking away.

With a fluid motion, I shifted my weight, placing one of my hands firmly on his mouth, the other over his nose.

"Katie!" Izzy gripped my shoulder. "What the hell are you doing?"

Davis pulled my other arm. "Stop! This isn't—"

But I was immovable, anchored to this moment. Shane's eyes held nothing but fear.

And I loved how it looked on him.

"No more threats. No more lies." My hands pressed down with the weight of every manipulation, every stolen dollar.

"No more Shane Sutton."

The resistance beneath me softened. His wide eyes faded into slack nothingness.

It wasn't violent or dramatic. It was quiet, almost gentle. Like turning off a light.

TWENTY-SIX

ISABELLA

The silk robe clung to my sweat-damp skin, sticky with guilt, and the lingerie underneath was the world's most inappropriate costume. What kind of idiot shows up to a crime scene in Agent Provocateur? I pulled the fabric tighter, hyperaware of how exposed I was—in every sense—but it offered no protection against the harsh stares of the uniformed officers. Radio static crackled from the cops' shoulders, undercutting the grim silence.

No more Shane filling the house or office with orders and lies. Shane was dead. Actually, truly dead. And I'd helped make him that way. Half of me wanted to puke, the other half wanted to high-five the universe.

"Which one of you found him?" a bulldog of an officer barked, notebook open.

I snapped back to the present. "I did."

He pointed at Davis. "And you didn't see him fall?"

“No.” Davis drummed his fingers nervously against his thigh.

“Shane was having balance issues since his skiing accident,” I offered, perhaps too fast. “The doctors warned him about stairs. He had a cane…”

“Right.” The officer scribbled. “And Ms. Valentine, you arrived after he was already…discovered?”

“Davis called me,” Katie said. “Shane and I are separated, but he’s still my husband.”

“And that was before or after the call to 911?”

A micro-hesitation. “Um, before, but she was only five minutes away.” He stopped. “We panicked.”

“Of course.” His tone was casual, but his eyes weren’t. “And your relationship with the deceased, Ms. Meyer?”

The word “relationship” sounded like a bad joke. What do you call it when you pretend to love someone while plotting their downfall? “We were…together,” I managed.

“I see.” Another note.

An officer circled Shane’s body, each squeak of his shoes on the hardwood scraping my spine. A camera flashed, a pop of blinding white light bleaching the scene. When the afterimage faded, Shane’s rigid body was still burned into my vision. He looked smaller. Pathetic. All that power and charisma reduced to a chalk outline waiting to happen.

I forced tears, though not all of them were fake. I was scared.

A paramedic gently touched my arm. “Ms. Meyer, is there someone who can stay with you?”

I eyed Davis. He stepped forward. “I’ll stay.”

The officer took notes. "We'll need statements from all of you. Here or at the station?"

"Here is fine," Katie cut in quickly. Too quickly.

The next hour blurred into a nightmarish montage of questions, photos, and more uniforms flooding in. The three of us eavesdropped on one another's conversations, trying to make sure the stories we'd thrown together in the moments after Shane died—for real—and the paramedics came in held up. Stick to the script. Shane and I were intimate. Davis happened to stop by. Shane got startled. Davis panicked and called Katie. We tried CPR, then 911. It was an accident.

A detective introduced himself as Amberg. He didn't ask questions so much as let the silence prompt them. He scanned our faces as we repeated the story again and again. He examined the stairs, Shane's cane at the top, then ran a gloved finger across the banister, searching for a secret that might give us all away.

"Tell me more about Mr. Sutton's medical history," Amberg said.

"Traumatic brain injury from skiing," Katie said. "He recovered, but still had balance problems."

"Any depression? Suicidal ideation?"

"No," I insisted. "He was looking forward to things. He had plans." Plans to destroy us, but still, plans.

When they zipped the body bag, Shane's face disappeared behind the black vinyl. A hysterical thought bubbled: he looked more peaceful than I'd ever seen him alive. The schemer was finally still. I bit my cheek, holding back the laughter clawing its way out.

What is wrong with me?

Davis's hand found mine, squeezing gently as they wheeled Shane away. The ambulance drove off without sirens. The dead weren't in a hurry.

"This is an active investigation." Detective Amberg turned back to us. "Ms. Meyer, I'll have Officer Langworthy supervise while you gather your essentials. The scene must stay secure."

The scene. Investigation. The words made my stomach pitch. Were they about to arrest us? Should I have changed out of the lingerie? How guilty did I look?

I could still feel his hot breath against my skin: "Your sister." He knew exactly who I was. And somehow, even with him dead, I wasn't safe from him.

Headlights swept across the window, slicing the dim room like searchlights. A car door slammed so hard the house rattled.

"Who's that?" Davis whispered, moving closer.

The front door burst open. Nancy Sutton stormed in, hair wild, mascara streaked. Less grieving mother, more banshee. Her eyes landed on the yellow crime scene tape.

"No," she said, before her voice tore upward into a scream. "Where is he? Where's my son?"

"Mrs. Sutton," Amberg said carefully. "If you'll sit—"

Katie stepped forward, palms out. "Nancy, I'm sorry. There's been an accident—"

"Don't you dare!" Nancy jabbed a finger at her. "Don't you dare pretend with me!"

Davis tried. "Mrs. Sutton, please, Shane fell—"

"Liar!"

"Nancy, you're upset," Katie spoke evenly. "This is a shock—"

"I should have watched him! I should have checked sooner!" Nancy fumbled for her phone. "I was too late!"

Watched him? Checked sooner?

"You killed my son!" Nancy shoved her phone toward Detective Amberg. On the screen: a paused video of Katie leaning over Shane's limp body.

No. It wasn't possible. We disabled the ring cameras. That angle, from the front door, in the foyer. How could it have recorded anything? And how did Nancy have the video? Ice raced down my spine. And then I remembered the things she'd said before, things she couldn't have known unless she'd been watching.

Shane had given his mother eyes in the house.

Amberg took the phone. His gaze flicked to Katie, then back to the screen, his former calm evaporating.

"It's not what it looks like," Katie stammered. "I was helping him—"

"You murdered him!" Nancy collapsed against the wall, sobbing. "She killed my baby! Arrest her!"

Davis moved toward her, palms up. "Mrs. Sutton, please—"

"Ms. Valentine." Amberg's voice was sharp. "We need you to come with us to answer some more questions."

Katie's eyes found mine across the room as an officer guided her toward the door.

"Wait." I stepped forward. "This is a misunderstanding—"

"Ms. Meyer," the detective raised a hand, cutting me off. "We will be in touch. For now, gather your things and leave. Both of you."

Katie paused at the threshold, eerily calm.

"Call Eric and Chris," she said.

She slid into the back of a cruiser without a fight, strobing red and blue lights painting her face in stripes. She didn't look like a killer. But she was. Like me.

Welcome to the club, Katie.

What did that camera show? Did it catch me pushing him? The argument? Every mismatch in our stories would be a nail in our coffins.

Officer Langworthy waited for me to head upstairs. Another cop blocked the door. Outside the crime scene tape, Shane's briefcase sat next to his phone, abandoned in the chaos.

Davis didn't blink. A silent communication passed between us, like we'd rehearsed it.

"I can give you a ride," he said smoothly as I followed the officer. "I'll wait in the car."

And just like that, Davis scooped up the phone and brief-case and walked out, casual as hell.

The clock on the wall ticked louder, each second pounding out the start of our race against time.

TWENTY-SEVEN

KATHERINE

I'd been staring at the same water stain on the ceiling for twenty-three minutes. The metal chair bit into my back, and my hands had gone numb from gripping the table. Twenty-three minutes of wondering if the officers behind the one-way mirror saw the truth written across my face: that I'd killed my husband and felt pure relief. Somewhere down the corridor, I heard muffled voices, phones ringing, the steady, indifferent noise of a police station at work.

The stain resembled a map of a foreign country, with irregular borders spreading across the cheap, Styrofoam tiles like spilled coffee. I counted the smaller spots that branched off from the main stain. Anything to keep my mind from replaying Shane's final moments.

I wasn't sure if I was avoiding reliving it out of guilt or because I liked it.

I closed my eyes. Behind my eyelids, I saw Shane's face as

the life drained from it, the shock, the fear, the final understanding that he'd lost. For a man who'd built his career on reading people, he'd completely miscalculated me.

I saw my own hands on his face, felt the resistance of his mouth and nose underneath them. My hands started shaking again, and I shoved them under my thighs to stop the trembling. The words wouldn't form, even in my mind. There were clinical terms: homicide, perpetrator. But they belonged to other people, people on the news, in movies, in orange jumpsuits. Not to mothers who packed lunches with notes and attended PTA meetings.

What kind of person had I become? A killer. Worse, a mother who killed someone. And perhaps worse yet, a wife who had killed her husband.

The words were foreign, impossible to reconcile with the woman who'd spent forty-two years avoiding confrontation, who apologized when other people bumped into me, who'd rather eat food I didn't order than send it back to the kitchen. Yet they were undeniably, horrifically true. For decades, I'd refined the art of making everyone happy except myself, and now I'd done the most selfish thing imaginable.

I'd taken a life to protect my own.

And I kept waiting for remorse that never arrived. Instead, I was gripped by terror for my children. What would this do to them when they found out? Emma would blame herself; she always did. Elliott would retreat into his games and pretend it wasn't happening. And Ethan…God, Ethan was still so young. CPS. Court. Custody. The letters rattled around my skull like dice.

But underneath that maternal panic, under the shock and

fear, was something else entirely: relief. The monster was gone, and he couldn't hurt us anymore. He couldn't manipulate another woman, gaslight another wife, or destroy another family with his lies and cruelty.

Or maybe he still could. In court. In headlines, the whispers at school. He could still take my kids away from me, even from the grave.

An officer opened the door. "Water?"

"Sure." I tried to keep my voice steady.

"It shouldn't be much longer," he explained, setting down the bottle. "You're not under arrest, but we appreciate your cooperation."

I was in limbo, somewhere between suspect and witness. Not under arrest, but not free to go either. I understood the unspoken message.

I unscrewed the water and took a sip. It was lukewarm and tasted like plastic. Sweat, stale air, and coffee clung to everything in the interrogation room while yellow lights pulsed overhead, making my head throb. I wrapped my arms around myself.

What mask should I wear? Grieving widow? Protective mother? If I look too calm, they'll think I'm guilty. If I cry too hard, they'll think I'm performing.

The silence of the room was a vacuum, and memories rushed in to fill it. Not happier times, but the beginning. The hook. I tried to keep the image of his dead body out of my mind by thinking of the first time I saw him, confident at the podium at Puget Academy's emergency parent meeting in August 2020. The world had fallen apart; kids were stuck at home since March, and I'd been out of work for five months.

He'd radiated confidence up there. Reassuring energy; and piercing blue eyes.

"We can't let fear make our decisions for us," he'd said. "Our children are depending on us to find creative solutions, and lockdowns are not proving to be more effective than masking and distancing in schools around the country that have remained open!"

I hung on every word. Everyone did. Here was a man who understood the impossible position parents were in, who had actual answers. I couldn't believe a man without children would be so passionate about having them return in person. And we were all behind him.

After his presentation, I thanked him for his passion, and his eyes seized mine, as if I were the first woman he'd ever seen. After months of feeling invisible and underwater, his focus was intoxicating. And I remember thinking back then, approaching forty, that my "catch a man" years were ending. I was flattered he'd chosen me. Wanted me.

"You must be overwhelmed with all of this. If you ever want to talk over coffee."

I said yes.

God, he was good.

The conversation had flowed more easily than I'd expected. He'd asked about the kids, told me how I'd raised mine so well. I remember choking up when he'd said that.

Then coffee became dinner, dinner became outings with the kids, Shane cheering louder than any parent at Ethan's games. He helped Elliott with Robotics projects and showered Emma with gifts.

My children fell for him first. I followed.

When I'd nearly run out of money, he suggested that we stay at his house. Salvation, not manipulation.

Then Valentine's Day arrived with roses and champagne and Shane on one knee with a ring.

I should have shoved it down his throat.

I ignored every warning sign. Other people got pandemic puppies, but I got myself a whole new life.

What a fucking lie.

The door opened with a jagged scrape that made me flinch. The detective returned, setting down a box of tissues I hadn't asked for.

"Thank you. Can I make a call?"

He pointed toward the phone on the wall.

All I knew was I had to protect my kids.

I dialed my mother.

And the irony wasn't lost on me—calling the one woman who'd failed to protect me from my father's destruction to protect my children from mine.

But she was the only person I trusted to shield my children from what was coming. For all her faults, all her enabling and excuses, she'd never let harm come to them. Maybe they were her redemption, her chance to do right by a generation she could still save.

Crisis stripped everything down to the essential truth. She was my mother, and I needed her the way I hoped Emma would always need me.

She answered on the first ring.

"Oh, honey, I heard the news. I've been worried sick! Are you—"

"Mom, I need you to do something for me."

A pause. "Yes, but Katie, what happened?"

I didn't answer. "Mom, I need you to go to Eric's and get the kids. The media will swarm as soon as this hits. I need you to protect them."

"Katie, you need to—"

"Make sure they stay away from the windows. Don't let them answer the door or check social media. And Mom?" My voice caught. "Tell them I love them. Tell them everything is going to be okay."

"Katie, you're scaring me. Where are you?"

"I'm fine, but please protect them. And if anyone asks, you know nothing, you haven't heard from me. Okay?"

"Katie—"

"Promise me."

"I promise. I'm getting in the car right now."

An officer poked his head in the door. "Detective Amberg will see you now."

"Mom, I have to go." I quickly hung up the phone.

The officer led me down a corridor lined with motivational posters: Integrity, Service, Honor. Each word a slight mockery. Through a window, I glimpsed the parking lot where news vans were gathering.

He opened a door to a small, windowless room.

"Please, Mrs. Sutton," he used the married name I had never assumed. "Take a seat."

The door clicked shut behind him, leaving us alone.

Detective Amberg sat across from me. He was my age, maybe a few years older, with tired eyes that had seen too many stories like mine to be impressed by any of them.

"I know this is difficult," he began, his voice emotionless. "But your mother-in-law is making some serious allegations."

"She's grieving," I said automatically. "She's lashing out."

"Sure." He placed a tablet on the table with a still shot of me over Shane's body.

"Why don't you tell me what you were doing here?"

TWENTY-EIGHT

ISABELLA

My hands trembled around the mug. The same hands that shoved Shane down the stairs. Funny how they looked the same as before I became a killer. The man I'd been playing—who'd been playing me harder—was dead. Because of me. Because of Katie. Because of all of us. My breath came ragged, like Shane's in those final seconds.

Davis's apartment was a shoebox with too much light and too much noise. Every siren down on the street sounded like it was meant for me.

Davis's voice pulled me back. "You okay?"

"Peachy." I set the mug down, and coffee splattered. "Nancy saw us. She's calling Katie a murderer, but I'm the one who—"

"Take a beat. Eric's on his way." He put his arm around my shoulders. "They didn't arrest Katie. Chris says that's a good sign."

Maybe not yet. This wasn't over.

My phone lit up with a text from my mom.

Bad news. The doctor said Pop needs a transplant within 6 months.

Six months. The words burned into my retinas. Six months to come up with the money. Six months I might not have had if I had gone to jail. I played savior and ended up a killer. The universe had jokes.

"Shit." I tossed my phone next to me like it was hot.

Davis looked over. "What's wrong?"

"Nothing," I lied. "Family stuff." I wondered if Shane had known about Pop's health, too, about the money we needed. What if he knew why I was there the entire time? Part of his cruel plan to make sure he destroyed another member of our family.

A knock at the door made us jump. Eric walked in, laptop under his arm, looking chewed-up and spit out.

"Sorry it took so long. Had some shit to handle." He dropped onto the couch. "You see the news?"

"What news?" Davis flipped on KING5.

BREAKING: SEATTLE BUSINESS LEADER SHANE SUTTON DEAD AT 45.

I cranked the volume.

"…tragic accident at his home," the reporter said, fronting our crime scene like a weather live shot. "Sources say Sutton, who had recently been recovering from a serious skiing accident, fell down a flight of stairs."

They cut to footage of Shane at a charity event, beaming that rehearsed smile. Then a shot of him with Katie and the kids, all of them picture-perfect.

Anger twisted on Eric's face. His children as Shane's props.

"Sutton was a pillar of the Seattle business community," the reporter went on, "known for his philanthropic work with Sutton Stars, which has provided college scholarships and job opportunities to underprivileged youth."

A pillar. A visionary. Try a predator with good PR.

But I already knew that. Because I didn't "fall" into Shane's orbit. I walked straight into it, eyes open, middle fingers up.

It was a job. A con. A way to buy Pop time.

At first, that's all it was.

Then came the sex—the kind you don't fake. The sex was supposed to be a performance. It was fire instead. And fire doesn't care about plans. It burns.

That's when he did what he always does. He turned me. Slowly, almost sweetly. He told me Katie was cold. That she'd been cheating on him first, not the other way around. He said I was the only one he could be honest with. As if his honesty meant anything.

Shane was a man who bent the truth until it snapped. And still, I let myself fall. Not because I trusted him. Because being desired by someone that powerful, that magnetic, was intoxicating in a way I'd never experienced. The fantasy he offered was better than the harsh reality I was living. And I was desperate and foolish enough, even with everything I knew, everything he did to my sister, to believe I could be the exception to his pattern of destruction.

The mayor came on the TV screen, doing the solemn-guy face. "Shane was a dear friend and a true visionary," he said. "This is a tremendous loss for Seattle."

They had no idea who they were sanctifying.

A tearful young woman appeared next. Sutton Stars recipient, pre-med, full testimonial. "Mr. Sutton changed my life. He believed in me when no one else did."

Sure, he did. That line had a thousand miles on it.

Hers, mine, Katie's, Jessica's, Misha's. All different. All the same.

Eric cleared his throat. "They're building the narrative. Makes things more difficult if—"

"If they figure out what really happened," I said.

"Right. So, we need to know what Nancy has."

Eric's fingers flew across his keyboard. He had Shane's phone cracked open, guts to screen, cables snaking to his laptop, code scrolling blue.

Davis leaned over to watch Eric's screen, his shirt riding up enough to make me forget how to breathe for half a second.

Focus, Izzy. Not the time.

"Well, well," Eric said, gesturing at the screen.

File names glowed on his screen like a hit list.

`Neil_boat_trip`

`Patrick_Jessica`

`Davis_Isabella`

`Tammi_karaoke`

Davis took a step back. "Holy shit."

Eric kept clicking. So many names. So many lives. An arsenal.

"This is how he stayed untouchable," he said. "Insurance."

"This is a folder full of ruined people," I muttered.

"Oh, get a load of this," Eric said, pointing to a file name: **`Alex_Collins_DA_undergrad`.**

"Of course. He had dirt on her, too." I wanted to scream. He'd never stand trial. He'd go down as a hero. Bullshit. "See any collateral on Bruce McFadden?"

Eric scrolled. "Nothing."

"Huh."

Eric continued typing away. "There's nothing on the ring server with the camera angle you described, so I'm looking to see if there are any other camera or video apps connected. If I can see the footage somehow... as I suspected. Cloud server. If I can get in…"

We waited in tight silence, with only the sound of clicks on the keyboard.

"I think I have it. Cloud Cam. It's an app used for local remote cameras, baby monitors, that sort of thing."

Davis stared at the screen. "Can you download the content?"

"Already doing it." Eric tapped on his keyboard. "And deleting the originals."

Davis paced. "Will that be enough? Nancy already has some of it."

"It depends. If we can see exactly what was captured, figure out what she saw, we'll know what we're facing. Give me ten minutes."

We moved to the kitchen. "Whatever happens," Davis said, "we're in this together."

"Is that supposed to make me feel better?"

"No. But it's true."

His honesty was the only solid thing I had.

"I should feel guilty," I said into his shirt. "But when I picture him down there, powerless, I'm relieved. What does that make me?"

"Human," he said. "Surviving. He would've destroyed us."

"That doesn't make it right."

"No." He pulled me closer. "But it doesn't make us monsters, either."

I wanted to believe we were just unlucky people who killed someone by accident, not murderers. But every time I blinked, I saw Shane tumbling down the staircase.

"I've got it," Eric called.

We crowded his shoulder. The timestamp was hours old. How was it still the same day?

Grainy footage filled the screen: Shane at the bottom of the stairs. Davis and I above him. I barely recognized myself. That woman was feral.

Then Katie appeared, dropping to her knees. The camera caught her from behind, leaning over Shane. Her shoulders shook. From the angle, it was impossible to tell what she was doing.

"It's record-on-demand," Eric said. "Not continuous. Someone had to trigger it remotely, from a phone or computer."

The frame showed the middle of the staircase and the

entry below, but not the top where I'd pushed him. There was no audio.

"You can't see the fall?" I held my breath.

"No. This is it." Eric's voice was low, like the camera could still hear us.

I exhaled. No shove. No hands on his face. Just three people over a body.

Eric outlined Katie's shape with his finger. "Nancy might think she saw something, but all I see is…"

"It looks like she's sobbing," I said. "Checking for a pulse."

"It does," Eric agreed. "No audio, limited angle. That's reasonable doubt. A lot of it."

Davis and I traded a look. Could we actually walk away from this?

"Are we sure that's all she has?"

Eric slouched. "We can't be sure about anything without Nancy's device, but this is all I see on the platform."

Davis fidgeted with his sleeve. "What about the autopsy? Won't they know how Shane died?"

"Stick to the story." Eric was calm again. "Shane fell. You thought he was dead. Katie tried to help. The end."

If Katie trusted him, I could too.

But I also knew Nancy was a loose end. And she liked me. I could exploit that relationship too, to find out what she knew. Because I doubted she'd stop until someone was in prison for this.

"Give me a couple of hours," I said.

Davis stepped between me and the door. "Where are you going?"

"I need to see what Nancy knows."

"Iz, that's crazy…don't." Davis pleaded.

"She likes me. Trust me."

"Likes you? She was ready to have Katie executed on the spot. What makes you think she won't turn on you?"

I grabbed my jacket from the chair, already calculating the drive to Ballard. "Because I'm not Katie. Nancy sees me differently, which is why I need to go now, while she's grieving and vulnerable."

Eric shuffled his eyes between us. "To manipulate a grieving mother?"

I looked over my shoulder on the way out the door. "To protect us."

TWENTY-NINE

KATHERINE

D*on't look guilty. Don't act guilty. You are a grieving widow.* The mantra played on a loop, a flimsy shield against my own image staring back at me. Kneeling over Shane's lifeless body. I tried to calm myself by picturing my children huddled at my mother's house, watching a movie, blissfully unaware that I was sitting in a cinderblock box, trying to remember how to breathe like an innocent person.

"Your lawyers are on their way, Ms. Sutton." His voice was even. "We can wait for them to arrive before we continue. It's up to you."

He was giving me an out. A lifeline. The smart part of my brain, the part that had binged every procedural drama on Netflix, screamed at me to take it. *Wait for Chris. Wait for the professionals.*

But I also didn't want him to think I had anything to hide. A grief-stricken widow would cooperate, right? Taking off the costume would mean admitting I had something to hide. And I had everything to hide.

This was a conversation. I'd spent my life managing difficult men; this was one more.

"It's fine, Detective," I said. "I want to help in any way I can. I want to understand what happened."

Amberg nodded and opened his notebook. "Let's go over your arrival at the lake house one more time. You said Mr. Clark called you?"

"Yes. He was frantic." I stuck to the script Izzy, Davis, and I had rehearsed in those stolen minutes before the sirens arrived. Before we knew there was video. "He said Shane had fallen, that I needed to come right away."

"And when you arrived?"

"I found him at the bottom of the stairs. Izzy…Isabella Meyer was there. She was very upset, understandably. Davis was on the phone, I think with 911." The details were fragmented, shrouded in the fog of adrenaline. Had they decided Davis was on the phone? Or was he trying to help? Shit. It was too late to change it now.

"So then what happened?" Amberg prompted.

"It's a bit fuzzy, but I took over, I suppose. I'm a mother. You see an emergency, you act." I took a sip of water, the plastic slippery against my sweaty fingers. "I checked for a pulse."

"And did you find one?"

The question was a precision strike. My mind flashed back to the faint, stubborn flutter under my fingertips. The gurgle in his throat. The smirk. I saw his eyes lock on mine, the empty space where his soul used to be.

"No," I lied. "I didn't feel anything, so I started CPR." I began to cry, surprised by my own tears, genuine though, not in grief. It was the terror of being caught, sour and sharp in the back of my throat. "Or I tried to."

Amberg scribbled a note. He let the silence stretch, a tactic, and I knew he wanted me to fill the quiet, to talk myself into a corner. I wouldn't.

"The thing is, Ms. Sutton." He looked up from his notes. "We're having trouble reconciling your statement with the video evidence."

My throat went instantly dry. "How so?"

Amberg folded his hands on the table. "You tell me."

He didn't elaborate, didn't describe what I was doing. He let the question hang in the air between us, forcing me to fill in the blanks with my own guilt. He hadn't played the entire video.

Did it see me cover his mouth? Did it capture the final, futile struggle? Did it show relief on my face when it was over?

"I told you, I was performing chest compressions," I said. "I was trying to save his life."

"Hmm." Amberg's beady eyes never left mine.

The walls of the small room closed in. He was painting a picture, and I was the killer at the center, defending myself against an accusation he hadn't even fully made.

"You mentioned to the officer on the scene that your husband had recently threatened you."

I did?

The shift caught me off guard. My bracelet clinked against the metal table as I trembled. I gripped my wrist to stop it.

"We were separating," I said carefully. "It was...difficult."

"Difficult how?"

The question was so simple. A crack in the door I could walk through and unburden myself. Tell him everything. The threats against my kids, the stolen money, the years of lies. *Justify what you did, Katie!*

"He was—"

I stopped mid-sentence, forcing myself to end the toxic dam of confessions.

Amberg's expression didn't change. He simply made another note. "Motive is an interesting thing, Ms. Sutton. But right now, we're focused on opportunity."

My composure cracked. "That's not what I meant."

"What did you mean?"

Fuck fuck fuck fuck.

"I want to help." My voice broke. "But I think I should have a lawyer present."

Amberg didn't blink. "Of course, Ms. Sutton. That's your right."

Why did he keep calling me that?

The door clicked shut behind him with a sound like a vault sealing. I put my head in my hands.

Idiot. Absolute idiot.

My mind was a blank wall of panic. I had no idea what Nancy's recording showed, or how she had it in the first place, but I knew what I'd done. I felt the life leave his body under the pressure of my own. How could I explain that away? The capable mom, the organized event planner—she was gone. In her place was a trapped animal, cornered and desperate.

I kept waiting for remorse. But when I thought of

Shane's final words, all that remained was the same fierce protectiveness as when one of my kids darted into traffic: you do what you must to protect the ones you love.

The door scraped open, and Amberg appeared again. "Your counsel is here."

Chris was pale. Beside him was a woman with sharp, intelligent eyes and steel-gray hair, and a younger man in a sharp designer suit with dark-rimmed glasses.

"Detective." The woman's voice was crisp, authoritative. "This interview is over. My client will not be answering any further questions."

"We are waiting for preliminaries, so stay close by for now," Amberg said.

The woman placed a hand on my shoulder, a gesture at once comforting and commanding. I looked from her to Chris to the detective, my breath coming in ragged gasps. I was safe, for now, but the damage was done. I'd flown blind into his trap and crashed spectacularly.

As they guided me from the room, Detective Amberg's eyes followed me. He hadn't gotten a confession. But I had a sinking feeling I'd given him something as good.

For the first time since Shane took his last breath, I was petrified.

The lawyers steered me into a small conference room down the hall, closing the door firmly behind us. The space was barely larger than the interrogation room, but the plain walls made it less intimidating. A scarred wooden table sat in the center, surrounded by mismatched chairs that had seen better days.

Before they could speak and tell me how badly I'd fucked up, I blurted. "Is it okay if I call my kids?"

"Of course." Chris gestured to the corner where my purse sat. I faced the wall, as if it would give me any privacy, and dialed Emma, who answered on the first ring.

"Mom?"

"Are you okay, sweetie?" I clutched my phone tighter. I wanted to crawl through the line and shield her from all of this.

"I guess." Emma's voice was small, nothing like her usual confident tone. She sounded as she had at six years old, when she'd fallen off her bike and tried not to cry. "It was crazy. As soon as Grandma drove us away from Dad's, the news trucks were everywhere."

"I know, honey. I know." Suddenly, I was fifteen again, pressed against my bedroom door while reporters with cameras shouted through our mail slot. History repeating itself in the worst possible way, but this time, I was the parent who had caused it. "Are you staying away from the windows?"

"Yeah. I don't think anyone knows we are here. We are okay, Mom. Grandma has all the curtains closed. We're watching a movie."

"Good. That's good." The team of lawyers in the conference room regarded me with sympathy while I soothed my daughter. "I love you all so much. Tell the boys I love them. And tell Grandma thank you."

"Love you, too, Mom."

I hung up and placed the phone on the table, fighting back tears. The lawyers waited politely as I patched myself together. My hands wouldn't stop trembling, and every breath was shallow, as if my ribs had shrunk overnight.

"My kids are at my mother's," I explained. "Hiding from the press."

Chris introduced the lawyers as Margaret Flagel, a stern woman with steel-gray hair and impeccable credentials, who hadn't smiled once since we'd met, and Jason Wentworth, a younger man whose expertise in forensic evidence had apparently gotten tech executives out of multiple jams. Jason kept fidgeting with his Apple watch, checking notifications every few minutes, while Margaret remained perfectly still, her hands in her lap. Chris sat with them, out of his league, but grounding me anyway.

"We're going to get you back to your family as quickly as possible," Margaret promised, her Boston accent clipped.

"I'm so sorry, I shouldn't have talked to the detective—"

"You did well." Margaret put up her hand. "You didn't say anything they can use against you."

"But I gave them motive. I told them about the money, the threats—"

"No, motive isn't proof," Margaret interrupted. "And the footage? Circumstantial at best. I've seen prosecutors try to build cases on stronger evidence and get laughed out of court."

"From a digital forensics perspective, we're in excellent shape," Jason added, pulling up something on his tablet. "The metadata shows multiple gaps in the surveillance timeline, and the compression algorithms used by this particular camera system introduce significant artifacts that would make any enhanced analysis inadmissible under Federal Rules of Evidence 702."

He caught my glazed look and simplified. "Bottom line? If this footage were enough to convict, we wouldn't be having this conversation," Jason added. "You'd be in arraignment."

"Right," I said. After all the prenup battles, after Shane drained our accounts and threatened my children's futures, none of it would matter if I were sitting in prison.

"Here's what they have." Margaret slid a tablet across the table. "This is the footage Nancy gave the police."

I watched myself from the camera's perspective. My back was to the lens, and my movements were obscured by grainy footage and poor lighting. Davis and Izzy placed their hands on my shoulders, embracing me, as if to console me.

It matched our story. We were trying to help him.

"They can't arrest you on this," Jason said.

I blinked hard, forcing myself present. "How did Nancy get it?"

"A private feed. Apparently, Shane told his mother to keep watch. He must have suspected something." Jason's face darkened. "Which raises bigger concerns."

"What bigger concerns?"

Margaret pushed paperwork aside. "Shane's political machine didn't die with him. Everyone he had in his pocket still has a vested interest in managing the narrative around his death."

"Why would they care?"

"Because Shane knew where the bodies were buried." She caught herself. "Metaphorically. Campaign finance irregularities, coordination between supposedly independent groups, and potential election-law violations. A criminal probe could expose everything in discovery."

"So, anyone who had a hand in his shady dealings will want it ruled an accident," I said.

"Yes, which helps us." Margaret adjusted her glasses. "But it means they'll be watching you—your movements, your statements. They need to know you won't rock the boat. They'll protect themselves, and that protects you, too."

"And then there's Nancy," Jason added. "She'll try to destroy you in the media. Your job is to say nothing to anyone. Keep your head down until the investigation is complete."

"Do not speak to anyone," Margaret said. "Not the reporters, not Isabella Meyer, or Davis Clark, not your ex-husband, friends. Nobody but us behind closed doors, understand?"

I stared at her, the dark irony landing like a punch. The same corrupt network Shane used to gain power would now scramble to protect itself. His powerful friends would want this to go away as quietly as possible.

Not in jail. But trapped. "So, what do I do?"

"For now, play along." Margaret squeezed my hand from across the table. "You have nothing to hide."

If only she knew.

When they stepped out to confer, I sat alone for less than a minute of silence. I pulled out my phone and searched Shane's name. I read his last text to me.

Don't wait up.

Perhaps the most honest thing he'd ever said to me.

I deleted him from my phone the way I'd deleted him in real life.

The door opened again, and Detective Amberg walked back in with the lawyers. "Toxicology and final autopsy will take weeks, but based on preliminary evidence, there isn't enough to keep you here. You're free to go."

Free. The word sounded impossible and precious. My lungs remembered how to work, drawing in air so sharply it made me dizzy.

"Thank you."

Chris drove me back to the lake in silence, the kind that was more companionship than discomfort. I was grateful he didn't try to fill it with platitudes or reassurances. There was nothing to say that wouldn't sound hollow.

The house came into view, and I sucked a breath. Yellow crime tape stretched across the front door, garish against the gray-blue siding. Police cruisers still lined the driveway, their presence making the whole scene look like a TV drama. Except this was my life.

My car sat where I'd left it hours ago, at an awkward angle, as if I'd been in a hurry. Which I had been.

Chris pulled up beside it. For a second, we both sat there, staring at the tape, at the officers still moving through the house with their clipboards and cameras.

"Thank you, Chris, for everything."

Chris's serious lawyer face slipped to reveal the concerned friend beneath. "Always. For now, lie low. Promise me?"

"I promise." I reached for the door handle, and my legs felt as heavy as lead as I stepped into the bone-chilling air blowing off the lake.

He drove away, leaving me at the scene of the crime, watching officers catalog the evidence of my husband's death.

The woman who walked into that lake house wasn't the same one who walked out. She'd died with Shane, and that was a fair trade. One death for another. Perhaps shock hadn't released me yet.

I started the engine and drove toward my children. Toward whatever came next.

I found myself making a list, the same way I'd planned birthday parties and fundraisers. Plans were my armor against chaos.

First: hold my children until they squirm away.

Second: call Eric.

Third: sell the homes I never wanted.

Finally: learn to live with what I'd done.

For now, I was a suspect on borrowed time.

THIRTY

ISABELLA

The Sutton family home in Ballard was a shrine to old money and older secrets. Brick and ivy, with leaded glass windows that seemed to judge you as you walked up the stone path. It was the kind of house where bad things happened behind closed doors, then got swept under antique Persian rugs.

Appropriate.

I rang the bell with a rehearsed "grieving girlfriend" face locked in place. My heart was a drumbeat of pure adrenaline. I was here to comfort the mother of the man I'd helped kill. More importantly, I was here to find out how badly she could burn us all.

The door swung open, and Nancy Sutton appeared like a ghost in a cream-colored cashmere tracksuit. Her eyes were puffy, her coiffed silver hair slightly askew. She looked like a woman undone, but now I knew better. Nancy didn't get undone; she did the undoing.

"Isabella, dear. Thank you for coming." She pulled me into a hug that was all bone and expensive perfume. A beautifully upholstered skeleton.

"Of course, Nancy. I'm so, so sorry. I can't even imagine what you're going through." My voice was thick with the fake emotion I'd been practicing in the car. It was disturbingly easy.

She led me into a living room that could be a museum exhibit on "Wealthy People's Grief." Towering floral arrangements, already beginning to wilt, crowded every surface. It smelled like bad perfume and death.

And Shane. Everywhere. Shane as a toddler in a sailor suit. Shane in his debate team blazer. Shane shaking hands with politicians. Shane, Shane, Shane on every surface.

I scanned the room twice before I spotted it: a single photo of Fred, tucked on a back shelf behind a vase, almost hidden. Their wedding photo: Fred young and hopeful, Nancy with that stiff, pageant smile.

"Please, sit." She gestured to a velvet couch.

"You sit, Nancy. Let me get you some tea."

Nancy's face brightened. "How thoughtful! I'd love some." She pointed to the kitchen. "The kettle is still hot."

I moved through the dining room, past more photos of Shane.

The kitchen was spotless, almost surgical. White marble countertops reflected the overhead lights. I fiddled with the canister of tea, filled a tea strainer, and poured water to steep while I scanned the room from this new vantage point. On the mahogany coffee table, next to a stack of sympathy cards, were dozens of amber-colored bottles, the same wellness products I'd seen at the lake house: Vitality & Grace.

So similar to the snake oil Mom used to give us, with better branding and a higher price point.

Nancy appeared in the doorway, making me jump.

"Sorry, dear, I wanted to make sure you found everything."

"Oh, yes, just letting it steep." I gestured to the bottles. "Quite a vitamin stash you've got here."

Her whole face transformed again. "Oh, these have been such a blessing! When my upline first approached me about the business opportunity, I thought, Why not? It's for a good cause." She picked up a bottle, cradling it like a holy relic.

"Upline?" I kept my voice light and curious.

"The woman who runs the whole operation." Nancy's eyes gleamed. "She said Fred's passing would be a good opportunity for a platform since I was using the products already."

Jesus Christ. Nancy was in a pyramid scheme. Of course she was.

She handed me a glossy pamphlet. The cover showed a disgustingly happy family in a field of wildflowers. I flipped it open, and an airbrushed photo stared back at me, with the title "President and Founder."

"Melanie Anderson," I said.

Nancy beamed. "Yes, you know her?"

"Uh, I think I met her once," I managed, handing her a steaming mug of tea. "Shall we sit?"

I followed her back to the living room, watching her settle into her chair like a queen on a throne.

"It's so unfair." Nancy's voice shifted back to grief. "My boy. My brilliant, beautiful boy. Taken from me. By *her.*"

The venom in that last word was pure and uncut.

"You were so good for him, Isabella," she cooed. "You understood him in ways Katherine never could."

She took a sip of her tea.

"Shane always needed someone who could keep up with him intellectually." She became distant, cold. "Fred never understood. He was too…soft. But Shane had ambition."

"That's for sure." I couldn't turn off my sarcasm filter, but she didn't seem to notice.

"I know you were trying to help him, dear." She patted my hand, her rings cold on my skin. "You made him so happy. It was that woman who drove him to this. All the stress she put him under."

"It's been hard on everyone," I said, a noncommittal response. I had to get her phone.

Then I remembered—the perfect narcissist can't resist playing the perfect hostess.

"Nancy, I am a little thirsty after all. Do you have anything other than tea?"

"Oh, goodness, of course." She lit up. "Our company has a new collagen drink. I have a whole tray of them in the pantry."

Blech.

"That sounds delicious. I'd love one if you don't mind."

She drifted out of the room, her slippers shuffling against the hardwood. The second she was out of sight, I lunged for the phone on the armrest.

I fumbled with the slick glass. No passcode. Another sign

of her bottomless arrogance. I searched: CLOUDCAM, the app Eric told me to find. I pressed play on the most recent thumbnail, my breath held tight in my chest.

The grainy footage was identical to the video Eric showed. It could be CPR. It could be murder. She knew nothing more, no different angles.

There were no other videos, nothing in her camera roll.

We were fine. We were actually, unbelievably, fine.

Relief washed over me so intensely that I was dizzy. I nearly dropped the phone.

"What are you doing?"

I snapped my head up. Nancy faced me, holding a small, gray-canned beverage. Her eyes were chips of ice.

My brain went into overdrive, scrambling for a lie.

"Oh, Nancy! I am so sorry," I gushed, holding the phone out as if it were a precious artifact. "You had such a beautiful picture on your lock screen. I just wanted to take a closer look. Is this you and Shane?"

I angled the screen so she could see the picture I'd quickly swiped to—a professionally shot photo of a younger Nancy and a teenage Shane.

The tension in Nancy's face dissolved instantly. "Oh, yes. That was the day he won his first debate tournament." She took the phone from my hand, her thumb stroking Shane's face on the screen. "He was always so brilliant. Destined for greatness."

She passed me the collagen water. I read the label: *Ultra-filtered grass-fed whey, formulated to neutralize cravings so that you can live your best life.*

She watched me like a hawk. I pulled the tab and took a

sip, the chalky, faintly sweet liquid coating my tongue. I fought the urge to gag. Fuck. "Mmmmm, thanks."

"I thought you'd like that," Nancy said, staring at Shane's face on her phone again. Then, a switch flipped, and her expression hardened. "She'll pay for this, you know. Katherine. I will see her rot in a prison cell for what she did to my son."

I gagged, then burped. Nancy didn't seem to notice. "What do you think she did?"

"She killed him. I'll prove it. I'll hire private investigators. I'll spend every penny Fred left me if I have to. Katherine Valentine will rot in prison if it's the last thing I do."

Her eyes were fixed on me, like a bug under a magnifying glass. But she never asked what I saw. My words would never matter to her. She would always believe what she wanted to believe.

"That's very determined of you, Nancy."

"A mother never stops fighting for her child." Nancy spat. "Never. Even when the world tells her to let go."

I set my can of cow water down. "I should let you rest."

"Oh, stay a little longer, dear." Nancy patted the cushion beside her.

I almost felt sorry for her.

Almost.

"I wish I could, Nancy, but I have to go."

"I understand." There wasn't an ounce of understanding in her voice. "I do hope we can stay friends through all of this, dear. It's so important to have friends."

The unspoken threat was crystal clear: *You're with me, or you're against me.*

"Of course, Nancy."

I had to escape the suffocating atmosphere of this house, this woman, and her promise of vengeance.

"Thank you again for coming." She walked me to the door, with her arm linked in mine.

As I stepped outside into the clean, cold air, she remained in the doorway, framed by the ivy and the judgmental window. She smiled. I smiled.

I said nothing, but screamed to myself, *I hope I never see you again.*

I got in my car and drove away without looking back.

Some loose ends tie themselves.

THIRTY-ONE

KATHERINE

I've been alone. Throughout my life, I've been alone quite a lot. But at certain times—when my father's scandal broke, after my first divorce, and now—it's been a completely different kind of alone. Scary alone. Aside from Piper, it was just me and my thoughts, and that was a terrible place to be.

With the media surrounding the case like vultures, we decided the kids should stay with Eric and Bridget full-time, at least until the full autopsy results came through. I was grateful they were safe somewhere the media couldn't reach, and yet I missed them with all my heart. The whispers from the rumor mill at school hadn't stopped, and I couldn't soothe my own children or protect them. It was worse than any punishment I could imagine. And I deserved it.

The life insurance payout was on hold, along with everything else, thanks to the investigation. Until then, I was living on fumes, watching every expense, counting down time like a prisoner. I spent my days hidden, boxing up memories in the meantime as I moved from one house to another.

I took a ceramic bowl off the shelf and read the worn but still legible sticker: **Emma and Katie Valentine, 2015**. It wasn't the most beautiful thing in the world; it was slightly crooked, an odd shade between blue and green, and had cracks from being left in the kiln for too long. When we first brought it home, I kept it up high out of reach, afraid it would break. We'd spent so much money on that pottery class when funds were sparse back then, but Emma insisted we use it. "It's a bowl, Mom! Why make it if we aren't going to use it?" Over time, I stopped guarding it. The risk of it shattering never left, but the fear did. Now, hiding it felt silly. Like the other things I'd overprotected—finances, jobs, relationships, reputation. And for what? Everything had gone to hell, anyway.

I wrapped it in newspaper, ink staining my fingers black. The headline smeared under my thumb:

Questions Remain In
Sutton Death – Anna Dollarhide

Three weeks, and the press still camped across the street. I'd stopped opening the curtains.

Tape screeched as I sealed the box, making Piper's ears flatten against her head, her nails clicking nervously across the bare hardwood. Even my poor dog was on edge.

My phone sat silent on the counter, a weapon I couldn't risk using. No calls to Izzy or Davis, too dangerous with Nancy's lawyers circling, and God knows who monitoring what. No texts about the case. I was on leave with Evergreen

Events "until this all blows over." Even my conversations with Chris happened in person, behind locked doors, in low voices. I'd nearly broken that rule a dozen times, typing and deleting messages.

I called Eric, my only touchpoint, though the only correspondence we could have was about the kids. Because the isolation was crushing me.

"Hey," he said after the first ring. "How are you holding up?"

"As well as can be expected, I suppose. How are the kiddos?"

"Fine. Well, mostly. They're hanging in there." He sighed, and I heard a door close, like he'd stepped outside for privacy. "Bridget got them all set up with therapists; they've been going a couple times a week."

"How are they feeling about it?" I said, though I wasn't sure I wanted to know. Being shut out of my children's healing felt like a punishment I absolutely deserved.

"Emma's…Emma. You know how she is. She's so matter-of-fact. Saw through him the whole time."

I closed my eyes, leaning against the counter. My brilliant, perceptive daughter. "Like you."

"Yeah, her therapist thinks that's actually healthy," Eric continued. "She's not in denial. She knows he wasn't who any of us thought he was. She just needs to work through it."

"How about the boys?"

"Elliott's the one I'm worried about." Eric's voice dropped. "He's completely shut down, Katie. Comes home, goes straight to his room, headphones on, door closed. Mr.

Morris says he's turning in assignments but is otherwise invisible."

My stomach dropped. "Fuck."

"Yeah. He feels stupid for trusting Shane, for looking up to him. And talking about it would mean admitting he was wrong, which Elliott hates more than anything." Eric's frustration bled through the phone. "I've tried, Katie. I've tried getting him to open up, but he just gives me one-word answers and walks away."

"He needs time," I said, though I didn't know if I believed it.

"Right." Eric didn't sound convinced either. "And then there's Ethan. Pretty oblivious, honestly."

"I guess that's good?"

"Hopefully," Eric said. "And he's not listening to those shitty podcasts anymore."

"How are they at school?" I managed. "Are the other kids…?"

"Some of it has died down. The media circus helped, weirdly—once the national news picked it up, it became less about local gossip. Most kids have moved on to other drama." Eric paused. "Though there are still whispers. You know how it is."

I did know. I'd lived it before.

"Katie, they're going to be okay," Eric said gently. "It's going to take time, and it's going to be messy, but they're tough kids. They're getting help. And they know you love them."

"Thanks for the update," I whispered. "And thank you for taking care of them when I can't."

"Always. Call you in a few days."

After we hung up, Piper nudged my leg, her liquid brown eyes pleading for a walk. "Not today, girl. Too many cameras."

Shane was dead, and I yet I'd become a prisoner in his life. His ghost controlled me. But the walls were closing in. I had to get out, even if it meant running the gauntlet of reporters and news vans waiting for me outside.

I wasn't supposed to talk to anyone, but there were things I needed to settle, aside from Shane. And I had to get the hell out of this house.

The reporters surged the moment the garage door rolled up. I flinched at the cameras, flashing lightning, while voices overlapped.

"Katherine! Did you kill your husband?"

"How do you respond to Nancy Sutton's allegations?"

"Were you having an affair?"

"Ms. Valentine! Is it true your own son was suspended for defending you?"

I kept my face neutral and pulled out of the driveway as if I were fleeing a crime scene. Again.

The drive to my mother's house took me past Lakewood High, where "pervert's daughter" had followed me through hallways. Past the 7-Eleven where my dad bought bottles in paper bags. Past the church where Mom still lit candles for his soul.

Each block looked smaller and shabbier than I remembered. Or maybe I was seeing it clearly, without the filter of childhood hope that things would get better.

They never had.

"Katie! What a lovely surprise." My mother appeared in the doorway with a practiced smile.

"I know I should have called first." I stepped inside.

We ended up at her kitchen table, the same Formica surface where I'd done homework while listening to my parents fight in whispered hisses. The table was cold under my palms. I was twelve the first time I sat at this table and understood what the whispered fights meant. My mother's blank face when my father slurred something under his drunk breath about the woman he'd been with that night. He ended up on the couch, and I asked if they were getting a divorce.

My mom barked back, "We don't do that in this family. We keep our promises." Even then, I wondered whose promises she meant. Certainly not his.

I grew up fluent in the exchange rate of beauty. My gorgeous mother earned his attention until she didn't, then it was his gorgeous young students. I did everything in my power not to be like any of them. I swore I'd gain respect, money, and love the right way. I cut my hair, added piercings, and wore grunge like armor. I earned everything the long, ugly way.

Then I met Shane, and for once, I let the door swing open because of my looks. I cashed in. I draped myself on his arm like eye candy, and I loved it, until I didn't. The interest nearly cost me everything.

Now, I pressed my palms flat against the same surface, channeling the courage of that girl who wanted to know why I had to be complicit in the lies just because she was.

"Are you hanging in there, sweetie—"

"Mom, we need to talk."

"Oh, of course, honey," she said, unbothered. "Do you want coffee?"

"No, I want answers."

Her smile faltered. "About what?"

"About you and Nancy setting me up with Shane."

"I thought he cared about you, honey. I did."

"Oh, really?" I said. "I saw the texts. You told him I was paranoid. You gave him ammunition to use against me."

"That's not what I was trying to do, Katie, I swear."

"How many women have to be 'crazy' before you consider that the men are the problem?"

The question hung between us, sharp enough to cut the air.

Her face crumpled, decades of willful blindness colliding with reality. Her mouth opened and closed, words forming and dying before they reached sound.

"I wanted to believe…"

"You wanted to believe the lie because the truth was inconvenient. Because admitting Shane was bad meant admitting you'd chosen wrong again, admitting you'd failed to protect me, again."

I remembered the day I divorced Eric and the cold words that followed: "*Well, kids are resilient. They'll adjust to a broken home.*" Those words haunted me for years, any time I struggled, every time the kids acted out, as if it were always my fault.

"I was so determined to prove I wasn't a serial divorcer, so desperate to be a good wife, I ignored every red flag."

My mother twisted her wedding ring, the one she never

took off, even during Dad's worst years. "Your father was sick, Katie. He had a disease."

Defending my father. Of course she was. "And what's your excuse? Dad had alcohol. What was yours?"

She lowered her eyes, and her lip began to quiver.

"Fear, honey," she said. "I was afraid of being nobody without him."

She stood abruptly, walking to the window overlooking the backyard where I'd once played. "You don't understand—I had no education, no money of my own, no family to run to. When your father's drinking got bad, when the affairs started, I convinced myself it wasn't happening. Because the alternative was admitting I'd trapped myself."

"But you had me."

"And that made it worse." She turned, tears streaming down her face. "Because then I wasn't only responsible for myself, I was responsible for you. And I thought a bad father was better than no father, and an unstable home was better than poverty. But I question every day whether I made the right choice."

She said it so quietly I almost didn't hear her. "Mom…"

"I was angry when you left Eric," she said. "Not because you were wrong, but because I was jealous. You did what I never could." She sat again, weary and resigned.

I suddenly saw her through a new lens, without excuses. I saw the scared girl who still lived inside her skin. A girl with no college degree, pregnant, terrified, making calculations she'd spend the rest of her life paying for. One who believed endurance was virtue and survival was love.

"Nancy was my friend, Katie. I trusted her." Her breath

caught. "Her son was so stable and devoted. I thought Shane was a good man."

I sat across from her the same way I had a thousand times as a child, searching her face for the mother I'd needed then. The anger I'd carried for so long softened into the realization I'd repeated her mistakes. I'd chosen others over myself. Maybe we were more alike than I wanted to admit.

Would Emma someday sit across from me the same way? Naming the inheritance I swore I'd never pass down? I pictured Emma in her forties, sitting in some kitchen with her own daughter, tracing patterns in the trauma I'd handed her like a family heirloom.

I'd break this cycle. Even if it killed me.

"I thought Shane was a good man, too," I said. "And I suppose, I wanted someone to save me."

She nodded. "Katie, I thought by staying loyal to your father, I was showing you how to persevere. But every day since he died, I've known I failed you. I was drowning, and drowning people don't always make good choices about who they pull down with them, do they?"

"No."

We sat in silence, two women who'd survived their own versions of hell. My mother reached across the table and covered my hand with hers. This wasn't forgiveness, exactly, but understanding.

"I won't make excuses for Shane, or for myself," she said. "But you need to know I'm proud of you for protecting your kids. I wish I could have done the same for you."

I squeezed her fingers, weathered and similar, marked by years of holding on too tight and letting go too late.

"We're going to do better." Even saying it, I knew it was a choice she might never fully make. So, it had to start with me, because Emma deserved a mother who broke the pattern, not one who excused it.

"Can I ask you something?" She looked up at me, timidly.

Here it was. "Sure."

"Did you…do what they're saying you did?"

I met her eyes, and saw fear. Fear for me, not of me.

"Mom, I'm not supposed to talk about the case, but I'll tell you the same thing I told the police: Shane fell. I tried to help him."

Warmth returned to her voice. "Okay."

"You believe me?"

"I believe you did what you had to do to protect your children." She squeezed my hands tighter. "And this time, I'm choosing you. No matter what."

Back in my car, I sat for a moment, processing. The conversation with my mother had drained me but also lightened me, as if I'd set down a weight I'd been carrying since childhood.

My choices, my mother's choices, and then Emma's. Her relentless questioning, her refusal to be silenced. I suddenly remembered shoving her article in my purse that day, the chaos of Elliott's suspension and Shane's death burying it under weeks of grief and legalities.

I reached past receipts and stray tissues until my fingers found the folded paper.

I unfolded it, smoothing the creases against the steering wheel.

Conflict of Interest? Parent Coalition Funding Raises Questions — By Emma Gray

Pride swelled. My daughter's name in print, even if it had never been published. I began reading.

The parent coalition pushing curriculum changes at Puget Academy received $50,000 this year from a Political Action Committee (PAC).

I frowned. A PAC. Eric had mentioned something called Puget Coalition while digging through Shane's files, but I never understood what it meant.

The PAC's largest donor is Vitality & Grace, a supplement company that donated $500,000. Vitality & Grace's president is Mrs. Anderson, who leads our parent coalition.

I suddenly remembered Todd, in bed, complaining about his ex's MLM. "Too expensive to fight."

And how Izzy had seen Melanie leaving the Puget Coalition office, looking nervous.

Here's what that means: Mrs. Anderson's company donated to a PAC. That PAC donated to the coalition Mrs. Anderson runs.

I'm not saying anything illegal happened. But I have questions:

- *Is that a conflict of interest?*
- *Are parents being told where this money comes from?*
- *Is outside political money influencing our school policies?*

I emailed Mrs. Anderson for comment. She said, "Everything is above board and legal."

Maybe it is legal. But is it right?

Students deserve to know who's funding the changes to our curriculum.

Emma had found something. A pattern. Melanie's company funding a PAC, that PAC funding Melanie's coalition.

I folded the article carefully, tucking it back into my purse. I was so proud of my daughter for asking important questions.

Soon, when the investigation was closed and I was free to speak again, this would matter, and someone could explain what Emma had found.

But today, it was just another thread I couldn't pull.

THIRTY-TWO

ISABELLA

My blood filled the vial, dark red, deceptively ordinary. A bored nurse made small talk I barely registered. I saved my lies for places that mattered, because my head was already crowded with the ones I'd told. Like the fact that I was about to sacrifice part of myself to save someone Shane Sutton could never hurt. Weeks of donation paperwork, legal hoops, and payment plan paperwork.

Shane's money would buy salvation…eventually. Mom would call it poetic justice if she still believed in such things. For me, it was the one clean thing to come from that bastard's death. Karma's a bitch, but sometimes she pays well.

Everything, Katie's freedom, the divorce settlement, the life insurance, still rode on the investigation clearing Katie of any wrongdoing. Nancy was doing her best to destroy her in public, but it was backfiring in a major way; most comments favored Katie over Nancy. Nancy had made herself the story, not for good reason.

When the nurse finished, she placed a cotton ball over the puncture site and bent my arm.

"The doctor will be in shortly."

Left alone, I slid off the examination table and changed slowly; my body aching from the extensive physical testing I'd already undergone. Everything here was cold as hell: the exam table, the vinyl chair, even the blood pressure cuff—tight as Shane's grip on my wrist that final day.

Dr. Morgan entered the room with my file open on her tablet. "All right, we are ready to move forward." She glanced down at the checklist. "I see you've already completed the psychological evaluation?"

"Yep," I said, remembering the show I'd put on for the hospital psychiatrist. Yes, I understood the risks. No, I wasn't being coerced. Yes, I had a support system in place during recovery. No, I wasn't experiencing any significant life stressors. Unless you counted murder and conspiracy. Tuesday activities.

Lying was easy. I'd been doing it for months. The truth? That I'd helped kill a man, and his widow would fund this surgery? Yeah, that stayed buried.

"Ms. Meyer?" Dr. Morgan was looking at me expectantly.

"Sorry, what did you say?"

"I asked about your recovery plan. The surgery will require significant downtime—about a week in the hospital, followed by bed rest at home for at least two weeks, then a gradual return to normal over six to eight weeks. Have you arranged for someone to help you during that time?"

"Yes," though, ironically, the people currently surrounding me had no idea this was happening.

"Good." She made a note in my file. "And you understand that while living organ donation is generally safe, it is a major surgery with all the associated risks—infection, bleeding, adverse reaction to anesthesia?"

"I understand." I'd read every piece of literature they'd given me, researched every possible complication. None of it mattered.

"The transplant team will go over all of this again before the procedure, but I want to make sure you're fully informed at every step."

Her expression softened. "It's a remarkable gift you're giving. Not everyone would undergo this for someone else."

If only she knew this "gift" was built on blood money. The man who'd destroyed my sister was, in death, saving Pop. He owed us.

"The waiting is often the hardest part. But try to take care of yourself in the meantime. The healthier you are going in, the smoother your recovery will be."

After a few more questions and instructions, she left me with a folder of information and prescription slips. I sat alone in the examination room, looking at a text from my mom.

Pop can't wait to see you!

I gathered my things and headed for the exit, stopping briefly at the reception desk to confirm the appointment.

"One thing, Ms. Meyer," the receptionist said. "Your license on file has a different last name. You'll need to be sure to indicate the correct one on the intake form when the hospital contacts you directly, closer to the procedure."

"Oh, yep, will do." Another reminder I'd be stepping back into an identity I'd temporarily buried.

Outside, the rain had started again, a mid-March drizzle that beaded on my jacket. I paused under the medical center's awning as people hurried past with umbrellas and raincoats, all caught up in their own lives, their own dramas. None of them knew what I'd done or what I was about to do.

I pulled out my phone and texted Mom back.

Eight more weeks! Finalizing everything. The end is near.

Another message appeared before I even reached my car. Jessica Banks this time, with a link and a single emoji: 😱

I clicked, already knowing what I'd find. Shane's obituary in *The Seattle Times*. Because, of course, he'd get a full-page spread.

"Shane Sutton, 45, visionary entrepreneur and philanthropist, passed away tragically on February 19th…"

I thumbed through, each word making my blood pressure spike like I'd mainlined three espressos, which was ironic, since coffee was one of the things I'd had to quit.

"…leaves behind a legacy of generosity through Sutton Stars, which has provided educational opportunities to hundreds of underprivileged youth…"

"...remembered by colleagues as a true innovator and mentor who saw potential in everyone..."

"...devoted son, caring husband, and friend to many..."

"Fucking bullshit." I slammed my fist against my car in the parking garage. Some lady with a designer stroller side-eyed me as she passed. Whatever. If she knew what I knew, she'd be dropping f-bombs, too.

The worst people always got canonized the second they stopped breathing. I'd love to see an honest obituary.

Hated kids and dogs. Never lit up a room; in fact, he brought darkness everywhere he went. Generally, a huge piece of shit, and nobody will miss him.

The photo they'd chosen was perfect—Shane at some charity gala, arm around a young woman who was maybe eighteen. Even in death, that bastard was hiding in plain sight. The Sutton Stars recipient giving the tearful testimonial? I wonder what NDA she'd signed, what price she'd paid for her opportunity. Another bright future Shane had probably tried to fuck with before building it back up in his image.

I texted Jessica back:

> OMG, they're practically nominating him for sainthood. Devoted husband?? I just threw up in my mouth.

Her response came immediately:

> The mentor part killed me. Interesting word for predator.

Right? And pillar of the community? More like a termite eating the pillar from the inside.

Jessica and I shared this burden. The Sisterhood of Shane Survivors. We didn't get T-shirts or a secret handshake, just matching trauma.

And there was Katie, whom I couldn't speak to until the investigation was complete. Chelsea. Rhonda. All the others. My sister. They'd never see true justice. The world would remember Shane Sutton as this generous, brilliant businessman, not as the predator who'd destroyed lives and careers. We were still living with the wreckage, while he got the simplest exit possible.

Death was too easy for him. He should have been forced to face those women in court, and for the world to see what he'd done. I wanted his entire image to crumble publicly, painfully, completely.

But now? Nothing. A beautiful lie everyone would believe because it was easier than the ugly truth.

McFadden was using Shane's death as a prop, fundraising off sympathy while his polling numbers continued to climb. Meanwhile, the women Shane destroyed stayed silent, still afraid of retaliation from the ghost who operated his political machine.

I slammed my car door harder than necessary, tossing my phone onto the passenger seat. Rain pelted the windshield, matching my mood.

I should leave town. Take the money and run. Nothing was keeping me here anymore. My job was done.

Except it wasn't.

The lights were on when I pulled up to Davis's apartment. I'd been staying with him since Shane died. My time with Davis was numbered, and I wanted to hang on as long as I could.

Every moment felt stolen. Not by Shane's ghost, but by the version of myself Davis thought he knew.

"Hey," Davis called from the kitchen when I walked in. The apartment smelled like garlic and tomatoes, rich and warm. "Hope you're hungry. I'm attempting homemade pasta."

"Starving." I dropped my bag by the door and followed the scent.

Davis was at the stove, stirring a pot of sauce, his dress shirt rolled up to the elbows.

"Did you see the obituary?"

A shadow crossed his face. "Yeah. Tammi showed me. Nauseating, right?"

"Total puff piece. Not a single mention of his hobbies: manipulation, blackmail, sexual harassment…"

Davis set down the spoon and pulled me into a hug. I rested my head against his chest, listening to his steady heartbeat.

"It's not fair," I said. "All those women will never get justice. He gets a hero's send-off while they're still scared to speak."

"I know. I wish there were a way to tell their stories without putting you and Katie in danger. I'm tired of carrying his secrets. It's like he's still haunting me."

Davis pulled back to look at me. "I probably have a couple

more weeks before everything is in probate and everyone is fired."

Nancy was appointed as interim president and locked down records, preserving Shane's reputation at all costs. Her lawyers threatened to sue anyone who defamed him. And McFadden sailed on the sympathy with no risk of scandal.

"Shane gets sainted, and everything gets buried."

"Yep." He turned back to the stove, hunched over. "And once probate clears, Nancy can do whatever she wants. Destroy evidence, rewrite history."

Then it hit me. The lightbulb practically visible over my head. "Wait. What if we flip the script?"

Davis set down his spoon. "What do you mean?"

I moved beside him, ideas tumbling over each other. "McFadden's using Shane's death as a talking point, right? Sympathy, raking in donations, honoring a visionary?"

"Yeah, they're acting like he was Jesus, and McFadden's followers are eating it up."

"But we know for an absolute, un-fucking-deniable fact that the campaign was taking dirty money, even if Bruce didn't know that himself."

"Okay…"

"So, he's vulnerable," I said. "We've been trying to take down the whole machine, but what if we turn McFadden against Shane?"

"I'm not following."

I pulled my laptop from my bag and opened it on the counter. "Remember the folder I found in Shane's desk? The Senate strategy?"

"I remember."

"What if Bruce learned that Shane was using his campaign as a 'test case' to build his own donor network?"

Davis considered this. "He would panic."

"Exactly. His whole brand is 'outsider businessman who can't be bought.' If it comes out that he was being used as someone else's stepping stone—"

Davis caught on, a grim smile forming. "He'd distance himself."

"And once he stops defending Shane's legacy…" I met his eyes. "He might be willing to tell the world what we already know about Shane, to save himself."

Davis rubbed his jaw. "Or Bruce could double down and call it fake news, and we'd be fucked."

"True," I said. "But his whole campaign is built on credibility. He can't risk voters knowing he was someone's puppet, or finding out he's been propped up by dirty money."

"All right, but we aren't supposed to touch anything involving Shane or the case right now." Davis slumped his shoulders.

"It won't be us." I pulled up Anna Dollarhide's contact information—the journalist who'd been hammering Sutton Strategy with scathing pieces back when Shane was alive. "We don't even need to make accusations. We give her the documents Alex wouldn't do anything with, nothing with your name on it or mine. A reporter asking the right questions would make McFadden freak out. He'd want voters to villainize Shane, not him."

Davis rubbed the back of his neck. "It's risky. These are powerful people."

"So was Shane. And he's dead." I held his gaze. "We're

not doing this for ourselves anymore. Once McFadden destroys Shane's legacy in the media, we don't have to tiptoe, and the women can come forward with their stories."

Davis nodded slowly. "Can I ask you something?"

I tensed. "Of course."

"Why are you doing all of this?" He gestured at my laptop. "I mean, I get wanting to help Katie, Jessica. But you've been relentless about this."

A dozen answers crowded my mouth. *Tell him. Tell him about Misha. Tell him everything.*

I clicked back to the complaint files. My finger hovered over the trackpad, and I pointed to a name. My heart hammered against my ribs. This was it. The point of no return. I braced myself for the pity or judgment I was sure would follow. "This one. Shelly Foster."

"I think I remember her. Quiet girl."

"We call her Misha."

Davis went still. "We?"

"She's my sister."

Davis took a step back. "Jesus Christ, Iz."

I kept my eyes on the screen. I couldn't look at him, couldn't see whatever was on his face.

"He was terrible to her," I said. "When I saw Katherine's posting for the server position at the fundraising event—"

"You targeted him." Davis moved beside me, grasping my hand. "Does Katie know?"

I shook my head. "No, and please, you can't tell her."

Davis pulled back. "Iz, she should know. She'd understand—"

"I know she would." That was the problem. She'd understand too much. She'd understand that every moment of our friendship had been built on me using her to get to Shane. And I still had to protect my family. "I'll tell her, I promise. Just let me figure out how to say it, okay?"

He squeezed my hand. "Okay. I'm so fucking sorry about your sister. Is she—"

"Don't be sorry. Help me finish this, please?"

I gestured to the email I'd started, tapping the keys before he could ask any more questions about my sister. I'd said more than I'd ever planned.

Ms. Dollarhide. I'm a source with access to Shane Sutton's internal files. I recently discovered documents suggesting Sutton had undisclosed political ambitions that may have compromised the McFadden campaign.

Attached are strategy memos outlining "Sutton 2026 Senate Run" that position the gubernatorial campaign as a test case and donor network builder for Sutton's own political future.

In addition, here are a few internal files suggesting that Mr. Sutton was funneling charity funds into his personal accounts.

Given your recent reporting on campaign finance irregularities, I thought you'd like to see this.

—A concerned citizen.

I turned the laptop toward Davis. "What do you think?"

Davis read it twice. "It's good."

As he was about to attach the files, my phone vibrated on the counter. A text from Nancy.

Thinking of you, dear. I do hope you're resting.

"She's trying to keep me close," I said.

Davis read over my shoulder. "This is nuts. What if McFadden calls her, and this whole thing backfires?"

"It's more dangerous if we do nothing," I shot back. "We have to give them a bigger monster to fight than her. It's the only way."

The cursor blinked at us. Then Davis reached over and clicked send. We both exhaled.

Davis closed the laptop. "Now we see if Bruce McFadden values his campaign more than Shane's legacy."

The silence stretched as the pasta sauce bubbled quietly on the stove. Outside, traffic hummed, oblivious to the atomic bomb we'd just lobbed into Bruce McFadden's world.

"You hungry?" Davis turned off the burner.

My stomach twisted in knots. "Not really."

"Yeah. Me neither." He turned toward me.

I reached up and put a hand on each side of his stubbled, beautiful face.

I kissed him, hard and desperate. He responded immediately, his hands sliding to my waist, pulling me closer.

"The sauce," I murmured against his mouth.

"It'll keep." He walked me backward toward the bedroom, fingers tangled in my hair.

We stumbled through the doorway, shedding clothes as we went. The urgency burned hotter each time, allowing me to escape the grief for my sister and the secrets threatening to destroy whatever this was between us.

His hands found the zipper of my jeans and slid it down. I pushed his shirt off his shoulders, needing his skin against mine. We fell onto the bed in a tangle of limbs, his body pinning me to the mattress.

"I've been thinking about this all day." His lips trailing down my neck.

"Liar." I laughed. "You were in meetings all day."

"Multi-tasking. It's called multi-tasking."

I let myself get lost in the slide of his hands across my skin. His touch brushed down my body, making me gasp while his fingers explored. My back arched as his mouth followed the same path, wet and warm.

"God, Davis," I whispered.

His dark brown eyes met mine. "I love watching you."

I couldn't form coherent thoughts as he made my hips buck against him. His strong hands gripped my waist, holding me in place as the intensity increased.

He knew how to make me fall apart. I clutched at the sheets, my breath coming in desperate pants. When the release came, he drew out every tremor until I was boneless and gasping.

Sex with Davis was more than sex. It was a reminder that my sexual awakening had nothing to do with Shane.

The power had been a turn-on, sure. But Davis? Next level.

Afterward, with my head on his chest, his fingers caressing

my back, I memorized every inch of him, storing it away for long nights when I'd have nothing to keep me company. I wanted to bottle it, to carry it with me wherever I went.

And like a snap, reality set back in. Soon, I'd disappear from his life as completely as Shane had disappeared from mine.

"You okay?" He kissed my forehead. "You seem somewhere else."

I squeezed him tight to avoid looking at him. "I'm… processing. Long day."

"Yeah. But we're going to be okay, Iz. Whatever comes next, we'll figure it out together."

I kissed him instead of answering.

"I've been thinking," he said, voice soft. "Why don't we make this official? Move in together for real, not because of circumstances."

In another life, this would have been everything I wanted. "Davis, I—"

"I know it's fast, but after what we've been through together… Life's too short to wait for the perfect time."

I swallowed, unable to form words. My lie had taken root and grown into something beautiful and terrifying.

"You don't have to answer right away." He misread my hesitation. "Think about it, okay?"

"I will."

"Oh, and I almost forgot to tell you." His eyes lit up. "I got us tickets for that concert you mentioned wanting to see. Memorial Day Weekend at the Gorge."

Shit. A few weeks after my surgery.

"That's…amazing," I lied, calculating recovery times in

my head. "But maybe we should hold off on making plans so far ahead? With everything still settling from Shane's death…"

"That's the point, though. To have something to look forward to, after all this insanity." He kissed my forehead. "Plus, they were hard to get. Like you."

"Right." I forced a smile. "It's perfect."

THIRTY-THREE
KATHERINE

Six weeks since Shane's death, and the phone hadn't stopped ringing. Today was no different. Chris. Then Margaret. Then Jason. The sound grated against my nerves, already frayed from weeks of sleepless nights and the constant low-grade terror that had become my baseline.

I turned the phone off. One more day of not knowing felt safer than whatever truth was waiting on the other end of the call.

Piper did figure eights through my legs, grounding me in the present. "One more day in this house, then we're done."

A sea of boxes swallowed the great room, each one labeled in my neat handwriting. Sorting through our lives had been unexpectedly cathartic, a physical act of deciding what deserved space in our future.

I'd talked to the kids earlier this week, brief, carefully managed phone calls that the therapists and lawyers had green-lit. Nothing too deep, nothing too complicated. They were surprisingly pragmatic about the move. Elliott and Ethan were relieved to learn we'd be closer to their friends and Eric and Bridget's house, and Emma said this place was "high-key cheugy," like side parts and skinny jeans. They'd seen what I'd been too desperate to admit: this home was never ours.

It was built for performance, not love.

Hearing their voices was enough to sustain me for a few more days of packing and isolation.

Emma told me about her Berkeley acceptance, her voice bright with excitement that dimmed only slightly when she asked if I'd be able to come to graduation. "Of course," I'd promised, hoping it was true.

Elliott was quieter, but Eric said he'd been more upbeat lately, less isolated. Small victories.

And Ethan went on and on about the latest drama at school, a new video game he was playing, blissfully ignorant in the best way.

The therapists said the distance had been necessary. That the kids needed space to process Shane's death and what he'd really been without having to manage my emotions at the same time. That I needed space to survive the investigation without the added weight of their pain.

They were probably right. But it didn't make missing them any easier.

I added more items to the donation pile. The new place was smaller, a four-bedroom rental. No soaring ceilings or Sub-Zero appliances or heated bathroom floors, but a large backyard on the water. When I'd first viewed it, the realtor apologized for the modest finishes. I almost laughed. As if I hadn't spent the last four years suffocating in a house that was

8,000 square feet of beautiful empty space. Too much space for the intrusive thoughts that continued circulating in my mind.

Because until the investigation was over, I still wasn't free.

My hand cramped from packing. I flexed my fingers. The same hands that had found a pulse I'd wanted desperately not to find.

I shoved the thought away and reached for another box. Covered in tape and Styrofoam remnants, I checked my phone. Several missed calls from Margaret. I returned her call.

"Katie," she said when she answered. "We need you to come to the office. Now."

"Is everything okay?"

"Not over the phone. See you soon." The line went dead.

My stomach plummeted. I looked out the window where the news vans were still parked like patient vultures. I had to leave, which meant running the gauntlet again.

Nancy's initial media blitz had been effective, painting me as a cold, cheating wife. But in the past few weeks, the narrative had begun to curdle. Nancy's increasingly erratic public behavior, rants to reporters, and wild accusations had started to backfire. Sympathetic pieces hinted at a troubled marriage and a man who was not the saint his mother claimed he was. I hadn't let myself believe any of it.

I grabbed my keys and pressed the garage door opener. A barrage of flashes blinded me. One reporter yelled, "Sources say the marriage was abusive. Do you have comments?"

I kept my eyes on the end of the driveway and drove forward slowly, forcing them to part for me.

With every red light, my mind replayed the scene at the lake house. I played through what the lawyers might tell me: that they had proof I smothered him, that I'd be dragged immediately to jail, that I'd never see my kids again. By the time I arrived at the office, I'd tried and convicted myself.

"Katie." Chris stood in the doorway. "We're ready for you."

I followed him into the sterile conference room where Margaret and Jason waited. None of their faces gave anything away.

"The final autopsy report came in this morning," Margaret began. "I'm not going to sugarcoat this, Katherine. The findings are complicated."

The floor dropped out from under me. "Is it…"

"The primary cause of death was a subdural hematoma, consistent with blunt-force trauma from the fall."

"But," Jason cut in, tapping his tablet and turning it toward me, "the toxicology report changes everything."

I squinted at rows of numbers that meant nothing to me, evidence of a life reduced to measurements and chemical concentrations.

"Ginkgo biloba, concentrated turmeric, high-dose fish oil." Jason read the names aloud. "Every single one of these is a blood thinner. And Shane was taking them in massive doses, way beyond anything recommended, even for someone healthy."

I sat up. "He was always ordering stuff from podcasts. I could never keep track of what he was taking."

Jason nodded. "According to the report, it could have been a major contributing factor. With those levels in his system, even a minor fall or bumping his head on a cabinet door could have caused a fatal bleed. A fall down the stairs was just… more dramatic."

I leaned forward. "So, nothing about his breathing or…?"

Margaret's eyes met mine. "With that tox report, he was a ticking time bomb. The official cause of death will be ruled an accident."

Relief washed through me, leaving me light-headed. There would be no dramatic courtroom scenes, no perp walks, no orange jumpsuit. The phantom handcuffs around my wrists had released. I was free.

"And there's more," Chris added, a smile breaking through the serious demeanor. "Nancy's lawyers dropped her this morning. It seems she accosted a local news anchor outside the studio. She's on an involuntary psychiatric hold. So, the civil suit is dead."

But my mind flashed to Fred, and Claudia's comments about the supplements Nancy had been pushing.

Nancy refused Fred's autopsy.

The moment passed. Whatever Fred had been taking, whatever had contributed to his heart attack, sadly, didn't matter now.

"I can't believe it," I said.

"Believe it. You're free. Start living like it." Margaret said.

"But first, will you please call Claudia and put me out of my misery? She misses you like crazy," Chris said.

"Will do. Thank you, all of you."

I drove home in a daze. The world looked different. The April sun felt warmer, and the colors of the city more vibrant. As I turned onto my street, I braced myself, expecting to see the news vans still camped out, a grim welcoming committee. But the street was quiet. Empty.

The media was gone. The news must have broken—investigation closed. The street was no longer infested with people craning their necks to see me and ask me questions. It was just a typical street.

I pulled into the driveway behind the moving van to see Eric's car parked beside it. He and Bridget stood on the porch, but they weren't looking at me. They were both staring intently at their phones, their expressions shocked.

"Did you see?" I said, "Investigation is over."

Bridget hugged me. "Yes, Katie, we are so relieved!"

"But have you seen this?" Eric turned his phone toward me. "It just broke."

On his screen, Bruce McFadden's face was frozen midsentence at a podium. The headline read:

Breaking: McFadden Addresses Sutton Charity Fraud Allegations

What on earth?

We went inside and watched the press conference on Eric's phone, huddled among the boxes.

Bruce McFadden gripped the podium flanked by American flags.

"Though his passing is truly tragic, I am shocked and appalled to learn that Shane Sutton was running a criminal enterprise while advising my campaign."

His voice was trembling, and it didn't seem manufactured.

Reporters shouted questions, and he held his hand up for silence.

"Shane Sutton lied to me and deceived me. While I trusted him as an advisor, he was stealing from his own charity, funds that were meant for students, and it's been brought to my attention that he was planning his own Senate run, and using my campaign as his test case."

His voice rose with righteous indignation. "I am as much a victim of his deception as anyone."

"No fucking way."

A reporter called out, "Did you know about the charity fraud?"

"I did not know about his egregious criminal activities," McFadden said. "None whatsoever."

Another reporter shouted, "Will you suspend your campaign?"

McFadden's jaw set, and his hands gripped the podium. "Absolutely not. I will not let Shane Sutton's crimes define this race. I'm staying to fight the very corruption he represents."

Murmurs and voices raised in the audience. He held a hand to hush the crowd.

"I'm cooperating fully with federal investigators, turning over all documents and communications regarding Sutton Strategy. The people of Washington deserve a governor who confronts corruption, not one who runs from it."

The feed cut back to the news anchor.

I shook my head in disbelief. "Is it actually possible that Bruce was oblivious to what Shane was doing?"

"Beats me," Eric said. "But he's torching Shane's entire legacy to save himself."

As Bridget put her hand on Eric's thigh, a flash of gemstone caught the light in a way that was impossible to miss. "Hold up, are you two engaged? It's about time!"

Bridget's face lit up as she extended her hand. "Last weekend. We would have told you, but with everything going on…"

"Not getting any younger." Eric gave a self-deprecating shrug, but his eyes never left Bridget's face.

"Speak for yourself, old man," she shot back. I smiled. There would have been a time when seeing Eric with another woman would have felt like a betrayal, even though I'd been the one to leave. But we wouldn't have what we had now. There wouldn't be a Bridget, and I loved the whole package.

"Congratulations, you two. I'm so happy for you," I beamed. Then I turned to Eric directly, unable to resist. "Don't screw this one up."

They both laughed.

"I won't, I promise."

He paused at the door. "You did well, Katie, getting through this."

I wanted to argue, to make a list of all the ways I'd failed and the mistakes I'd made. But he stopped me.

"Forward, not backward."

After they left, I was alone again in the empty great room. But the silence pressing against me no longer felt hostile. I could go anywhere, be anyone.

Who do you want to be, Katie Valentine?

Legally, I was innocent.

Morally…I didn't know.

But I promised myself to start new patterns.

I typed a text message to my mom.

Want to help me unpack tomorrow? It will suck, but I could use the company.

Her response came quickly.

I'd love that, honey. What time?

How about 10? I'll make coffee.

I walked through each room one last time: the great room with the two-story windows, the chef's kitchen I'd barely cooked in, the master bedroom with the California King I'd slept alone in more nights than not.

These walls witnessed my unraveling, as I pretended everything was fine while dying inside.

But they'd also witnessed my survival.

I secured the last box with tape and marked it with a black Sharpie.

The empty house echoed around me as I carried it to the moving van and didn't look back.

THIRTY-FOUR

ISABELLA

The fairy lights strung across Katie's new backyard danced like fireflies against the darkening sky. Seattle had delivered one of those rare, perfect mid-April evenings—the kind that made you forget the nine months of gray that earned it.

I stood by the makeshift bar, watching Katie flit between clusters of guests with the energy of a hummingbird on espresso. She'd found her element again. Valentine Event Planning logos decorated every napkin as proof this wasn't a simple housewarming, but a branding event for a whole new life. The woman who once apologized for existing was now professionally unavailable for your bullshit. That's what you call character development.

Davis sidled in beside me, pressing a seltzer into my hand. His fingers brushed mine, a tiny spark I stole for later. I'd been hoarding them, tucking them away like contraband for the drought ahead.

Around us, life had rebuilt itself. Eric and Bridget swayed together near the water, her head resting against his chest in a way that should've been nauseating but was kinda sweet. Emma laughed with friends by the firepit, Elliott helped pass trays, and Ethan tried to make the dog perform tricks she had zero interest in.

It was all so normal. So violently normal it hurt. Like sunshine directly in your eyes after months in the dark.

Jessica held court near a dessert table, blushing every time someone congratulated her on the book deal. After McFadden threw Shane to the wolves, she wrote an op-ed in the *New York Times*, and dozens of women came forward with their stories under the hashtag #FallenStars.

Tammi quickly pivoted into podcasting. *The Women on the Side* was already trending in true crime. Rhonda's episode made people cry. Chelsea's made them furious.

Davis was rebuilding Sutton Stars as Seattle Stars. Actual students this time, revolutionary concept.

Sutton Strategy was long gone. Neil and Patrick had retired, probably golfing more than they'd ever worked.

Everyone was celebrating their own modest victories like we'd won the whole war. I overheard a snippet of Jessica talking excitedly about her book tour, while Tammi debated the ethics of sponsored content. Each victory felt like a reminder of the one victory I could never claim aloud.

And McFadden was still running, still polling well with the parental rights crowd, out there with his promises to make kids healthy and clean up schools and streets.

Same shit. Different day.

I smiled. I hugged people. I made small talk and pretended everything was fine.

I wondered if I ever would be.

Suddenly, everyone's phones seemed to explode at once. Buzz. Buzz. Buzz. Like a swarm of mechanical bees.

Every conversation died. The music screeched to a halt.

My head snapped up, not toward my own purse, but across the lawn to Katie. Her reaction was the only one that mattered. Her face went white.

"What?" Claudia did a double-take at the screen. "Holy shit."

Eric showed Bridget his screen. "Is this for real?"

Davis turned his toward me:

McFadden Suspends
Gubernatorial Campaign

My stomach dropped.

"He owned the supplement company?" Tammi scrolled frantically.

Eric's voice rose. "BM Holdings LLC. Bruce Michael McFadden. He owns eighty-seven percent of Vitality & Grace."

"Bruce McFadden is a boss babe?" Claudia cackled.

"Wait—" Davis scrolled. "His campaign platform promised supplement deregulation. He was literally running to deregulate his own business."

Katie sank into a chair. "Jesus Christ."

Bridget called out, "Public documents listed Seattle resident Melanie Anderson as the company president; however, investigators found she was a brand rep, not an owner or officer."

"Fucking Melania?" Claudia cackled again.

"Holy shit." The cunty bob leaving the PAC office. The hush-hush donation. Of course.

So much for a decent guy.

"Wait, wait—" Emma's voice cut through. "It says a student journalist from Puget Academy first identified the V&G to PAC connection."

Katie looked at her daughter. "Emma, I sent them your article. I didn't know what it meant, but—"

"Emma fucking Gray took down a governor," Claudia yelled. The backyard exploded. Chris started a slow clap that turned into full applause. Eric lifted Emma off her feet, spinning her around.

I stepped back, overwhelmed, and moved to the water's edge, listening to the waves lap on the shore.

I shoved my shaking hands in my pockets before anyone noticed.

If Misha were here, I'd grab her hand, squeeze until it hurt. We'd scream and cry together. This was all for her.

But she wasn't here. She'd never be here again, anywhere again, and I was in a backyard full of people who had no idea what this really meant.

"There you are." Katie found me hiding away from the celebration. "We did it."

I studied the ground. "That was all you and Emma."

"No." Katie took hold of my hands. "You got McFadden to turn on Shane, so all those women could come forward. I emailed an article I didn't even understand." She laughed.

"Emma is the GOAT," I said, still avoiding her eyes.

"Who would have thought?" Her words came out soft. "We were all so focused on Shane's fraud, we completely missed McFadden's."

"I know."

She squeezed my hands. "We make a good team."

I opened my mouth to say something, anything, but nothing came. Then Emma materialized, and Katie was gone, again, celebrating, congratulating.

I returned to a table next to Davis when Claudia appeared, heels hanging from one finger, dragging Chris by his necktie. They sat next to us.

Davis put his hand on my back. "I'll get you ladies drinks. Another seltzer for Izzy, and what are you having, Claudia?"

"Oh, same for me, please, and thank you!"

"Not drinking, either?"

"Nope. I'm not pregnant, not Mormon, not on antibiotics, and I didn't hit rock bottom." Claudia listed, counting on her fingers. "Those are the usual guesses."

I smirked. "People are dicks."

"Yup. My dad died of cirrhosis, and I see what alcohol does to people's health as a nurse, so I've never touched the stuff."

Chris slid in beside her. "Can you imagine her drunk?" He laughed until Claudia elbowed him hard.

She turned back to me. "How about you?"

"Oh, sometimes. But I have…a medical procedure coming up. So not now."

Biggest understatement of my life. Three weeks until they

carved into me, until I gave away a piece of myself for someone I loved more than breathing.

Then Claudia leaned closer, conspiratorially. "Hey, sorry I wasn't nicer to you. I didn't know you were helping Katie. Also, it's annoying how hot you are."

I laughed. "It's fine, I get it."

"Okay, so tell me, what's your birthdate?" Her expression softened.

"July 5."

She grinned. "You're a Cancer! Empathetic, intuitive. I bet you read people like a psychic."

If you only knew. "I'll take it."

Davis returned, setting drinks down.

"Thanks," Claudia said. "Hey, what's your birthdate?"

Davis squirmed. "Uh, October 30th."

"Scorpio." Claudia flashed her teeth. "Two water signs. You two must have the best sex."

"Babe, inside thought." Chris pulled her back to the dance floor.

"She's wild." Davis angled closer. His breath was warm against my cheek. "Speaking of wild, want to get out of here soon? I have plans for you that don't involve small talk about Zodiac signs." His hand slid under the hem of my dress, making me want to jump out of it.

"I'll go find Katie to say goodbye."

Inside, the house was everything the Magnolia mansion wasn't—warm, lived-in, Katie's. Photos of the kids plastered the fridge, a calendar crowded with orthodontist appointments and graduations—futures, sketched neatly in ink. Dog bowls on a mat with "Good Girl" written in curly font. A world I'd never thought I wanted, until I realized how much it hurt to walk away from it. Katie could build this kind of life. Not me.

Katie appeared. "You sneaking out without saying goodbye?"

I jumped, guilty. "Oh, no, of course not."

Davis joined us, arm sliding around me. He kissed my neck, and Katie rolled her eyes. "Oh, would you two get a room already?"

"I don't need hotel rooms anymore," I joked. "Too soon?"

Davis laughed. "This was great, Katie. Really."

She smiled, radiant. "Thanks, both of you, for being here. It means a lot."

"I'm going to pull the car around." Davis handed me my bag and left the room. The handle slipped as I tossed it on my shoulder, scattering receipts, lipstick, straight-up trash, and the small photo I always carried. My reminder, my reason for everything.

I lunged for it, my fingers brushing the edge just as Katie's plucked it from the mess. The photo sat so innocently in her manicured fingers—a little girl with wild red hair and bright blue eyes, grinning at the camera.

"Aww, who is this little cutie?" Katie's voice went soft and maternal, the tone reserved for puppies and toddlers.

"My niece."

Katie tilted her head and squinted at the photo. "I didn't know you had siblings?"

Shit. I still hadn't told her about Misha. Soon, I wouldn't have to keep the lies straight.

"I used to. A sister, but she passed away." For one reckless second, I almost told her everything, the whole brutal truth.

Katie softened. “Oh, I’m sorry.” She reached out, squeezing my hand.

I squeezed back. “Thanks. Tonight was amazing.”

“Coffee soon,” she said. “After we get back from spring break?”

“Yeah, for sure,” I lied. I hugged her before she could see my face, burying myself in the scent of her expensive perfume, like I could take her with me that way.

Someday, she’d understand why I had to disappear, and why my sister and my niece had to remain a secret until it was safe.

“You sure you’re okay?” Katie pulled me back to study my face. “You’ve been weird all night.

“I’m always weird.” I forced a laugh. “Just tired.”

“Oh, here.” Katie passed me the photo. “What’s her name, your niece?”

I swallowed hard. “Poppy.”

THIRTY-FIVE

KATHERINE

"I know you loved me, Dad," I whispered.

The cemetery always smelled like earth and endings. I kneeled beside my father's headstone, my jeans soaking through on the muggy ground. The dampness pulled me down, heavy, as if it would never leave me.

The granite was rough under my fingertips as I traced Dad's name and the date underneath: William Aaron Valentine, June 15, 2002. The day Eric and I should have been opening wedding gifts. I never saw his body. I refused. I wanted my last memory of him to be of him being full of life at my wedding reception.

He'd been proud, insisting on giving a toast with ginger ale, despite my mom's worried glances.

"My little girl," he'd said. "I'm happy you've found someone who deserves you."

Had he known it was goodbye? Had his toast already been a eulogy cursing my marriage before it even began?

I was adjusting the flowers in their holder when the memory hit. Not a dream this time, but Shane's actual face. His eyes dilating and emptying as I pressed down.

I pitched forward, and my palms hit the wet grass.

"Ma'am? You okay?"

A groundskeeper approached me.

I forced myself upright, wiping my hands on my jeans. "I'm fine, thanks."

I waited until he was out of sight before I let myself breathe again.

Did my dad have these terrors too?

Though my childhood was a minefield of feelings, before the scandal, in between his benders, before my classmates started whispering and teasing me when I walked down the hall, my father and I were pals. He had the patience to teach me to throw a softball, though I had little natural talent, and the strong will to watch me fly down a snowy mountain on a sled and cheer me on instead of screaming "slow down" as my mom would. He wouldn't judge me when I doodled and daydreamed during church or tell me I wasn't taking things seriously if I didn't keep my room spotless or have perfect manners. With him, I could be myself; messy, distracted, imperfect. And yet, I hardly knew him at all.

And now, I hardly knew myself.

Standing over my father's grave, I wasn't haunted by guilt. I was haunted by how easy it had been.

The movies made murder look passionate and frenzied. But pressing my hands over Shane's face was methodical, almost clinical, as if I was timing cookies in the oven.

That's what terrified me. Not that I'd done it, but how calmly I'd done it.

My father's destruction was messy and public. Drinking, fucking his students, losing control. I'd destroyed mine with perfect control.

Which one of us was the real monster?

"I wish you could have gotten your shit together earlier, Dad."

My voice caught. I wanted him to see Emma's first birthday, to listen to Elliott's first clarinet solo, or to wrestle with Ethan as a toddler. But he didn't. He never would.

"I wish you'd chosen to stay."

My mom found him on the bathroom floor. Her scream through the phone still crawled across my skin. He'd downed a bottle of whiskey and a bottle of painkillers. Mom insisted then, and every day since then, that he was medicating a sore back, and he would have never taken his own life.

He'd been sober for two years. We thought he was healed, better. My mom was forever convinced it was a tragic coincidence. I wasn't so sure. Perhaps he never got past the shame, and the weight of his choices always felt heavier than we could see.

I understood him more than I ever did growing up because I carried that weight now, too.

"I miss you. And I'm mad at you. And I love you."

We'd never be sure if he took his own life. And I'd never be sure what exactly killed Shane. Like being in a firing squad, none of us would ever know who fired the fatal shot. Not knowing should feel like mercy, but it didn't.

"We're more alike than I ever wanted to admit, Dad. And I hate that."

I traced his name one final time.

I wouldn't let Shane destroy my family, and I wouldn't let the shame of what I'd done destroy me either. My father never understood that.

My kids would never know what I was capable of. And that lie would let them sleep at night.

I came to my feet and wiped grass from my knees.

"I'm not free of what I did. But my kids will be."

Back at home, I stepped over three suitcases still overflowing with unwashed clothes and Disney merchandise. The spring break trip was perfect: Emma genuinely laughing with her brothers on Pirates of the Caribbean, Elliott conquering his fear of Space Mountain, and Ethan's pure joy when he saw a room full of Stormtroopers. Everyday family moments made us all feel like kids again. And now they were dumped on my floor like sandbags, waiting for me to unpack everyone's joy and fold it neatly back into drawers.

Piper nosed through one suitcase, emerging with Micky Mouse ears in her mouth.

"Drop it." I tugged it free. A souvenir from the Happiest Place on Earth, covered in drool. Perfect metaphor for my life.

I lost myself in organizing as I often did. There were bills to sort, forms to file, and endless paperwork proving I was still a functioning mother despite what had happened.

Elliott burst through the front door.

"Hey kiddo—"

"Mom! I passed!" His voice exploded into the air, pure teenage triumph.

"Elliott, that's awesome, bud!" I wrapped my arms around him.

"I only hit one cone parallel parking. Dad said it was a record for our family."

I laughed. "Well, I'm proud of you. Let's celebrate this week, okay? Talk with Dad and Bridge about a good night to celebrate with dinner out. Anywhere you want."

"I will. Thanks for not giving up on me, Mom."

My heart swelled as he marched proudly to his room. "Never, kiddo."

Current favorite.

My phone hummed. Emma's name with twelve exclamation points.

Mom!!!! It's live!!!! I'm published!!!!

Below, a link:

Student Journalist's Investigation Exposes Deadly Supplement Scheme – By Anna Dollarhide, Contributing Journalist: Emma Gray, Puget Academy.

My daughter's name in *The Seattle Times,* in print.

I scrolled, my eyes catching fragments.

"...dozens of consumers reporting adverse reactions to products from Vitality & Grace, a wellness MLM..."

"...internal emails show McFadden suppressed safety complaints for over two years..."

"...Melanie Anderson was allegedly unaware of the consumer complaints; however, she knew she was committing electoral fraud..."

"...McFadden indicted on seven counts, including campaign finance fraud and self-dealing..."

You're amazing, Em!

I set my phone on the desk, but it lit up again before my hand had even pulled away. Davis's name filled the screen.

I swiped to answer. "Davis, did you see the news—"

"Katie, thank God." His voice was stripped of its usual calm. "Have you heard from Izzy?"

The question threw me. "No, we got back a couple of days ago, so I haven't...Why?"

I heard the faint, sharp sound of him tapping something against a hard surface. "She told me she was visiting her family for a week. That was two weeks ago. She won't answer her phone. She's just...gone."

"Gone? Maybe she wanted some space, after everything—"

"I went to the address on her employment forms, Katie." His voice dropped. "It's an empty lot. Gravel and a chain-link fence. I knocked on every door on the street. Nobody has ever heard of Isabella Meyer."

My knees felt weak. "There has to be a mistake. Maybe she gave a fake address for safety."

"It's all fake, Katie, her whole file. No driver's license, no social security number. The corporate lawyers have nothing." His breath was jagged.

I slid into my chair. "That can't be right—"

"Did she tell you about her sister?"

The air in my lungs went cold. "What…sister? Yes, she mentioned that she had passed away."

"Died? She never told me that." Davis's confusion was a mirror of my own.

"Yeah, at the housewarming party, I saw a picture of her niece—"

"Niece?" Davis said. "No, she never mentioned that. But her sister was Shelly Foster."

The name was meaningless. "Who?"

"Michelle Foster," Davis said flatly. "One of the interns."

My grip went slack. The phone slipped from my fingers, clattering against the floor. Davis's distant voice became white noise.

An empty lot. A fake name. A sister Shane destroyed.

The niece with those impossible blue eyes.

The smooth wire transfer of half of everything.

I hadn't hired an ally in a dark closet during a fundraiser. I was scouted.

Izzy wasn't my weapon.

I was hers.

THIRTY-SIX
ISABELLA

Number forty-seven had a crack like lightning. Forty-eight was perfectly round. Forty-nine looked stabbed with a pen.

I counted the ceiling tiles because thinking about the scalpel, the anesthesia, or blurting out a murder confession under drugs was worse. The betadine burned my nose, dragging me back to nights with Pop in hospitals like this. Full circle. Or maybe just punishment. My heart kept time to its own soundtrack—Britney's "Oops, I Did It Again." Disturbingly on-brand, considering I was about to get sliced open after helping kill a man.

"You're going to feel a little pinch." The nurse slid an IV needle into my arm.

I barely registered the sting. My fingers drummed restlessly, my mind on the little girl in the pediatric prep room down the hall, the text messages I'd ignored, the people I'd abandoned. So I kept counting. Fifty. Fifty-one.

"Your blood pressure's elevated." The nurse said. "Pre-surgery jitters?"

"Something like that." But I wasn't nervous. This was the first truly good thing I'd done in years. Everything else was survival, revenge, or both. "How's Poppy?"

"She's doing great," she said. "Your mother is with her. Doctor Haught says she's a real trooper. She's been showing everyone her stuffed bunny."

"Mr. Floppy."

"That's the one. We told her we'd get him a liver, too, so that they can match." The nurse chuckled. "Quite the imagination."

Another physician entered, clipboard in hand. "Ms. Meyer? I'm Dr. Tierney. I'll be administering your anesthesia today. Any questions before we get started?"

"Nope." A million questions, none of which he could answer.

"All right then. The surgical team will be in shortly. Try to relax. I gave you a medication to help." He pushed something in my IV line, patted my shoulder, and left.

My phone lit up on the side table. I reached for it, surprised to see a text from Davis. I hadn't answered a single one since vanishing from his life. But this one cut deeper than any scalpel.

I miss you. I love you. Please, call me.

Three knives, straight to the chest.

In another universe, I'd have called him back. Maybe I deserved him there. It could have been us against the world.

But not here. Not in this one. Here, I'd used him like Shane used me. Let him fall in love with a lie. The woman he missed wasn't real.

And some truths were too big to send in a text.

I set the phone down and closed my eyes as the medication took effect, the antiseptic smell fading into the scent of woodsmoke, herbs drying in the rafters, and rain on tin. Our kitchen table. Last September, the night I stopped running from the truth and decided to hunt it down instead.

The memory pulled me under like warm water…

"We can't afford this." Mom's hand trembled as she set down the invoice—the same hands that brewed tinctures she swore could cure anything, the kitchen light glinting off new threads of silver in her red hair.

$575,000. It might as well have been written in blood.

"All those nights I chose herbs over doctors…"

"Mom. Stop."

"I know. I know. I blame myself every day," she whispered —same litany as always. "If I'd only gone to the hospital with Misha when she was struggling, with Dad when he was coughing blood, with Poppy when she wasn't getting better…"

"Stop it," I said, before the self-loathing began. "That's not helping Poppy."

The memory still haunted us, always would: Mom dosing Dad and Poppy with her homemade concoctions while they burned with fever. By the time Dad died, and Poppy's little eyes turned yellow as the sun, the damage was done.

She wiped away a tear. "I've been putting aside what I can, but it's not enough. Not nearly enough."

We didn't have a network to raise money. Nobody cared about people like us.

Her conspiracies were wrong, but she was right about one thing: the system was rigged.

I reached across the table and took her hand. Her skin was rough, callused from years of clinging to soil she trusted more than doctors.

"Mom, I need you to listen to me. I need you to do what's right."

"Anything," she whispered, and for once, I believed her. For all her flaws, for all the damage her paranoia had done, she loved Poppy fiercely. She'd finally seen the pain she'd caused. Another death on her conscience would kill her, too.

"Take care of Poppy while I'm gone. Keep her safe. Take her to all her appointments. I'm going to get the money we need."

"How? Isabella, what are you planning?"

I glanced out at the overgrown fields where Misha and I grew up under Mom's paranoia. I'd left at eighteen, dragging my fourteen-year-old sister with me. Four years of double shifts, petty theft, and raising her into a brilliant young woman who earned a full scholarship and internship.

She was so fucking smart. Too trusting.

And when the pandemic destroyed both our jobs, we'd been forced back here. It's where Misha discovered she was pregnant and gave birth to a beautiful baby girl. Where, three months later, I found one of Mom's toxic tinctures spilled across the sink, and my sister cold in the bathtub. Her final act of surrender.

I waited for my mom's eyes to meet mine. "I'm going to make Shane Sutton pay."

Someone adjusted my IV drip, pulling me back to the present. The fluorescent lights overhead reminded me where I was and what came next.

Last night, I studied the papers I'd read every day since Misha died. Her journals—each page a descent into depression and postpartum psychosis. She wrote about the night she showed up to confront the father of her baby, hoping he'd feel something. Anything. An ounce of paternal instinct or responsibility. Instead, he called the cops.

Her final journal entry was a letter to Poppy, explaining why she couldn't stay and who was to blame.

He was easy to track down, but I didn't have a way in to his posh social circles until I found the job listing for waitstaff at an event in his upscale home. I wasn't sure what I'd do at first, find out secrets to ruin him, maybe? Or steal something valuable—jewelry, art, a code to a safe, anything to help pay his share of Poppy's mounting medical bills. Instead, I found a woman as desperate as I was, for different reasons, offering me her blessing to bleed Shane dry financially.

Katie never knew I'd been hunting Shane before we met. She didn't need to know about Misha's tear-stained face or Poppy's sickness haunting my dreams.

If she could exploit my desperation, I could exploit hers.

A doctor's voice came from somewhere distant, discussing the surgery. Time was running out. I read Davis's text one more time before the nurse took my phone.

"Any messages you want to send before we go in?"

I waved a hand, dismissively. What could I possibly text?

Some truths were too jagged to share, even with someone you literally loved.

The surgical team entered the room. The lead surgeon's eyes crinkled above her mask as she spoke.

"Ready to be a hero, Ms. Foster?"

I managed a smile. "Yes."

In the hallway, another gurney appeared, so small, like a toy. My heart stuttered.

Poppy.

Her bright red hair peeked out from beneath the tiniest, cutest blue cap. Mr. Floppy dangled from her arm. Her blue eyes—Shane's eyes, though I tried not to see him there—lit up when she saw me.

"Auntie Izzy!" she called, her words high-pitched and clear. "Look, we match!"

"That's right, Pop."

So brave and innocent. The one good thing Shane Sutton ever created. The only thing I'd ever been willing to die for.

"I love you to the moon," she yelled, our bedtime ritual finding its way to the quiet space.

"And back again," I finished, as they wheeled her away, her small hand waving until she disappeared.

I'd killed for her. Lied, manipulated, destroyed, burned every bridge. And I'd do it all again tomorrow, twice, without blinking. That's the thing about love nobody tells you, how it makes monsters of us all. How it can turn a sister's grief into a weapon strong enough to end a man's life.

The anesthesia began to pull me under. The room softened, ceiling tiles bleeding into one tapestry, sounds distant, like floating underwater.

My last conscious thought was a promise I made to the sister I couldn't save:

"I'll do it right this time, Misha. I'll save her."

And then, in the space between consciousness and darkness, Misha was there. Not sunken-eyed and desperate, but radiant. Eighteen again, and full of life.

"You did it, Iz."

She reached for my hand, and her touch was warm, real, forgiving.

I wanted to say I was sorry I hadn't saved her, hadn't seen how bad it was. But in that in-between place, words weren't necessary. She knew. She always had.

"Take care of her," Misha whispered as the darkness claimed me. "And yourself, too, this time."

I surrendered to the darkness, more peaceful than I'd been since I learned the name Shane Sutton.

THIRTY-SEVEN
KATHERINE

Eric's voice caught. "Damn. Graduation. Wasn't she in kindergarten last week?"

"We made a great kid," I said. "Three great kids."

A corner of his mouth went up. "Jury's still out on Ethan."

I laughed. Bridget tapped my elbow. "We picked a date. End of August. Vegas. We can celebrate your birthday, too!" She made a "glug glug" motion with her thumb and pinky finger.

"Wow, that's fast! Vegas wedding?"

"No!" Bridget rolled her eyes. "Bachelorette party!"

Before I could answer, the orchestra tuned its instruments. Rows of seniors lined up to march in, ready in their red and blue caps and gowns. The second *Pomp and Circumstance* started, so did the tears.

The students processed down the middle aisle. A few of

Emma's friends passed, and I choked up with each one. Josie waved at Chris and Claudia, a few rows back.

Brock Anderson passed us, cap and gown too large on his body, which looked somewhat deflated. The cocky swagger was gone. I felt a pang of sympathy. Yes, Brock had called me a gold digger. Yes, he'd parroted his mother's venomous words like a wind-up toy. But he was a kid. We all had our parental damage. Some just wore it differently.

A few rows back, Todd caught my eye and gave a warm smile. He'd mentioned over coffee last week that authorities had subpoenaed their divorce records and they were, in fact, shady as shit. Melanie remained at home, under house arrest, awaiting her fate. I couldn't help but feel empathy for her, too. Conned by a crooked man.

"There she is," my mom said.

My little girl. Her platinum hair peeked from beneath her cap, tassel swishing. Sequined sneakers sparkled with the late May sun, scattering tiny beams of light. I wasn't prepared for the flood of self-reflection the ceremony would spark. Looking at her was like looking in a mirror.

As her eyes met mine, her lip quivered, the same small lip that curled in the bath as a baby or pouted as a toddler. I reached into the aisle, and she squeezed my hand as she passed by. The surge of love was beyond words. A first and last all at once.

She stepped on stage, taking her place at the podium.

"Welcome, friends and families," Mr. Morris boomed. "We will start with an opening speech from your class president, Emma Gray."

Emma cleared her throat. "Thank you, Principal Morris,

and please let me be the first to say, and I think I'm not alone, that we will all miss your leadership and fun, possibly inappropriate T-shirts."

She paused for laughter, then took a deep breath. "We made it, everyone! Looking out into the crowd, I see the kids I grew up with. Every single one of you helped make Puget Academy unforgettable. Through all the chaos, two things kept me sane: my friends and family. My ride-or-dies, showing up in class, at football games, or at 2 AM TikTok dances Josie forced before finals."

Josie bowed dramatically.

"This year tested us. We lost people. We questioned things we thought were certain. I learned that asking questions is scary, especially when powerful people don't want you to. But thankfully, I have my mom, who taught me to stand up for myself," she caught her breath. "My dad, who showed me second chances are always possible, and my little brothers, who manage to be both the most annoying and most awesome people I know. I see you, I appreciate you, and I love you, even when you drive me nuts."

Her words landed like a punch—a bitter, beautiful irony. The boys laughed and beamed at their big sister.

My kids. Against all odds, they were healing.

They'd visited Fred's grave twice since Shane died, but they'd never once asked to visit Shane's.

I'd worried about that at first, but their therapists assured me they'd processed Shane, seen him clearly, and decided that he didn't deserve their flowers or tears.

Fred had earned their remembrance. Shane had earned their absence.

It was a lesson I was still learning myself.

Emma continued. "So, here's my advice: Ask questions. Follow the money. Don't accept no for an answer when you know something is wrong, and fuck the patriarchy! Let's go change the world!"

Cheers filled the stadium, and tears fell down my face.

Eric slipped his arm around me. "You did good."

"You too," I said. But inside, I wondered if Emma would still look at me with such admiration if she knew what I'd done? Or would she turn cold, as I'd done when I learned my father's secrets? Would she understand the lines between victim and villain can blur until they disappear entirely?

Yet seeing confidence, I couldn't regret it. My darkness had shielded her light, even if it stained me forever.

After half a dozen speeches, names called, diplomas handed out, and tassels shifted from one side to the other, Mr. Morris announced the graduating class.

Caps filled the sky, red and blue confetti raining down. Everyone cheered.

It was such a surreal, magical moment, yet an unspoken ache gnawed at me, like a gaping wound. I caught myself scanning the crowd during the ceremony, searching for a flash of red-gold hair among the sea of proud parents. Twice, I thought I spotted her, my heart leaping before reality crashed back—just a woman with similar coloring. The third time, I forced myself to stop looking.

It made no logical sense. Izzy was in my life for less than a year, through deception and petty theft, wormed her way into my trust, and then vanished last month. But she was the only one who could possibly understand the weight of what I carried and how my relief was inseparable from guilt. I found myself reaching for my phone to text her sarcastic commentary, imagining her eye-roll or the joke she'd make to pull a laugh from me. I had more questions than answers. I'd called her number so often I had it memorized; each unanswered ring was a cut I kept reopening.

"You okay?" Eric whispered.

"Fine," I lied, trying to pull my thoughts back to Emma. Today was about her, not the ghost of a friendship built on mutual destruction.

My phone vibrated in my purse. I glanced down—Davis calling. Weird timing. I sent it to voicemail, but he called again immediately. And again.

I slipped into the aisle as families found their graduates.

"Davis? I'm at Emma's graduation—"

"I found her."

I stopped walking. "What?"

"I found her, Katie." His voice cracked. "I found Izzy."

THIRTY-EIGHT
ISABELLA

I sat on the wraparound porch of our new farmhouse, watching Poppy chase butterflies through the wildflowers Mom and I had planted. The weathered wood creaked with every rock of the chair—a sound I never thought I'd find comforting, but here we were. The whole scene was so fucking wholesome it could have Momfluencers drooling.

Poppy's laughter carried across the property, a sound I never tired of hearing. Three years old and already so resilient. After six weeks, the scar on her belly had healed completely, while my own pulled uncomfortably. Why did little kids get all the collagen? Not fair. But it had all been worth it. Every twinge was a reminder Poppy was alive because of what I'd given her—a small price.

My mom appeared at the screen door, holding a glass of lemonade. "You need to hydrate more." The conspiracy theorist turned hydration police. Growth, I guess.

"Thanks, Mom." I took the glass, our fingers brushing.

These small, everyday interactions were new, like tender shoots growing from scorched earth.

She lingered, gazing at Poppy. "I never thought we'd have this," she murmured. "After your father, after Misha…"

"I know."

We'd both failed my sister in different ways, but damned if we were going to fail her daughter.

"You saved us," she said. "All of us."

Mom sank into the chair opposite me. The paranoia that had defined her for decades was giving way to a fierce, focused determination to care for her granddaughter. She still had her quirks, her suspicions, her moments of retreat from reality. But Dad and Misha's deaths and Poppy's illness had anchored her in a way nothing else could.

"So, you still haven't answered their calls?"

She'd asked me every day since I'd been home from the hospital. "Not yet. I'm still waiting for the right moment."

"You should tell her and Davis," Mom said. "They deserve to know the truth."

"Yeah. But it's scary. You should know what that's like."

Mom chuckled, a dry rustling sound. "I do. But I was wrong about a lot of things, Izzy. For a long time." She patted my knee. "Fear made me small. Don't let it do the same to you."

"I know, Mom." But I couldn't, not yet. Not until I was sure no one could ever threaten Poppy again.

"Anyhoo, I'm going to start dinner." She rose to her feet and disappeared back inside.

I closed my eyes, letting the late afternoon sun warm my

face. The doctors had said my recovery would take longer than Poppy's, though I was getting stronger each day.

A car engine rumbled in the distance. I craned my neck and winced at the pull in my side.

A red car I recognized immediately came into view, kicking up dust along our newly graveled driveway. I'd known this day might come, but I wasn't prepared for it to be this soon.

"Pop," I called, trying to keep my voice steady. "Come here, sweetie."

She bounded toward me, cheeks flushed. "Who's coming?"

"An old friend," I said, though I wasn't sure if that was true anymore.

Katherine Valentine stepped out, looking effortlessly elegant in jeans and a simple white blouse. Her eyes found mine immediately, and I saw the question in them before she even closed her car door.

"Stay right here with me, okay?" I said to Poppy, who clung to my leg.

Katie came closer, her gaze darting between the child and me.

"Izzy." She reached the bottom of the porch steps. "It's been a while."

I didn't trust myself to speak.

"The Seattle Stars Foundation received a generous donation. This address was listed."

An oversight, or a Freudian slip? Maybe I wanted them to find me. "Oh, right."

"I did try calling first. Several times," she added. "Davis has been worried sick. We all have."

"Hi." Poppy peeked her head from behind me.

"And who is this?" Katie crouched to Poppy's level.

"I'm Poppy," she announced proudly. "I'm three."

She held up three tiny fingers with the confidence of someone declaring they've solved world hunger.

"It's very nice to meet you, Poppy. I'm Katie." She extended her hand, which Poppy shook with gusto.

I held my breath and studied Katie's expression. First came the smile, then a slight narrowing of her eyes, the way someone looks when trying to place a familiar face—a subtle tilt of her head. And then—there it was. The recognition hit like a storm breaking.

She knelt as if her legs had given out, gazing at Poppy, then back at me, then back at Poppy. Her eyes. The unmistakable, piercing blue that had once held her focus from across a pillow, at a dinner table, and from the bottom of a staircase.

In that split second, everything I'd tried to hide was out there. All my lies, all my schemes, all my secrets, lay between us like cards on a table. Game over. No more bullshit.

"Poppy, why don't you go help Grandma with dinner?" I squeezed her shoulder gently.

"But I want to stay with you and your friend," she protested.

"We'll be right in," I said. "But we need to talk about grown-up things first."

She sighed dramatically but obeyed, skipping up the steps and into the house. So innocent and unaware of the blood and lies that had brought us to this moment. The screen door slammed behind her with a bang.

"Katie—"

"She's Shane's daughter."

I gestured to the porch swing. She sat next to me.

"Do you remember the woman who came to your house? Shane told you it was Jessica?"

"Yes," Katie said.

"That was my sister."

The color drained from Katie's face.

"Misha. That's what we called her." I picked at my cuticles. "When she got pregnant, I always assumed it was another coed from the program, but she would never tell me who he was. I think she was scared." I sucked my teeth. "And he told her to 'take care of it' like it was a parking ticket."

Katie's mouth hung open.

"She thought once the baby was born, he would change his mind. It's why she went to your house. But he didn't even want to see her. That's when she told me what happened."

"I can't believe that was her. The one he'd called 'crazy.' He'd convinced me it was Jessica." Katie covered her mouth with her hand and leaned back in the chair.

I flinched at the word "crazy." "When he called the police on her…on the mother of his child, it broke something inside of her that could never be repaired."

Neither of us said anything for a moment. Because we both knew what came next.

"After she took her life, I did everything in my power to find him. And then, Poppy got sick, and we needed money, fast."

I couldn't read her expression. There were so many layers she didn't know, like the fact that after his accident, my first morbid thought was that Shane Sutton might do one good thing in his miserable life and be a donor match for his own daughter, but he wasn't. Of course, he wasn't. Same eyes, wrong blood type.

"That's why you took the job," she said. "Izzy, why didn't you tell me?"

"You know why. Because I couldn't risk Shane having her taken away from us. He didn't care about hurting people."

Katie blinked. "No. No, he didn't."

"And even after he was gone, there was Nancy. If she'd known she had a biological granddaughter?" I stammered. "There wasn't a safe time to talk about Poppy. To anyone, even you or Davis. I couldn't risk it."

Katie bit her bottom lip. "I assume you heard about Nancy?"

"No, about what?"

"She is at Western State Hospital. She had a complete mental breakdown."

The deafening silence sat between us, a sound I'd once hated but had grown to accept.

"There's one thing I never expected," I said.

"What's that?"

I shook my head. "I never expected to care about you. That wasn't part of the plan." I placed my hand on the swing between us, as an invitation, not a demand. "I figured you were…collateral damage. A means to an end."

Katie's eyes dropped to my outstretched hand. "And now?"

"Now, I know we're more alike than different. We both did what we had to do to protect the people we love." My voice dropped. "I don't regret what happened on those stairs, Katie. Any of it."

She faced me, and I saw everything reflected there—the shared trauma, the blood on our hands, the impossible choices we'd both made.

A tear fell from her face. "God, she has his eyes, doesn't she?"

"She does," I said. "But not his soul."

Her hand clasped mine.

EPILOGUE

ONE YEAR LATER

Katherine Valentine smoothed her hands over the ivory silk of her dress, her fingers catching briefly on the delicate beadwork. The late June sunshine warmed her shoulders as she beheld the majestic and snow-capped mountains in the distance, presiding over the perfectly arranged rows of white chairs on the verdant lawn.

She took a deep breath as her eyes swept over the meticulous details: the arch of wildflowers framing the mountain view, the string quartet tuning their instruments, the champagne flutes waiting to be filled. This event had to be perfect. Absolutely perfect. Like all her best work, even this joy was choreographed.

Emma appeared at Katherine's side, stunning in a sleek blue dress matching her girlfriend Charlotte's. "Mom, everything is ready if you are."

"Okay." Katherine pressed a quick kiss to her daughter's cheek. "You look beautiful, by the way."

Emma's first year at Berkeley had transformed her, softening edges while strengthening her core. The teenager was gone, replaced by a confident young woman who FaceTimed three times a week, sharing stories about classes, journalism projects, and activism. When Emma came out, Katherine joked she hoped Emma hadn't chosen girls since Katherine had ruined men for her. Emma assured her that wasn't how sexuality worked, but appreciated the attempt at humor.

Emma took her seat beside her brothers. Elliott waved from where he sat with Ethan, both boys looking surprisingly comfortable in their suits despite their usual aversion to formal wear. In two months, Elliott would be off to the University of Washington; his decision to study finance made perfect sense for the quiet, analytical middle child, who had found his calling in the patterns of numbers. Ethan, now the tallest, still exuded teen angst but was clearly eager to rule the roost.

Across the lawn, Eric caught Katherine's eye and winked. He'd protected her and their children against all odds. The kids would never know how close they'd come to losing everything, nor how many lies had been buried to make this view possible. And his new bride, Bridget, never needed to speak the truth aloud for it to be understood. The cover-up of Shane's death had been staged as neatly as one of Katherine's events—reports altered, timelines tightened, evidence tucked away like silk ribbons.

The truth was both simpler and more complex than any investigation could have uncovered: Shane Sutton had been killed by the very qualities that defined him in life—his arrogance, his cruelty, his belief he could control everything and everyone around him. He had created the circumstances of his own demise, and his empire collapsed faster than his body had.

She'd learned the difference between complicity and authorship. From the outside, they can look the same, with clean hands and neat timelines, but inside, there's a pulse: *I chose this.*

Though sometimes, late at night, Katherine still felt the phantom weight of a face beneath her hands, and saw eyes meeting hers. She'd wake gasping and tell herself she was okay.

Most of the time, she believed it.

The string quartet began the processional music, and Katherine took her place in the back.

Someone might have mistaken the nervous energy in her posture for bridal jitters, but when she pulled a clipboard, her true role became clear. Katherine was the architect behind the scenes, the creator of perfect moments for others. Valentine Event Planning had taken off spectacularly in the past year; her calendar was booked solid six months in advance.

The altar framed Mount Rainier like a painting. Katherine gestured to Davis to make his way down the aisle, flanked by his proud parents. He gave each of them a hug and adjusted the cuffs of his suit. In the back row, a small group of fresh-faced scholars looked on proudly. Seattle Stars, formerly Sutton Stars, students who were no longer selected for malleability, but for their academic potential and commitment to their communities. Rebuilding the nonprofit had nearly broken him, but he'd done it: transformed Shane's corruption into a genuine force for opportunity. Shane's fortune was funding the very institutions he'd worked to undermine. Fred would be proud. Shane would be furious.

Shane's empire had collapsed faster than his body had tumbled down those stairs. Melanie Anderson began her three-year federal sentence quietly and without fanfare last month. The parent coalition she'd built, where she'd convinced parents that control was protection and supplements were salvation, had dissolved overnight. Vitality & Grace was gone. She'd performed empowerment while a man pulled her strings, and discovered too late that she'd been a pawn, not a player.

McFadden himself awaited trial. But the movement hadn't died with its architects.

Congressman Grant Halloway adopted the entire playbook and nearly pulled off the impossible in Washington State's gubernatorial race. The closest Republican margin since the '80s was carried by the same red wave that swept the nation, all under the guise of wellness and godliness.

Katherine shivered. Shane was dead, his co-conspirators faced consequences, and yet his ghost still whispered through school board meetings and campaign rallies across the country. The lies he'd told were too profitable to die. Someone would always pick them up, polish them, and sell them to the next desperate, angry parent looking for someone to blame.

They'd killed the man, but not the movement.

The music shifted, and a hush fell over the gathering. Everyone turned to the tiny little girl in a white dress. Four-year-old Poppy made her way forward, her red curls bouncing with each precious step, her haunting blue eyes wide with concentration as she tossed rose petals from her basket. She was thriving, a living promise the Suttons could no longer touch.

Katherine sent the bridesmaids down the aisle next. The women were all familiar faces: Tammi, whose popular podcast shot to the top of the charts before being picked up as a docuseries; Jessica, whose new book hit the *New York Times*'s bestseller list last week; and Claudia, who had declared she and Isabella were "cosmically destined for friendship" and bonded over their equally twisted sense of humor. The most unusual wedding party, a perfect revenge party.

Finally, came Isabella, radiant in a snow-white gown that flowed like water around her curves. Her arm was linked with her mother's, the two women walking in perfect step.

As Isabella moved down the aisle, surreal lightness lifted her. She was the same woman who was determined to make Shane Sutton pay for what he'd done to her sister. The same woman who became his victim, and then a co-conspirator in his death. Today, she was walking toward a life she'd never dared imagine with a man who knew her darkest truths and loved her anyway.

The scar on her abdomen pulled slightly, still tender after a year. The permanent reminder of what she'd given Poppy. What Misha couldn't give.

Some nights, she still woke gasping, watching Shane careen down the staircase. Davis always woke when she did. He never asked. Sometimes he was up with the same nightmares.

Katherine and Isabella had visited Nancy at the hospital the month before. Nancy sat by a window, hair brushed into obedient waves, eyes everywhere and nowhere at once. She didn't recognize any of them.

Isabella waved at Poppy, who gave her aunt a wide smile of pride. Reaching the altar, Isabella took Davis's hands in hers, noticing the slight tremor in his fingers that mirrored her own. Their eyes met. Bonds like theirs didn't need words. Davis would never be able to repay her for finishing what he'd started.

But his heart still raced every time he passed a staircase.

"Dearly beloved," the minister began, his voice carrying across the lawn. "We are gathered here today…"

A hand slid across Katherine's back, and Todd kissed her temple. Their relationship had evolved slowly, cautiously, both wary of commitment after their respective experiences. But there was comfort in their understanding, in the absence of pressure, in the simple pleasure of companionship without expectation. He was fun. But so was Mark. And Isaac. Katherine knew one thing for sure. She could stage a wedding to perfection, but for herself, the idea was dead and buried.

If there were a procession in her future, it would lead to her grave, not to an altar.

As the ceremony concluded and the newlyweds sealed their vows with a kiss, the summer breeze carried away the applause, and with it, the last lingering shadows of fear. Katherine embraced what was once impossible. The revenge party had survived. The law had chosen blindness, the whispers had dulled, and time had done its quiet erasing.

They were free, not because they escaped justice, but because in their own imperfect, messy way, they had achieved it themselves.

That, perhaps, was the greatest revenge of all.

ACKNOWLEDGMENTS

No book is written alone, but this one especially wasn't. It was written in conversation, in laughter, in frustration, and in moments when someone else stepped in to hold the belief for me. These are the people who made that possible.

To my husband, Kale, one of the good ones: thank you for your steadiness, your humor, and for believing in my work even when it took over my calendar and my brain. I couldn't do this without you.

To my children: thank you for cheering me on, for asking how the book was going, and for reminding me why hope matters. You are my loudest, proudest team, and everything I do is better because of you.

To my dog, Buddy, the best, most handsome, goodest boy: thank you for keeping me company in my office, for the daily walks that pulled me out of my head, and for reminding me to stop typing and live once in a while.

To my friend Brooke, who has appeared in all three of my books in various forms, some fictional and some pulled straight from real life: you drew the short straw on husbands, but telling me to write about your experience is the reason this book exists at all. There aren't words for what you are to me. *Friend* doesn't feel strong enough. You are the toughest person

I know. Also, my favorite TikTok influencer. My life and my closet are better because of you.

To my early readers, especially Celeste Yvonne: you read so many goddamn drafts that I genuinely don't know why you still speak to me, especially given my stance on dragons. I'm insufferable, but profoundly grateful. Thank you.

To my friend Laura McKowen, who reads my work whenever I ask, answers every call or text no matter the hour, and has agreed to the insurmountable task of deleting my browser history after I die: thank you for your loyalty on every possible level.

To my fiction writing group—Laura Cathcart-Robbins, Lara Love Hardin, Christie Tate, and Reema Zaman: thank you for your support on this wild ride through publishing. I am in awe of you to the point of awkward fangirling that I constantly remind myself to suppress.

To my local writing group in Bend, Kelly Kearsley, Joey Roddy, Ashley Redwood, Kerry Chaput, Tracey Lange, Holly Klein, and Nicole Meier: you inspire me and make me laugh. Just a few more writing retreats and we'll have the patriarchy solved. The memory of Boss Rambler lives inside all of us.

To my local book club: you push me to keep reading books that make me a better writer. Books I love, books I hate, and books that sometimes make me cringe. You know the one. Thank you for all of it.

To Sarah Edmondson for so graciously agreeing to narrate the audiobook. I'm proud to call you a friend and be in the revenge party cult with you!

To my early blurb-ers. Jo, Tia, Laura, Christie, and Reema, I can't thank you enough. You know how annoying the blurb industrial complex is, and yet you graciously said yes, even with your own busy writing schedules. Thank you.

And to everyone who told me to keep pitching, keep revising, and not quit when over one hundred agents rejected this novel: thank you. You were right.

To Kristen McGuiness at Rise Publishing: holy fuck. This book was a ride. I honestly couldn't have done this with anyone else. Lauren, Raya, and the entire team, including Kerry, my amazing cover designer, those behind the scenes—thank you for everything you poured into my debut novel.

This book is a work of fiction. The feelings behind it are not. I wrote it as a woman in America between 2024–2026, out of catharsis and out of hope. Hope that things can change. Hope that truth still matters. Hope that stories like this still have a place. Remember, women outnumber men in this country. Don't let yourself be dismissed.

And if push comes to shove, I'll meet you on the top step.